The Awakening of Thomas Hunter

Clay Alexander

ISBN-13: 978-1979711159

DEDICATION

I am dedicating this novel to my mother, Janet Hutchinson Alexander, a world traveler and published photojournalist who focused on saving fish and wild animals. She was way ahead of her time. I am grateful for her DNA as it endowed me with a sense of humor, a love of words and respect for Earth's wild creatures.

To a VERY special woman who is a Real artist. Life is good so... "cumquat may, make THE best of it!"

Clay

"I could well imagine that I might have lived in former centuries and there encountered questions I was not yet able to answer; that I had been born again because I had not fulfilled the task given to me."

—Carl Jung

"My magic has always been about stories. It's not about fooling people; it's about showing people infinite possibilities."

—David Copperfield

"It's taken all of my life to understand it is not necessary to understand everything."

—René Coty

"It is always in season for old men to learn."

—Aeschylus

Chapter One

The first sensation I had when I awoke was that I was cold. I had my eyes closed, but I knew I was floating in—I supposed—water. There was a soft rumbling sound around me and an occasional gurgle and splash. I was rocking back and forth and the right side of my body was bumping against something rough. I opened my eyes, but the sun's glare was too much. I had a brief glimpse of a tree that had fallen into the river and was keeping me from floating downstream. The banks were not high and the terrain beyond was flat.

I managed to free my right arm and hand and kept the sunlight out of my eyes when I opened them again. Upstream I saw a large boulder in the middle of a strangely familiar river that briefly split the water into two streams. The fallen tree disrupted the flow on my side of the boulder and caused a whirlpool to form next to the bank, eight feet upstream from where I lay. The river was about a hundred feet wide and I could only conclude I had floated down from somewhere and was lucky enough to be on this side of the boulder. If the tree had not been there, I'd have floated on down the river to God knows where. Relief and anxiety mixed in my mind. What was I doing here?

I looked at the rest of my body and could not imagine why I was naked. Everything seemed to be intact, except for a sizeable defect in my left forearm. The strange appearance probably came from my arm hitting a submerged rock on the way down. Skin and fatty tissue were missing and I could see muscle fibers, to a depth of about two inches. The tissue in the cavity was irregular, but totally sealed so there was no blood visible. Maybe cold water did that.

I was shivering and knew I had to get out before hypothermia set in. The current was moderately strong, but I managed to stand upright in the four-foot deep water. It was shallower upstream of the whirlpool and, holding on to the bank, I slowly moved in that direction. The whirlpool was six feet in diameter and I could see silt swirling up from the bottom as well as yellowish leaves, grayish flecks, and brown twigs circling around. The debris disappeared into the center vortex and then reappeared on the outside, until it was again swirled towards the middle. My upstream progress through the whirlpool disrupted its action for a short time. My left arm drifted into the whirling center, although the suction was not enough to cause any harm. When the water depth decreased enough, I lurched onto the bank and crawled out.

I collapsed in the grass, exhausted and numb from the cold water. I guessed it was late summer as trees in the distance had a hint of red and yellow in some of the leaves. Happily, the air was still warm and the sun felt good. I pushed to my feet and stood, making sure of my balance. I felt someone might be nearby and turned slowly around. Nothing.

There was a farm in the distance with the house painted off-white and a dull red barn to one side. Between us, there was tall meadow grass that had turned to hay. I didn't see any animals, but thought the hay was used for something. I needed to get to the farm although I was concerned what they would think when a naked man, dripping wet, approached the house. Farmers usually kept a shotgun or two in their homes. Good guys are usually not stripped and thrown into rivers.

I stumbled through the field for several hundred yards and then sat down to rest. I tried again to figure out why I ended up naked in a river. What the hell? My memory was gone, even my name. It was as if my memories were deleted and I'd been magically transported to a copycat planet. I suppressed panic, knowing it would impair my thinking. Once I got to the farm, with access to the outside world, I'd get the answers. I rose and continued on, looking around and searching for something, anything that might be familiar. When I came to a gentle rise, I could see a dirt road about a quarter-mile to my left. It might be safer to walk to the farm on the road, rather than approaching through a backyard.

When I got to the road, I had to sit down again, as the cold was still deep in my muscles. My shivering had stopped and my skin felt better, but it was an effort to move my limbs. At least I wasn't going to die of hypothermia. I walked a couple of hundred feet towards the farm before I heard the sound of a motor behind me. I sat on the edge of the road as I figured a naked sitting man would be less alarming than a walking one. A battered old silver pickup stopped before it reached me, raising a cloud of dust that blew over me, turning the river droplets on my skin into little brown warts. The fellow driving must have been a brave soul to get out of his truck.

The man was early middle aged and tall, I'd guess about four or five inches over six feet. He was well muscled and his soiled overalls showed he was used to heavy farm work. The fellow came over and stood looking down.

"Whatcha doin'?"

"I know this sounds strange, but I have no idea what happened. I woke up in the river with no clothes on. I have no idea how I got there. Can you lend me a shirt and a pair of pants? I'll pay you back when I get a job."

The man's face wrinkled up and he moved his lips from side to side. The frown marks between his eyes slowly relaxed and he said, "I'll talk to Papi. We'll be mowing in a coupla days and could use some help baling. My clothes are too big for you, but Mama saves everythin'.

3

My high school stuff might fit." He looked over at the farmhouse and then back at me. "Get in the truck and stay there 'til I bring out my old clothes. Papi would probably shoot both of us if I bring you near the house."

I thought, "Oh shit. I was afraid of that."

As we got closer to the house, the big guy kept looking at me and then all around the area, probably making sure his father wasn't nearby. "You slouch down and make sure you don't look up 'till I get back. I don't know where Mama put those things."

"I sure appreciate this. I've never been naked like this in my life. By the way, what's your name and where are we?"

The man parked the car a hundred and fifty feet away from the front of the house. He opened the car door quickly and jumped out. About ten feet away, he apparently remembered my question, came back and leaned in through the window. "Idaho, east of Boise, and name's Jeff."

If anything would call attention to the truck, his coming back and saying something to an empty seat would do it. I prayed Mama or Papi was not looking out a window. I scrunched down even further, trying to get my whole body under the dashboard. It wasn't easy with my stiffened joints.

It was a good fifteen minutes before I heard someone's footsteps. I didn't know who was coming and panic hit me again. My head came up quickly, thumping loudly as it hit the bottom of the glovebox.

The door opened and Jeff said, "I told you to stay down and be quiet. I don't want nobody to see you if you're naked." He shoved some clothes onto the driver's seat and stood by the open door, smoking a cigarette.

"I can't get dressed under the dashboard. I've got to get outside."

"Come outa there and get behind me. I'll keep the door open."

With some effort, I untangled my limbs, crawled across the seat, and slid headfirst to the ground. I pulled on a patched pair of jeans and a thin plaid shirt. Jeff must have been bigger than I even in high school. Papi was bound to notice I was wearing his son's old clothes. What then?

Jeff looked casually over his shoulder. "I gotta know your name. It's important."

I could feel the hairs on the back of my neck popping up. I had no idea what my name was. Jeff, obviously irritated, turned around and said, "Hurry up. Papi's gonna to be back any minute. Don't you even know your name?"

"It's Tom Hunter." Where that came from, I didn't know. I also thought I'd better find out the date from Jeff before I got to the farmhouse. It would be too weird otherwise.

Jeff said, "It's 1955, August. What happened to your arm?"

I saw him staring at it in the car and was ready with my best guess. I glanced down at my left forearm and my mouth opened to respond. It remained open, as did my eyes. There was only a thin jagged line where the large divot had been.

"I cut myself on barbed wire when I was a little kid." It was the only thing I could come up with at the moment. I could not imagine what might have caused it to heal so fast. Maybe I was on another planet where the air kept everyone healthy.

There was no time to think about it as Jeff pushed me ahead and closed the door of the pickup. He put his long arm around my shoulder for a moment and we started walking toward the farmhouse. Just before we got there, I caught a glimpse of a face looking out of a second story window. It might have been a woman, but I wasn't sure. Jeff opened the front door and, ducking slightly, walked into a big front room. "Hey Mama, this is Tom. The man I told you 'bout."

I heard a pot clatter from the back and a painfully thin woman entered, wiping her hands on a stained dishtowel. She stared at me for quite a while, mostly looking at her son's shirt, which was obviously too big for me. "Jeff told me you was in an accident and got your clothes torn up."

"Yes, I was minding my own business and a truck came by, ran a stoplight, and hit a post. The back was full of fertilizer and it got all over me. I fell down and somebody stole my wallet with all my cards and money. I really appreciate you and Jeff helping me. I'll work off the debt and maybe I can make a little money."

"Stealing ain't no way to treat a person," said Mama. "We need help every Fall so this is good for both of us. You can sleep on the floor in Jeff's room. Jeff, go get Tom some cushions and a blanket. Papi will be anxious to talk with you."

I wasn't sure what Papi would think about all this and glanced over at Jeff. I could tell he was as worried as I was. We didn't have to fret much longer because the back door opened with a rasping noise as the spring stretched and then slammed as the door closed. Papi entered the room a half second ahead of his footsteps.

Papi took one look at me and stopped dead in his tracks. "What the hell?" He was a big man too, but not as tall as his son. Maybe six foot two, but he outweighed him by forty pounds, most of it in his belly.

"We got lucky, Papi. I was in town and saw the accident. Tom, here, almost got killed and his clothes mostly got tore off. I brought him . . ."

"I don't like foreign folks, especially when they're standing in my house wearin' your clothes."

"We're going to need help with the baling. He'll buy his own clothes."

"That don't make no never mind. We don't hire strangers." Papi turned to me. "Take those clothes off and git outa here."

Mama stepped in front of him. "You gonna put him on the road naked? Once a year we gotta do a little kindness. Those boys you hired last year hardly did a lick of work. Jeff and I did most of it."

Papi stared at his wife and then twisted his head to the right. You could see he was sniffing the air. I think I was saved as much by the aroma of a pungent stew bubbling in the kitchen as by Mama's talk.

"Lemme see your hands, boy."

Papi grabbed each hand and pushed my too long sleeves up. "This kid won't do a lick of work either. Those hands never did no baling."

I didn't think I was a kid, but I'd never looked at myself and had no idea how old I was. I hoped there was a mirror somewhere in the house. As scared as I was, I had to come up with something. "I worked all my life, but you're right, probably not on a farm. I learn quick and I'll wear gloves if I have to. If you find I'm not doing my share, I'll walk out of here naked." Papi was working his mouth and shifting his eyes.

Once again, Mama stepped in: "He's had some learnin', I can tell."

"Who's going to pay for his sleeping and eating?"

"After work, he can help Chinny with her homework. Maybe she can get her diploma by the end of the year. That would be a real blessing."

I now knew the person looking out the upstairs window was a woman, probably trying to get a college degree. However, it turned out to be a high school degree and she had been at it for eleven years. My neck got bristly again because I had no idea if I had a high school degree. I knew Papi would throw me out if I couldn't teach his daughter something in the next month or so. It was ominous no one else in the family was capable of helping her. Anyway, I became a temporary, if reluctant, addition to the family.

Chapter Two

Mama knew how to cook. The dinner that evening was a stew with tender meat, carrots, onions and potatoes, all simmering in tasty thick gravy. Jeff smiled at me before we sat down, carefully choosing a time when his father wasn't looking. Papi, on the other hand, spent considerable time staring at me with angry eyes. I offered him a nod and a cautious smile, but soon gave up as it seemed to irritate him. I planned to spend my waking hours doing anything he wanted around the farm. It was essential to have a place to stay and earn a little money until I could figure out who I was and where I came from.

I had my first look at Chinny at the dinner table. She had honey blonde hair in a ponytail and huge brown eyes. She looked at me often during the meal and I was quite uncomfortable at the end. Having both Papi and his daughter staring at me was a recipe for disaster. After learning about her high school efforts, I wasn't surprised she was moderately retarded. I would have to come up with a totally different teaching method if she was ever to get a diploma.

The other problem poor Chinny had was a receding chin. Her chin went back well behind her lower lip and made her retardation look even worse than it was. Her facial defect was undoubtedly evident at birth and Papi probably gave her the unkind nickname. Mama taught her how to cook and she was a happily involved sous chef at every meal. Chinny also did little chores around the farm and I felt she was happiest when she was busy. I can't imagine why the family thought a high school diploma was necessary and it certainly increased her stress.

The family went to bed about eight thirty because Jeff and his father were up two hours before sunrise to bring the three cows in for feeding and milking. Human hands did the chores and took quite a while. There were dozens of chickens that needed feeding and their eggs collected daily. Jeff told me his father also kept pigs as his field of yellow corn would take care of both them and the family. They killed one or two hogs every year for the meat. They kept one boar and half a dozen sows and made some money selling most of the piglets. They had a large hay field and sold the bales to neighbors who had livestock and horses. Mama and Chinny tended a garden that provided corn, cucumbers, melons, tomatoes, onions, beets and potatoes. Jeff told me he spent a whole summer digging a root cellar and mama kept potatoes, canned goods and cider in that cooler environment.

The day after I arrived, I got up with Jeff and had serious blisters on both hands at bedtime. I talked Jeff into lending me some gloves, although he didn't want to be too helpful in front of his father. Papi seemed to enjoy inflicting punishment on anyone who stepped out of line. I knew I would suffer the worst so when he ordered me to do something, I always called him "Sir" and obeyed instantly. After I wore Jeff's old shirt for four days running, Mama was kind enough to wash it for me. She gave me several more shirts, pants and socks from Jeff's high school collection. Shoes were a problem as both men's feet were bigger than mine. Jeff found an old pair of large boots with laces I could tighten and that did me for the whole time I was there.

Chinny was a different story. After supper, I sat at the dining room table with the woman and tried to get her to understand simple math, basic history and how to write an essay. It was all totally beyond her. After eleven years, the sight of a textbook would make her cry or have a hissy fit. I dreaded either one as Papi would come stomping into the dining room in a rage.

"What the hell you doin', Tom? Chinny ain't going to learn nothing when she's raising a ruckus. You get her settled down and start learning her something."

"Yessir. Right away."

I decided the only way to get her through high school was if I became her ghostwriter. After eleven years, the mail-order staffers probably had no previous connection with Chinny. The way she was behaving, Mama probably had not sent in any exams for years. I found a coloring book and set her to work on the dining room table with a few crayons while I prepared to take the senior examinations. In the evening, Papi was usually working on something in the barn and mama sat in the living room, watching a black and white television. Jeff had a 1936 Ford coupe, which he found in a junkyard, and was trying to get it in running order. My calm and reasonable arrangement with Chinny lasted almost a week.

I largely ignored Chinny beside me at the table with her crayons and concentrated on trying to figure out answers to test questions. The company mailed them to her years before. Happily, there were a number of texts in Chinny's room, most of them unopened. My study was laborious, stressful and took my total attention. I didn't notice Chinny began moving a little closer to me every day so I was shocked when I felt her hand high on my right thigh. I jerked upright and slid to my end of the bench. Chinny started to follow and I held up my hand to keep her at bay. If Papi ever saw this, I was a dead man.

"Chinny, you're supposed to be coloring your books. It is very bad to touch other people like that. It's okay to give your father, your mother and your brother a hug, but not me. Never do that again. Do you understand?"

"I like you, Tommy. It's okay if you like somebody. Papi likes Mama and he touches her all the time. Sometimes he whacks her."

I wasn't sure what Chinny meant by "whack." It could go either way. Secrets didn't exist in an un-insulated farmhouse. Regardless of her intelligence, there was no doubt her ovaries were working normally. I didn't want to make my cheating for the diploma obvious to the family, so I couldn't put Chinny in the living room with her mother or ask her to go to her room. I decided to put her on the other side of the table and try to be more aware of my surroundings.

During the first few days in the farmhouse, I spent some rare alone time upstairs in Jeff's bathroom. It was scary to look at myself in the mirror, but at the same time, intriguing. I didn't recognize my own face and wondered if it was different from my original. My eyes were brown and there were substantial lines, usually called "crow's feet" around the eyes. I prefer to call them "laugh lines" and that was supported by the lines around my mouth. My bottom lip was full which made me chuckle. I remembered my mother told me, on several occasions to, "Beware of a man with thin lips." Just thinking about my mother caused me to push back from the mirror. I didn't know who my mother was, yet I had the picture in my mind of an attractive slender woman.

Later visits to the mirror showed brown hair over a high forehead with a hint of gray at the temples. I could be anywhere from thirty-five to forty-five years old. For some reason, perhaps not quite ready for the next decade, I chose thirty-nine. When I began to get complaints from Jeff about having to wait to relieve himself, I ended my narcissistic bathroom habits.

When the mowing started, Papi drove a green John Deere tractor out of the barn. As soon as I saw it, I felt big arms squeezing my chest. When he stopped at the edge of the field I ran over and caressed the hood. The sound of the engine. That same green color. I shook with the memory of it. I went around to the front and looked down, searching for the crank opening.

Jeff appeared beside me and Papi started yelling at me. "Git the hell away from the tractor. You crazy?"

I shouted back, "Where do you put the crank?"

Jeff pulled me away from the front. "Daddy was cranking it when I was a little kid. You push a button now."

Papi shoved the gearshift forward and took his foot off the clutch. Jeff and I were about ten feet in front of scissoring blades that came at us like angry sharks. Jeff said, "Shit", and ran ahead at an angle to escape. I waited the three seconds it took for the moving teeth to get to me and then jumped over it. Papi never looked at us. Jeff and I exchanged looks and that said it all.

Jeff and I, using pitchforks, raked the cut stalks into piles. I kept asking myself if I'd ever been a farmer; my blistered hands said no. Papi hired a local teenager in the weekends to help. He worked hard for a couple of hours and then spend time plunging the pitchfork into the earth and examining the dirt on the end of the tines.

"Hey Dubo," I said, "whatcha looking for on the pitchfork?"

"Someday I'm going to get a mole. I've eaten squirrel, rabbit and a big rat, but I've never tasted mole. They're blind, you know, so they must be superheroes to find their way around under the ground. I think they'd be real tasty."

The kid was bigger than I so I didn't want to ask him about his nickname. He had big ears so maybe one of his classmates mispronounced "Dumbo." Just plain "dumb" was also a valid option. Anyway, his two hours was time I didn't have to sweat so much in that damned field.

There was a modest wind blowing and alfalfa seeds would fly into the air every time we moved a bunch of hay. It was not long before Jeff and I, who were shirtless and shiny with sweat, were covered with seeds and other fragments. Scratching only made the itch worse. Dubo kept his shirt on so maybe he was smarter than he seemed. We took a break at midday, drank a gallon of water, and ate a ham and cheese sandwich. No one dared go inside for a shower and dry clothes while Papi was mowing. He never stopped for anything. He had a couple of canteens strung over the gearshift. I didn't think they both held water as, at quitting time, the tracks of his tires began to wander off line.

The mowing took a week and then we pitchforked the piles of hay into the back of a large truck that Papi borrowed from a neighbor. He had to pay for the gas and throw in some money for the generosity. Getting rid of the hay took many more days because Papi, when the truck was full, drove it to several cattlemen's ranches. To fill up the truck with as much hay as possible, someone was in the truck bed to stomp it down. Everyone took turns, as this was a devilish place to work. We used an old door that we put down over several piles. We then stomped on it to pack the hay down. I think the door was oak as it weighed a ton. No problem for Jeff, or even Dubo, but I was the smallest one. I guessed I was about 5'10", but I didn't have near as much muscle. I put a bandanna around my mouth and nose because, stomping on the door, really made those seeds fly. We all got to coughing after a while, regardless of the protection.

We were now into October and Papi gave me thirty more days to get a high school diploma for Chinny. I was about halfway through the learning process and figured another month would do it. I had no idea what I was going to do after that, but he promised to pay me the going wage, seventy-five cents an hour, so I'd have a little cash. He also had me doing chores around the farm and I was Mama's dishwasher for many dinners. Mama loved my company and I loved hearing her stories. I did not realize there was a dark and evil spot in her life until the very end of my stay at the farm.

Chapter Three

Several weeks went by and Chinny continued to be a problem for me. She was a woman, still in her early thirties, who I didn't think had ever been with a man and probably had no idea how to please herself. She knew better than to come into my bedroom as Jeff was only a few feet away from me at night. However, she watched me when I wasn't in the fields or working with the animals. One day, when I was in the barn cleaning the metal buckets after milking, I saw a shadow darken the light reflecting off the pails. I turned and there was Chinny, the straw on the floor silencing her footsteps, about three feet behind me.

I got to my feet in a hurry and started toward the open barn door. Chinny was faster. She cut me off and pushed me into a pile of hay stacked against the wall. I fell backwards and the woman was on me in an instant. In the act of falling, she raised her skirt so her naked crotch landed right on my ding-a-ling. If I hadn't been wearing jeans, she would have impaled herself. I panicked. I had no idea where Papi was, but I knew he would go for the shotgun if he caught me.

"Get off me, Chinny. Your father will kill us both if he comes in here." I kept my voice to a hoarse whisper, hoping it was strong enough to intimidate her, but not to leak out of the barn.

"I'm tired of Papi. I want you."

My brain was turning in every direction. If I simply shoved her off me and ran out, she was certainly capable of yelling after me and alerting the family. I'd be done. Reasoning with her would take far too long, since she was on top of me and working hard at my belt buckle.

I pulled her head down and put my lips next to her ear. "Chinny, if we do this here we only have thirty seconds. It will be much nicer on a bed and we can take all night. Let's wait for a better time."

Chinny's hands stopped moving and she looked up at me. "Can we do it a lot?"

"Yes, four times and Papi won't be anywhere near us."

Her eyes glazed over and she looked up at the door, motionless. I knew she was thinking and I had to use all my willpower not to shove her off me and bolt for the house.

"When?"

"One week from today. I'll borrow Jeff's pickup and we'll go into town."

That did it. She didn't think about what would happen when the rest of the family saw Chinny and I driving off in the truck. She put her hands on my chest and pushed herself to a standing position. I got to my feet and brushed off all the seeds I could. I'd have to take my shirt off and shake it before I came out of the barn.

I gave Chinny a quick kiss on the cheek to seal the deal and said, "Now you walk back to the house and help Mama do something. Do not run. Act normal so nobody knows what we're going to do. Do you understand?"

I could see she wanted to kiss me so I turned around and picked up a bucket and held it between us. It always took a little time for Chinny to grasp concepts, and I started to sweat. Then she smiled and twirled around twice before leaving the barn. There were only two buckets, but I took a long time cleaning them. My fingers trembled and sweat kept dripping off my chin. I went back over our conversation several times because something was picking at me. "I'm tired of Papi" went round and round in my head, but I couldn't make it out. Hell, I was tired of him too. I took my time walking back to the house.

I deliberately chose one week, as my thirty days were over in five. I'd get Jeff to drive me to the bus station in town on day six. I'd be finished with the mail-order high school exam in twenty-four hours and Chinny should get her diploma back before I left. The test company assured me on the staff checked the answers and the results took no more than three days. I wasn't going to get all the questions right but seventy-five percent ought to do it. I had the bus schedule and planned to arrive at the terminal with no more than five minutes to spare. I'd tell Chinny I was only going with Jeff to help him bring back the groceries, but there was always the chance she'd panic and reveal our "plan" to be together the next day. Papi would come after me like a rabid hound dog.

The following morning, Chinny and I were in the dining room, pretending to work together. I was finishing the last few questions and I glanced up to see the woman, a little girl really, bright eyed and smiling at me. Her mouth was half-open and her tongue began to move out over her lower lip. She reached out to me across the table with her left hand and, if anyone entered the room, it would be obvious she was in heat.

"Not now, Chinny, in a few days. We have to keep this a secret."

Her facial features dropped, as if a puppeteer had released the strings. A wave of irritation passed across her face so I smiled and kissed the air in front of me to appease her. She relaxed and I was safe for the moment. Her moods were unpredictable and she was certainly capable of screaming at me if I did not constantly reassure her. I went back to the test questions and Chinny got up from the table and wandered off.

Before I darkened one square on the test, my long-standing concern for Chinny shot to the surface. When she slid her hand across the table, the loose sleeve of her shirt moved up her arm, almost to the elbow. There was a vivid red bruise around her wrist as if somebody had held it or pulled it with intent. I had wondered, especially in the warmer days, why she always wore long sleeves. Knowing Jeff for this length of time, I didn't think he was capable of hurting his sister. Papi was another matter.

Occasionally at night, the creaks in the creaking old house became louder and more rhythmic. I assumed the muted squealing that often accompanied this was Mama and Papi getting it on. Now I was not so sure. Chinny was simple and honest and, under the right circumstances, I resolved to ask her if she was being "whacked" by someone else in the house. Disgust flooded my face. I began to plan a little farewell gift for Papi on the day Jeff would take me into town. I'd stop off at the police station before boarding the bus.

Chapter Four

Two days went by before I found Chinny alone in the house. She was in the kitchen with her hands covered with flour, baking cookies. Mama was in the garden and Papi and Jeff had gone to town in the pickup.

"Your cookies are so good, Chinny. Are we going to have them after dinner tonight?"

"I guess so, Tommy. I have to wait 'til Mama gets back because she wants to put them in the oven herself."

"I'm looking forward to being with you on Saturday, Chinny."

The woman's face lit up and she stuck her chest out at me. I could see her nipples through the thin fabric. Her rolled up sleeves showed that the red marks on her left wrist had turned blue. On her right arm, there were also bruises high on her forearm. Her collar on the right side had slipped down as she was working the dough and the yellow of an old bruise peeked over the top. "Whacking" had multiple meanings where Chinny was concerned.

"Do you know how to 'whack', Chinny?

She looked up at me so abruptly her hands flew out of the big bowl and flour scattered over the table. "I don't like to talk about it."

"You can talk to me. You and I have secrets so it's safe to tell me."

Chinny stared at me with an intensity I'd never seen before, at least in the alien world I was in since climbing out of the river. Papi's gaze was ferocious, but this was different. The woman wasn't angry, it was more of a searching for trust.

"Papi said not to tell. He would hurt me bad."

I had my answer and I did not need to cause her any more pain. "You don't have to say anything. I'm sorry I asked the question. Now we can look forward to our time."

I saw the puppeteer was at work again as the corners of her mouth lifted and her eyes opened with anticipation. Mama was not capable of calling the sheriff, as she knew penalties would result. He might even kill her. Jeff was bigger and stronger than his father, but he was intimidated all of his life and had undoubtedly closed his ears to the squeaking.

When the mail came on Thursday, seventy-two hours was up and I was sure Chinny's certificate would arrive. It didn't. I called the Educational Mail Company and they said they'd received and scored it. They would not tell me whether I . . . I mean Chinny . . . passed or what the score was, but said the results were on the way. I didn't want to stay in this place any longer than I had to, but Papi made the rules.

At breakfast on Friday, we were all sitting around the table and I felt safe in speaking up. "Good morning, Papi, I'd appreciate it if you would pay me today. Jeff is going to drive me to the bus station tomorrow." We'd agreed on seventy-five cents an hour after Jeff told me it was the accepted minimum.

"You got big ones, kid, I'll hand you that. You're not finished here 'til Chinny gets her high school diploma. You work pretty good for a city boy, but we made a deal. If it don't come, you get nothin'."

"I called the company and it should be . . ."

"Changed my mind, Tom. If it don't come, you ARE going to get something. You and me behind the barn."

"I'm not going anywhere, Papi, even if you pay me today. I can't get to town unless you or Jeff drive me."

Jeff said, "He's worked very hard, Papi, and spent every evening working with Sis."

"You stay out of it, boy. This between Tom and me. He got weekends off and Chinny paid for his room and board."

I couldn't believe Jeff kept talking. "Tom worked most weekends too. It's not fair to cheat him." I thought he'd get out from under someday.

Papi stood up, leaned forward, put his hands on the table and glared at his son. I did not want Jeff to do battle while I was in the house. I'd be too tempted to do something I'd regret. I said, "I've been here for forty-nine days and although I worked more, I'm only charging you for eight hours a day, five days a week. That comes to $294"

"I'll pay you $200 and that's a bargain, son. Take it or leave it."

Jeff put his hands on the table and I could see his muscles tensing. Before I could step in, Mama came to my side with a huge stack of pancakes surrounded by homemade link sausages. I knew she had an herb garden and I could smell the rosemary, oregano and sage in the sausages. She stood at the end of the table with the food steaming in front of her, making no motion to set the platter down. I knew Papi could smell it too and everyone at the table knew Mama's cooking was his Achilles' heel. In the end, it was Chinny who broke the ice.

"Please, Daddy."

"All right. I feel generous today and I'll pay you what you said. But you're getting nothin' if Chinny don't get her diploma."

I could hear muscles sighing with relief as everyone relaxed and watched as Mama put the platter down at the head of the table. There was no further conversation as mouths and tongues were busy with other things. No one wanted to do much after such a feast and everyone, except me, settled down in the living room. I went out and fed the chickens to show everyone I was a standup guy. When I came back, Papi went into his bedroom and came back with my money in a paper bag.

"Here it is, boy. I'm going to keep it until I see a diploma. After that you can have it and Jeff will get you on a bus." He looked puzzled for a moment, and said, "Where you going to?"

That was the question I had no way of answering. I did not even know where I came from. "I'm going to look at the schedule and find someplace I remember. Maybe if I see things I know my memory will come back."

Papi rolled his eyes and shook his head, but the others all looked at me with various emotions: Mama with genuine caring, Jeff with a sense of loss and Chinny licking her lips with anticipation.

At the end of the day, it was ninety-six hours since I mailed in the test questions.

Chapter Five

It was Saturday, the day I was supposed to leave. Chinny, whenever the rest of the family was elsewhere, would look at me and rub her crotch. Shaking my head at her did no good and my anxiety level soared. I must have lost several pounds of sweat by the time the mail arrived at noon. Mama went out to the mailbox and started back with a paper, a couple of catalogs and an official looking envelope. She shook her head at me halfway back to the house.

I was terrified. I had to get my money and get away. Chinny would not be able to contain herself if I told her we had to wait until Monday. She had no understanding of my agreement with Papi. She would scream bloody murder and reveal everything if I broke my promise. Papi was itching to rearrange my face and he would use any excuse to pull me behind the barn. Maybe Jeff would save me, but I couldn't count on it. It would require him to do battle with his father, which I don't think he was ready for yet.

Mama came into the kitchen and sliced open the envelope. I was still standing by the front door, paralyzed by my situation. She said, "Good news. The bank's not going to raise their interest rates on our loan for next year."

It would be rude not to say something, but there was a storm going off in my head. I muttered, "Nice," and started for the stairs.

I heard mama say, "Oops, musta got stuck in the catalog." There was a buff colored envelope on the floor and she bent over and picked it up. I leaned back against the wall and found myself sliding down until I was squatting. The knife made a zipping sound as it cut through the flap. My elbows were on my knees and I covered my face with my hands. I thought the darkness would help, but it didn't. "Well, lookee here. It's from the testing company." Mama's face was working as she was reading and, after a while, she looked down at me, frowning.

I came up with a plan. Papi always carried his keys with him on a ring, which he had fastened to his belt with a thin chain. I'd never get them. However, I knew where Jeff kept his car key and I'd wait a couple of minutes, take his truck, and head for town. Before I left, I'd take the distributor out of Papi's pickup and then pull the phone out of the wall. Hopefully, a bus to anywhere would show up before Papi ran six miles to the next farm. With any luck, he'd have a heart attack on the way.

Mama was shaking my shoulder. "You in a coma or something? I've been talking to you."

"Sorry, I've been thinking about stuff."

"I don't know why these company people can't speak plain. It's about Chinny, but they talk about college and her future. Can you figure it out?"

Standing, I read the letter over and over until my knees gave out and I was sitting on the floor. Educational Mail Company, among the verbiage, was pleased to inform me Chinny was now a high school graduate and she could frame the enclosed diploma. They went on and on about using their company to educate Chinny further so she could become a college graduate. I could see why Mama got muddled. I stood and teased the envelope out of mama's hand and looked inside. There was another paper, a diploma with a lacy blue border. I turned it around and pointed out Chinny's name. Mama let out a whoop and ran out to the barn to show Papi and Jeff.

Jeff came in and shook my hand; I thought my fingers would break. It took a while for Papi to come in and I'm sure he was disappointed not to have an opportunity to alter my features. He disappeared up the stairs, came back with the paper bag, and handed it to me.

"Here's your money, boy. Now get the fuck out of my house."

I ran up the stairs, counted the money and offered Jeff some for his clothes and boots.

"Nope. Don't see reason to take money for stuff I don't use no more."

"You're a good man, Jeff. I'm counting on you to look after Mama and your sister. It's not Chinny's fault that she was born a little short. She is a decent person and needs protection from persons who might want to take advantage. I know you love her and will not let that happen."

Jeff's head dropped and I could see his mouth tense until his lips turned white. I knew he got the message. He never said a word, but when he looked up into my eyes, he gave a nod so subtle, I would've missed it if I'd blinked.

My bus would be there at 3:10 and it was almost 2 o'clock. Jeff gave me more of his things in an old tote bag. I hugged Mama and shook Chinny's hand. She held it while she stared at me and smiled. I spoke to her nicely in a loud voice, congratulating her on her high school diploma. I whispered, "Later," to her before Jeff and I got into his truck. I dreaded the scene that would occur when Jeff got back without me. I should be a hundred miles down the road by the time Papi roared into the bus terminal parking lot.

After we arrived, I told Jeff to spend some time in the town, maybe have a beer and do some shopping before he went back home. He was happy to do that as he was usually with his father and it was all business and no fun. I had the number for the Society for the Prevention of Cruelty to Children at the farm and after Jeff left me, I

24

found a public telephone. The woman on the other end was all ears once I described the marks on Chinny's wrists and the bruises on her neck and arms. I told her what the poor woman called the sex act and that she told me who was whacking her. I made sure Jeff was totally in the clear.

Although I was confident in the SPCC, I wanted to make sure Papi got his due and decided, in the ten minutes before the bus arrived, to tell the sheriff what was going on at the farm. Halfway through my story, I was in trouble. The sheriff's face darkened. "I've been sheriff here for a long time and the man you describe was a friend of mine for fifty years. Went to school together. I cannot believe he do anything like that. However, since you've worked there for a while and have an opinion, I'm going to follow up. The best way to do that is to put you in my cruiser and take you back to the farm. We can sit down with Papi and discuss it together."

I knew he thought I'd been boning Chinny myself and he'd leave me there for Papi to mete out justice. Even if he suspected his friend of fifty years, he was not going to do anything about it. After all, Chinny wasn't normal and probably enjoyed it. Right?

"Great idea, Sheriff. I was hoping you'd suggest that. I came into town with Jeff for a little shopping and a quick beer. I want to go back with you so I can tell you more, but I need to let Jeff know so he won't wait here all afternoon. I don't want that big boy mad at me." I went around the sheriff's desk and he was obviously surprised at finding himself shaking my hand and listening to me saying, "Bless you" over and over.

I'd been into town several times and I knew the name of Jeff's favorite bar. It was close by, in the opposite direction from the bus terminal. I gave the Sheriff the name of another bar, some distance away and told him I'd be back as soon as I spoke to Jeff. I said I could not wait to tell him what I saw Papi doing to Chinny in the barn. I could almost hear the Sheriff's mouth watering with the expectation of a steamy story he'd share with his deputies. Many chuckles, right?

It must have been sensational acting because the sheriff was still standing behind his desk when I left the building. I headed to Jeff's bar and told him about my visit to the sheriff. He assured me he would act very surprised when you never returned and then he gave me a bear hug and shoved me out the door. I doubled back out of sight of the sheriff's office and got to the bus station with minutes to spare. When we first got to the town, I asked Jeff to buy a ticket with the name Tom Hunter going north to Grangeville and I bought one with a fake name going to Boise. The wait before the bus took off for Boise was agonizing. I pretended to have trouble tying my shoelaces until we were outside the town limits. I hoped the sheriff would think I was heading to Washington or Montana, which would be much safer than Boise. He, of course, could easily call the bus terminal in the capital and have me arrested. I was sure he couldn't wait to teach me a lesson in a jail cell before we headed back to the farm where he would hand me over to Papi.

Chapter Six

I kept looking at the cheap watch I'd bought in the station and estimating the miles from the city. After forty-five minutes without the sound of a siren behind us, I figured I would at least get to Boise. Knowing Papi, he would have no trouble persuading his badged schoolmate to follow me to hell if necessary. The bus line only went in two directions, to Boise and away from it. I'd try to lose myself in the city and then take some form of transportation north. I had some money, but still no ID. If the police were waiting at the Boise bus terminal, I was dead. I needed a plan B.

There were only two more stops ahead for me and I was sitting in the front of the bus, not knowing what was going on behind me. I knew there was an airline type lavatory in the back and I got up and walked down the aisle slowly, as if I needed a new hip. It was only a third full with passengers and I searched for a good candidate. I spent a minute in the lavatory thinking about how I was going to do it and hoped for a little luck.

No one turned around or paid any attention when I sat down next to an older man who had taken the last seat in the bus. He was leaning against the window, snoring with his mouth open. The fellow was wearing rough clothes and a worn leather jacket, which he'd unbuttoned to get more comfortable. I eased closer to him and put my head back, looking at the other passengers and the driver's rearview mirror. There shouldn't be a problem if I kept my head visible. I moved six inches to the right and stretched my hand into the chest pocket of the jacket. I thanked lady luck as I pulled the man's wallet out and searched through his cards. My new friend, Jessup, had a driver's license, a local bowling club card, a union card and one for Blue Cross insurance. The license was in a sleeve with a plastic window and I knew he would use that to show the police. I took his bowling and medical cards and carefully replaced his wallet. Since sitting, I pretended to be talking with my sleeping friend and after I got up, I gave him a wave goodbye, walked forward, and resumed my seat. Would taking the front seat again turn out to be mere luck, or did something else have a hand in my destiny?

The sheriff was good at his job and, after sending deputies racing to stop the northbound bus without finding me, he alerted Boise about a fleeing rapist. As we approached the terminal, I saw three cruisers parked outside and when the bus stopped, there were six cops by the door, two with drawn weapons. I made sure I was the first in line so the officers could see me limping toward the exit. I stepped down seemingly oblivious and then looked up at the armed group. I said, "Bless me, Lord", and showed them trembling open hands. I looked back at the bus with my eyes wide, hopefully indicating to the police someone still on the bus was the one they were looking for.

The police told the rest of the passengers everyone's ID would be checked and to form a line. I pulled out my bowling club and insurance cards.

"Show me your driver's license."

"I gots epilepsy, 'fore my teens. Couldn't never drive." I said this in a halting high voice that suggested epilepsy was not my only problem. Chinny had no idea how much our relationship helped me. "My last fits was more than two years ago. Could you help me get a license?"

I heard one officer say to another, "Make sure to check the driver's ID, we're looking for a 'Tom Hunter'."

My interrogator looked at my dull pleading eyes and then down at my cards. As he handed them back to me, he said, "Good luck to you, fella."

I felt badly for the old man as I could imagine the hurdles he would have to jump over to get a replacement for his medical card. He'd be the last one in line, but as soon as the police realized there were two passengers with the same name, they'd close down the city. I walked quickly to the Lost and Found and told the woman in charge I'd found these on the ground by the last bus. I suggested she make a public announcement if Jessup didn't come into her office in the next five minutes. It did not matter if she could ID me as the cops already had a good look. I took off my green jacket and held it, inside out, over my arm as I strode to the nearest exit. Hold on, getting in a taxi would be a mistake. I walked a block before I realized what I needed to do. Nobody liked a rapist and the police would soon close down the city exits and have plain-clothes officers covering bus terminals and the airport. All taxi drivers and car rental agencies would be on the lookout. I only had a few minutes to think this out.

I went back into the terminal by a different entrance and bought a ticket under a false name heading north. I'd have to wait thirty-seven minutes for the next bus, but I couldn't imagine a rational rapist wouldn't want to get lost in a city with almost two hundred thousand people. To a criminal, that seemed a lot safer than never leaving the terminal. If they did check inside, it would be cursory. I bought a New Yorker magazine and put Jeff's green windbreaker under my seat. I made no effort to conceal myself when I saw a cop crossing fifty feet in front of me and entering the restroom. He came out quickly, looked around, and left. If I didn't get an ulcer now, I'd never get one.

As I waited for the bus, I looked at the cover of the New Yorker and wondered why I picked that. Wouldn't Life magazine have been more appropriate? Was I only trying to throw the police off my trail or was I involved with publishing, writing or journalism? The newspapers said the date was 1955 and I tried to guess when I was born. The number didn't help. My memories were tingling, but I did not have an answer.

Many hours later, and a jerky dozing on the bus, I arrived in Glasgow, Montana. It was a town of about three thousand people with the requisite retail shops, healthcare clinic, basic entertainment and restaurants. There was a rumor an airbase was going to be built to house B-52s, but construction hadn't started. Too bad for me. It seemed everyone in the town had a job and, after two days of searching, I wondered what brain fart had brought me to this place. My sleep the night before was intermittent and sweaty.

I decided to leave the next day and go west. It was Sunday morning and I was having breakfast in the café across the street from my motel. I could not help bitching to the waitress about my plight. She and her husband owned the café and she said he was the foreman of a construction job in Howes. It had something to do with school renovation and he couldn't find enough workers. He came home on the weekends and, as chance would have it, he was in the back restocking shelves.

"I hear you're looking for a job. Done any construction work?"

"I'm a farmhand and used to hard work. I'm as good with a hammer as anyone." I had a deep tan and muscles now, especially around the arms and shoulders. I held out my hands and they were thick with callus. "Things are always going wrong on a farm and I've done a bit of plumbing, painting and electrical."

"Well, it's my lucky day. I thought I'd have to settle for a truant teenager. We're doing an addition to the school to accommodate a gym and equipment room. There's only a few hundred folks live up there so athletics is very important for the kids. It gets well below zero in the winter. Now they won't have to travel to play basketball. Call me Lomus"

"Lucky for me too. I was planning to leave tomorrow. What's the pay?"

"I'd pay seventy-five cents an hour for you, unless you're putting me on." He gave me a look and I knew what that meant.

"We're taking a chance on each other, Lomus. I have an idea we're both going to be very happy at days end. Name's Tom."

Chapter Seven

Howes was north of Glascow, about twelve miles from the Canadian border. It was a paved road for the first twenty miles, then dirt. There was a ditch on each side of the road and I could see the builders had simply scraped up the earth on each side and piled it up in the middle. A steamroller must have spent considerable time packing it down. As we drove through town, I saw a gas station, three bars and a combination grocery and hardware store. The men apparently hung around in the town for entertainment and the women went to Glascow. The school was an easy quarter mile walk from most of the little houses scattered about. I noticed sizable garden plots behind some homes and several barns in the distance.

The construction company had put two long trailers and one short one next to the school. The first long trailer contained a table for eight and a kitchen with a large storage area. The second big one held eight bunkbeds with a space in the middle for clothes storage. There was no heat. The smaller trailer had steps going up to separated commodes with sinks and showers. The workers brought water in from the school and there was a thirty-gallon propane fired water heater. I was the fifth construction worker and it was going to be a long winter unless the other four knew what they were doing. I had not lied to Lomus, but I had not done any actual construction work.

I was not fond of the cold, especially at 20° or 30° below zero. The sleeping quarters was not going to be a happy place.

"Most of the guys ought to be back by now, if they didn't get too sloshed over the weekend. If I say it's a mixed bag, I'm including both of us."

"Lomus, your sense of humor may be the saving grace for me."

We were both chuckling when we entered the bunkhouse. A short wiry man in his early thirties slid off a top bunk and landed deftly on the floor. He had a cast on his right arm running from below the elbow and including his hand. The tips of his fingers look like little red marbles.

"Welcome to heaven, Boss. How far did you have to go to find that geezer?"

Lomus said, "To hell and back, Dicker. Wake up boys, this is Tom. Now we can cut our working hours to fourteen." There were four men in the trailer and they all turned to look at me. The man in the bottom bunk, under Dicker, was enormous. The man everyone called "Heavy" must have weighed over three hundred pounds and had a happy grin on his face as we shook hands. Ian was a tall blonde man with smooth skin, serious eyes, and fine features. He turned out to be the smartest and quietest of the bunch. The cook, nicknamed Sossie, wore a soiled T-shirt and an open fleece jacket. I learned his nickname came from the SOS branding of his cooking: same old shit.

As I was standing there, as uncomfortable as an outsider can be, a memory flashed in front of me. I was in high school and my math teacher, Mr. Muldoon, was sitting at his desk. Above him, with a hook in its mouth, was a two foot long stuffed fish. Underneath was a plaque that read: *"This fish would never have been caught if it kept its mouth shut."* I'd kept that lesson with me all my life and I simply smiled and nodded at everyone.

Dicker asked me what I did for a living and I told him farming, but I was tired of dirt.

"Then you've come to the wrong place, Tommy. We're the dirtiest bunch of guys you've ever met." Gruffaws all around.

I hated the name "Tommy," but I made sure to smile. "What did you do to bust your hand up?"

"I was on the boxing team in the Army until I got out six months ago. Twelve years is long enough to take sass from bastards with an extra stripe. Busted my hand in a bar a month ago when someone with no stripes got in my face. Not too smart to keep getting up after I broke his jaw. Hit the side of his head with my last one and paid the price." Dicker waved his hand around, doing hooks and uppercuts. "Comes off in two weeks and it'll be stiff and sore." He looked at me at an angle. "If you want to take me on, that would be a good time to do it."

The other men were looking at me with varying expressions, some amused, some worried. "Dicker, I wouldn't sass you unless I had four stars on my shoulders." Dicker laughed and put his left arm around me. I could see the rest of the crew relaxing.

There wasn't much to do in Howes unless you liked to drink and play pool. Three of the crew had cars, but the rest had to hitch a ride if they wanted a night or two in Glascow on the weekends. I'd never played much pool and some of the fellas in the bar were quite good. I began to study the angles and was better than most by the time we finished the job. *I wondered if I'd studied geometry.* I forced myself to like beer as nobody ordered martinis or whiskey sours.

Friendly physical competition was the off–time activity of our group. This included Indian wrestling, arm wrestling and wrist wrestling. I had slender arms so everyone beat me at arm matches. I was quite good with the Indian style as I had long arms and good balance, but Ian was the ultimate champion. Heavy was a lot of fun. We used to shadowbox, with Dicker yelling instructions. I was much too quick for him, but if he grabbed me and forced me down it was all over. He would sit on me, all three hundred and twenty-five pounds, and laugh as I squirmed helplessly. I laughed harder than he did.

For some reason, as I did not have big muscular forearms, I excelled at wrist wrestling. Perhaps it was the psychology involved, which no one else seemed to get. Two men would stand facing each other and interlock their fingers high in front of them. The winner was the first one able to bend an opponent's hand back. The nerves to the fingers run along the sides, and when each competitor is straining as hard as he can, the pressure squeezes those fibers. The pain begins slowly, but becomes excruciating and opponent's faces grimace with the agony and effort. I keep my face totally bland except for a slight smile. Almost everyone is right-handed so I simply hold steady with my left and, in a minute or so, slowly increase the power in my right. I never lost. The whole crew was as amazed as I was.

My knack for wrist wrestling almost doomed me when we all, except Sossie, went into Glascow for a weekend. None of us made much money so Dicker suggested he and I get one room in the cheapest hotel in town. It was not easy for either of us to sleep well in one double bed without colliding from time to time. Dicker's power with his fists, in spite of his size, kept everyone from asking if we were gay. In the evening, we would go to a bar, sit around with beers, boast and tell jokes. It was fun until Lomus pointed out a tall very muscular young man two tables away. Everyone called him "Gravy" and he was the fist-fighting king of the region. If he challenged you, you had to fight him outside in the street. I think his nickname had something to do with cemeteries, not sauce. Nobody wanted to be called "chicken" so Ian was forced to fight him a couple of weeks before I joined the team. It was no contest. Ian told me he hit the King in the head as hard as he could, but the guy didn't even blink. Two or three blows later, Iain found himself on his back, trying to figure out what happened.

Dicker could be nasty when drinking and this was one of those times. He got up from the table, went over to Gravy, and told him I was a champion wrist wrestler who had never lost a bout. The tall guy turned his head slowly and looked over at me. I was five inches shorter, sixty pounds lighter and twice his age. Although he must have found this amusing, his only change of expression was a brief raise of his eyebrows. He rose very slowly, walked into the empty area in the middle of the bar, and beckoned to me. I tried to figure out whether his ho-hum movements reflected supreme confidence or was an attempt at intimidation. As I rose, I hoped his brain was not as fast as his reflexes.

All talk ceased in the bar and everyone looked at Gravy awaiting his little challenger. I admit I was scared because I felt I was doomed if I won and doomed if I didn't. Regardless, I wasn't about to throw the match. We faced off and I put on my bland mask with the slightest of smiles, quite a contrast to his growing scowl. We interlaced our fingers and waited an instant before bearing down. I think Gravy thought my wrist would bend quickly and when it didn't happen, his lips whitened over his teeth. I stared expressionless, straight into his eyes throughout the match and his frown deepened. His eyes would wander off and sometimes close tightly. As the bout progressed, it was all I could do with my left to hold off his attack. I began to ramp up the grip on my right and this increased the pain in my fingers to where it was almost unbearable. I kept going by reminding myself Gravy was feeling the same thing. Sweat drops began appearing on his forehead and some were running down his face and into his eyes. His left wrist was trembling as it began to weaken and I knew I had him. I could tell by his eyes he was furious and I hoped he wouldn't kick me after he knocked me down. The silence in the room thickened.

He jerked his fingers away from mine so quickly that I remained standing with my hands in the air as if I was surrendering. He knew he had lost and wanted to stop it before he was humiliated in front of his neighborhood buddies. Regardless, everyone in the room knew who won.

"Wanna arm wrestle?"

"Sure." What choice did I have?

It took him about three seconds to slam the back of my hand onto the oak table. I'm sure he enjoyed the audible "cracking" sound when my knuckles hit the wood. I was tempted to say, in a loud voice, "We're tied now, Gravy, let's Indian wrestle for the championship." I knew if I happened to win, the next contest would be out in the street so I said nothing and returned to the table. Dicker slapped me hard on the back and Iain shook my hand. We all had another beer and that was good enough.

Chapter Eight

Our whole crew hustled because the cold had settled in—it was late October—and being active kept us from freezing to death. There was one more week to go and Dicker said he was tired of Glasgow on the weekends and had another idea. It would be a celebration of our friendship and finishing the job.

"I have a surprise for you, Tommy. We're going to Coyote Cairn."

"What's there?"

"We're going to get laid."

I was stunned. Surely I had been with a woman, but I couldn't remember who or when. Or even if. Maybe I was married. Children?"

"What's the matter, Tommy? You a virgin or something?"

The truthful answer was yes, I was a virgin in my amnesic life. I was not about to tell Dicker about my cold aquatic entrance into this alien world, but I had to say something. "You know some women over there?"

"I know a lot of women over there. You can have your pick."

I was going to a whorehouse. I felt my neck stiffen as a list of sexually transmitted diseases flashed into my mind: syphilis, gonorrhea and herpes. I knew about all of them. Maybe I worked in some government lab.

I felt a shove on my right shoulder that spun me halfway around and I fought for balance. Dicker was standing in front of me with a frown and a raised upper lip. "What's with you, man? You are not paying attention to me. I'm giving you a surprise opportunity and you're off in another world."

Dicker had no idea how right he was, but I didn't want to upset him. If he had given me more time I probably wouldn't have been pressured into a quick answer. "Sounds great, unless I come down with syphilis." I laughed to make him think I was joking, which I wasn't.

"We'll leave after dinner. It's fifteen bucks." He turned away with a sour look on his face.

Surely, the "ladies of the night" weren't all the same price. I wondered if a twenty bucker would be safer. I'd pay her thirty bucks NOT to tell Dicker we didn't mate. However, that might hurt her feelings and she would tell Dicker anyway. I didn't eat much dinner, but that didn't set off any alarms as everyone knew I didn't like Spam.

Dicker had a 1936 Ford coupe and I envied him. It was repainted maroon with the original eight-cylinder engine and seats. It was the love of his life and he spent a significant percentage of his paycheck upgrading the engine and making sure his custom muffler sounded ferocious. When he turned the key, you feared for your life. I concluded some men believe the hallmark of an alpha male was how loud a noise he could make. It didn't matter what made the noise. It could be a muffler, a radio or a rectum. Or all three.

Dicker was drinking much of the afternoon and he had two beers with dinner. He seemed irritated about something. It's usually a mistake to get a boxer mad so I didn't feel I could get out of the evening's entertainment. I got in the passenger seat sweating bullets and tried to act thrilled. I could not have gotten excited even if a naked Marilyn Monroe was sitting on my lap. Dicker started out driving fifty miles an hour on the dirt road to Coyote Cairn. He was hunched over the wheel and breathing through his mouth. Every so often, he turned and looked at me with spooky eyes. The muffler note changed a little bit and continued to go up. The slight smile on his face scared the hell out of me.

I raised both fists in the air. "I love this car, Dicker. If I had the money, I'd offer you anything you wanted."

He looked over, nodded vigorously, and pushed the speed up to seventy miles an hour. I broadened my smile and pounded on the dashboard. I felt the car suddenly decelerating and wondered if he'd passed out.

"You're a ballzie guy, Tommy. If you'd said anything to me I'd have hit ninety. These dirt roads are a bitch, but that makes it more fun. I'm going to take a little nap in the back and let you drive for a while; it's only another hour. Just before you get to the town, there's a big white sign. Take the second left and keep driving for a mile or so. It's a big green house on the right with a revolving door. You can't miss it." We both laughed at his door joke.

With Dicker asleep behind me, I could enjoy driving this classic car. It had excellent acceleration and good brakes. I kept the speed at fifty. The muffler note took me back a few decades. Did I have a hot rod when I was a kid? An hour later, there were cars on a paved road. I made a left two streets after the white sign and drove through mostly uninhabited countryside until I saw a glow in the distance. I expected a large Victorian house lit by red and yellow neon signs. I was wrong.

I smelled smoke before I saw the fire. It was a large house painted green, half consumed by flames. There were men and women scurrying back and forth carrying luggage, boxes and bags of stuff. There was some furniture on the grass and women hugging each other. The absence of firefighting equipment was startling until you realized most of the volunteer fireman probably had wives. There was no way a wife would allow her husband to rescue such a temptation.

I allowed myself a moment of delight and relief before I shook Dicker awake.

"Dammit, Dicker. The place is on fire."

"Wha . . . Jesus . . . lookit those bitches go. A sight like this is worth more than fifteen bucks." There was silence for at least a couple of minutes while we both looked at something we would never see again. It was what an emergency room must look like: frenetic activity that appeared to be total chaos but was, in actuality, quite organized. The local firemen, no doubt.

"Move over. Let's go home."

I searched for something to say to Dicker, something that would please him and keep him calm so he wouldn't roll the car over on the way back. "I'm grateful for your trusting me. In the end, you got a nap and I got a chance to drive this wonderful car. It was a strange kind of adventure, my friend."

"Shit, what am I gonna do now?"

"Take a shower, soap your hand and dream."

Dicker started shaking and then backhanded my left shoulder, hard. He had done this before so I knew it was how he bonded. He began laughing so vigorously I had to take the wheel to keep the car on the road.

"You're really something, Tommy. You got a way with words. You read a lot I guess. I'm not smart, but I know when something should be appreciated."

"When we get back, Dicker, the beer's on me."

Chapter Nine

Two days later, we finished the school's sports addition and I rode with Dicker back to Glasgow. We hit three bars until Dicker could hardly walk. I put him to bed at our usual hotel and joined him an hour later. I had one glass too many myself as I thought it would help me sleep. I learned the hard way that no one sleeps when they're dizzy.

The bus to Spokane pulled in at nine fifteen the next morning and this time I took the last seat in the back. It was a long trip, with multiple stops and other drivers along the way. I had money now, but still no ID. That was a priority and I spent a lot of time stretched out on the back seat figuring out how to get a driver's license and birth certificate. The idea that came to me was risky, but desperate times required desperate solutions. I had put on a good show at the farm and with Dicker so I had some confidence in my acting ability.

The first thing I noticed about Spokane in February was it was warmer than Howes; 35° above zero is a lot better than 10° below. I hoped it had a comparable crime rate compared to other Washington cities, as I needed to locate a particularly bad spot downtown. In the bus terminal, I put most of my money and Jeff's high school clothes in a small duffel and placed it in a keyed locker. I then went to a ticket window and asked the woman behind the glass what parts of the town to avoid. She gave me an earful. It was about midday and I ate a ham and cheese sandwich with ice tea at a nearby bistro. I got a map with bus routes and headed to the city's most dangerous location.

My plan would save me a lot of trouble and avoid the risk of arrest on an Idaho warrant. However, it would be dumb luck if I ran across the right people wandering the streets in the middle of the afternoon. I hadn't shaved for five days on purpose and I wore torn jeans, Jeff's extra-large T-shirt with a skull on it and a John Deere baseball cap. In the "place to be avoided", there were homeless people in doorways and mixed groups on street corners. My confidence wavered and it was all I could do to keep my hands steady. For what I needed, I figured the biggest group would have the most information. I took a deep breath and sauntered over to a mean-looking bunch.

"Hey, fellas, I need a little help. Worth your while."

The conversation among the seven mostly young men ceased fifty feet before I got close enough to say anything more. Every one of them looked the same. They had that "What the fuck" expression on their faces. I stopped ten feet before I reached them and broke the ice. "Got jumped and lost my ID. Just as well, 'cause there's a warrant out. Know anybody who can get me a new license and turn me into a law-abiding citizen?" Sweat ran down my back.

The biggest and oldest guy chuckled, sauntered over, and got in my face. "I'm Big Boy and you look like a pussy, little man. Who'd need to put out a warrant on you?"

I feared I was making a big mistake, but I stood my ground and brought my hands up to eye level, palms in his face. The thick calluses turned white and bulged out.

"Whoa, watcha been doing with those beauties?"

"Folks call me 'Farmer' way south of here. I dig holes in the ground, plant stuff, and sometimes it grows. Sometimes it don't." I let the implication hang in the air for a while and then said, "If one of you guys is undercover, I'm in deep shit."

Big Boy jerked his head at the group and they all came over. "Which one of us is undercover, huh?" He had a broad grin on his face and everyone laughed. "Lobo, what's the name of that dude gets IDs for the new bitches?"

Lobo looked over at me with a scowl. "You talking 'bout Pinny?" He turned to Big Boy and said, "You trust him?"

"Show him your hands, Farmer. No cop, even weightlifters, looks like that." He turned to me. "We know a guy. What's it worth?"

"Thirty for you and half that for Lobo." I could see they were about to laugh so I added, "and I'll take care of anyone bothering you. Nothing will grow."

I could see the attitude change in the eyes and the smiles vanished. The large man nodded and said, "You ain't going anywhere for a while." I understood it wasn't a question. He squinted at me. "Might be some work for you." He put two fingers, none to gently, into Lobo's chest. "Go get Pinny and bring him to the cave."

Lobo, walked off with another guy and muttered, "He don't look like no hitman, Snag."

"That's the beauty of it. He can get up close and personal. Can't imagine what he does with those hands. Maybe a wire."

"More likely a shovel." They laughed and pushed each other, looking back at Big Boy.

I thought to myself, "In for a Pinny, in for a pound." Thank God for the farm, the thick calluses and muscular hands were tickets to places I would never get to otherwise.

The cave was a two-bedroom apartment on the third floor of a decrepit residential building with no other tenants. I could see why the gang had chosen it as there were three bolt locks on the steel front door, a fire escape in the back, and stairs to the roof. Someone had taken a sledgehammer and knocked a two foot opening in the low brick wall that surrounded the roof. It was about a dozen feet to the flat roof of the adjacent building. There was a reinforced fifteen-foot board propped up against the low wall next to the opening. It was obviously the means of getting quickly to the next building, and someone would remove the "bridge" from the other side.

Pinny arrived at the apartment fifteen minutes later. I expected a small bespectacled man of advanced age, but the forger was exactly the opposite. He was young, two inches taller than I and a hundred pounds heavier. He was sweating which I could relate to, having been in the gang's company for a while. I wondered if Big Boy told him I was an assassin. I couldn't help chuckling at that.

Lobo looked at me with evil little eyes. "What's so funny?"

"I was thinking Pinny looks like a former client of mine." I made a big show of looking at my hands, flexing and contracting my fingers. "Someone that big takes a lot of effort."

Pinny looked at me oddly and said, "What do you need?"

"I'd like a driver's license and birth certificate. You can throw in a National Farmers Union card for the pleasure of my company." I ignored the titters from the group in the room.

"Licenses are tough and expensive."

"Show me one of your licenses, Mr. Pinny. I don't expect it to pass muster at the Department of Motor Vehicles, but every other spot."

Pinny suggested we all go to his place, which was number 64 in the same neighborhood. Once there, he opened a folder and extracted three licenses. In a casual inspection, they seemed identical. After studying them for a while, I was able to pick out the two forgeries. "Not bad, Mr. P, let's do it. My current name is Tom Hunter and I was born thirty-nine years ago in Chicago, on June 2. Just so you know, I'm going to be working with Big Boy and his friends doing a little job or two. I think that qualifies me for the family discount."

Pinny glanced from me to Big Boy and his face contracted when he saw the quick nod. I had no idea what forgers charged and I only had two hundred and fifty dollars. It was a good time to step in.

"I don't carry my wad with me, but I'll bring forty dollars down whenever you're ready."

"I'm afraid my price is . . ."

"My friends call me, 'Farmer', and you do not want me digging in your garden. I will owe you a favor, but I am not going to pay you any more money."

Pinny, squirming in his seat, looked at Big Boy appealingly. He sighed when he saw the head shake and pointed to a chair set up in front of a tripod. He took my picture with a Polaroid Land camera, got my signature and we discussed the birth certificate and the union card. He told me to come back in two days and I shook hands with him and Big Boy. The group wanted to take me to a pizza place and get me laid, but I told the group I was having my "period." Humor works wonders in all sorts of situations.

As I started for the bus stop to find a place to stay uptown, I didn't notice Lobo writing something in a little notebook.

Chapter Ten

I awoke early the next morning, anxious. At first, I thought it was a dream, but it was not. It was a nightmare. How could I be so stupid as to give Pinny my "real" name? At least it was a real name in this alternative universe of non-memory. Not only could the sheriff find me, but also anyone in Big Boy's pack of wolves. I dressed hurriedly and bussed down to Pinny's apartment. Someone had drilled a half inch hole in the steel door and after I knocked, I put my mouth there and said, "Farmer." I could hear Pinny opening a closet and muttering to himself before the door opened.

"Good morning, Mr. Pinny. Have a seat. I have a special order for you, for which I have brought an additional twenty-five dollars. As you are aware, an 'order' is not a request. It is actually a 'demand,' but I always start out being nice to people.

"I need an additional driver's license and duplicates for the other cards. This time, the name will be, Darren Tubeeh. Wacky eh? Well, you have to be a little off to do what I do. It would bother most people. I assume Big Boy has told you my business so when I tell you this is confidential (which means ONLY between you and me), you get the picture."

Pinny was sitting down and he simply stared at me. His small downturned mouth was half-open and saliva collected in both corners.

"Our private deal is like a contract, my dear friend, and there are severe, sometimes very unfortunate, penalties for breaking a contract. A steel door is no deterrent because you'll have to come out eventually. Tell me you understand." As I said the last sentence, I raised my palms and slowly moved them toward his face. "Put all my cards in one letter size Manila envelope."

Pinny lurched back in his chair, still staring at my calluses, and whispered, "I understand." He said this over and over until I dropped my hands and began to smile. I gave him forty dollars in cash and told him he'd get the rest the next day when I came to collect all the IDs. Big Boy and his minions would be present when I came to #64 to collect and pay for my stuff. I'd have to be careful to be sure no one noticed the extra cards.

I spent the rest of the morning acquiring two objects that I needed to cement the idea of my line of work. I looked through the Yellow Pages and was annoyed that the dive shop, the toy store, the sports center and the hardware store were not close together.

The scuba shop had exactly what I wanted, a hefty diver's knife I could strap above my right ankle. At a local toy store, I started looking in the isle with cowboy stuff. I wanted a toy revolver, and it took a while to find something that looked like a more compact 38 caliber pistol. The toy handguns were painted pink, light blue or yellow. I could fix that.

The sports store had a special area with handguns, rifles and shotguns, as well as an annoying clerk. He said, "Good morning, sir. We have an extensive collection of long guns and handguns. I can supply you with all the information necessary to make a smart purchase that will last a long time and won't leave you short of money." He giggled.

"I need a shoulder holster that will accommodate a 38 caliber pistol."

"We have several to choose from, but you will need a revolver to fill it. If you want the best weapons, I can sell you a half-dozen." He giggled.

"I need a shoulder holster that will accommodate a 38 caliber pistol."

"May I suggest you buy your handguns first so we can choose a holster that would best serve all of them. Here, let me show . . ."

I slapped both hands down hard on the glass counter and then, after turning the palms up, glared at the clerk.

"Oh, my dear fellow. How did you burn your hands?"

"I burned my hands throwing an annoying sporting goods clerk into a flaming barbecue pit."

Within three seconds, there were two shoulder holsters on top of the glass. I took each holster in turn, turned my back to the clerk, and thrust my light blue plastic revolver into it. "This one works best. I'll pay for it up front and tell them you are the world's best salesman." Before I left the building, I glanced across the room at the gun section and the clerk was still staring at me, standing silent behind the counter. I loved my hands.

The hardware store was only four blocks away and I bought a can of spray paint. When I painted my blue toy black, it became a real handgun from a distance or if you are only allowed a quick look.

I did some sightseeing in the afternoon and went to a nice Italian restaurant for chicken parmesan. I liked the city, and was sorry I could not spend more time there. I went to the bus terminal and got two tickets to Seattle, one at noon the following morning under the name Darren Tubeeh and a second one for Tom Hunter at half past three in the afternoon. I changed my hotel room for a pricier one and slept like a log, knowing I was safe.

* * *

Lobo was a deeply suspicious man. He had gotten involved, in a very bad way, with an undercover cop when he was with a biker gang. Happily, he was not the one who shot two members of a rival motorcycle club, but the police arrested Lobo with the rest of them and he spent several days in a cell before release. He thought Tom, in spite of his clothes and beard, was too smooth and too smart to be an itinerant hitman who joined their group by accident. Didn't make sense. He called an informer, who was playing both sides of the fence with the police, and found out Tom Hunter had an active warrant in Idaho for rape. Lobo overheard Tom telling Big Boy the name of his first hotel and planned to visit him. He had all sorts of ways to make a man talk, especially a rinky-dink clown like Tom. Those hands were not magic. They didn't shoot flames like in the comics.

Lobo was furious when he went to the hotel and found that Tom had signed out that morning with no forwarding address. His concern had mellowed a bit when he found out Tom had an arrest warrant, but now his suspicions returned with a bang. He was hiding something. Lobo planned to get it into the open at Pinny's the next day.

I arrived at number 64 at a quarter to eleven and waited outside. I knew the whole gang would arrive ahead of time and I wanted to be sure Pinny wouldn't give me away when I wasn't there. Sure enough, Big Boy arrived five minutes later with Lobo. Snag and the rest of them sauntered in separately with their usual attitudes.

"Big Boy, you and Lobo have helped me out and I'm going to owe you after this payment. To show my appreciation, I'm raising your cash by forty dollars and twenty dollars." I doled out the cash and while they were counting it, I turned to Pinny and snatched the manila envelope out of his hand. I reached in quickly, found the Tom Hunter license, and took it out.

"Well, Pinny, you did good. Lookee here boys, I had no idea I was so good-looking." I noticed everybody laughing except Lobo and wondered what he was going to come up with. I made a big deal about reaching into my pocket and pulling out the rest of the money I owed the forger. To make sure no one questioned me about that I said, "I'm even raising his price."

"Let's celebrate tonight. I'm the only one who's gonna be without a date and I wonder if one of you could help me with that. You pick the place and everything's on me."

Lobo moved to the front. "Something ain't right. I don't trust this tomcat. He does have a warrant out, but it's for rape. He wasn't at his hotel last night." He looked over at Big Boy and then glowered at me.

"I moved because I can't stand sleeping in dirty sheets. I stomped on two cockroaches after I put on my shoes yesterday. I'll tell you all where I moved and you can check on me all night if you want. However, if you want to sleep in my room, it's going to have to be on the floor. Again, everyone laughed except Lobo.

"What's this about rape? I didn't know killers like you went around raping women."

"I admit, Lobo, I made a mistake there. Her brother was a construction worker and died in a nasty accident two days before. Nobody knew he was loansharking on the side and he owed a lot of money to a friend of mine. He was on a Sunday job checking cracked rafters in a school gymnasium. I went with him to help and he lost his grip. Terrible thing. He didn't turn up for breakfast and his sister went looking for him. I was shocked like everyone else and told the police I wished he had called me because it's much safer with two people.

"The sister never liked me and told the cops to check me out real good. It never occurred to the police it wasn't an accident, but I knew they'd follow up after talking to that bitch. The girl was a gorgeous piece and she pissed me off. She lived alone and I came by later and gave her a more personal reason to hate me. I got out of town with the sheriff hot on my ass." I could see Lobo getting steamed up so I looked at Big Boy, shrugged, and casually unbuttoned my jacket as I moved back several steps.

"I don't believe it, you bastard." Lobo came at me.

I raised my right leg, which lifted the hem of my jeans, and whipped the diving knife out of its sheath. At the same time, I let my jacket open up so Big Boy's pals could see the shoulder holster and the butt of a snub-nosed 38. Lobo saw the knife at the same time that Big Boy swung his left arm around Lobo's neck. I could see the surprise and fury in his eyes.

Snag said, "Holy Shit," and crouched down, reaching into his jacket pocket.

Big Boy swung Lobo around so he was facing his mob. He raised his right arm and said, "Be cool, brothers. One hothead is enough." He whispered something to Lobo and shoved him toward the rest of the gang. Then he turned back to me saying, "What's this with the knife?" I buttoned my jacket and the knife was back under my jeans.

"I could've taken him out with the 38, but where would you be after a gunshot in this neighborhood. Finished, that's what. I hoped we'd all be working together for a while."

Big Boy was not slow. He turned to his pack. "Tom owes us and is going to pay his debt. You don't have to like him, but we all know a couple of things he can help us with." The big fellow then turned sideways so he could keep an eye on everyone and said to me, "Get the fuck out of here and keep to yourself. Practice your digging. I'll call you later and tell you about a cactus I'd like you to plant."

I left the room and headed to the bus terminal. I was careful not to look at anyone on the way out. That was a mistake because, if I'd looked at Lobo, I'd have been much more alert in the days to come.

Chapter Eleven

Alone on the bus, I had time to think. I was numb inside and it took a while before I stopped shaking. My emotions were a crazy mixture of happiness with my new name and IDs, and fear of what might have happened if Pinny had given me away. Every one of those felons was packing and Lobo would have taken his time with me. It didn't help that the sunshine in Spokane turned into an overcast sky and misty air as the bus approached the Bellevue suburb of Seattle. The pull was strong and I sensed I'd been here before, probably more than once. Maybe I was a living jigsaw puzzle and my memory would come back to me in little bits and pieces. If I went deeper into the city, walking by the fish market might open a door and all would come flooding back.

The fellow in the ticket booth was no help this time so I bought a tourist book and a newspaper in the terminal. I checked into an inexpensive rooming house and started looking through the classifieds for a job. Farming was out, but my eyes stuck on a help notice for a garage job. I was not a mechanic, but, for some reason, I felt I could handle everything else. I walked a little over a mile before arriving at a small local garage. There were no gas pumps or fancy signs. The name "Gulliver's" was above the two open bay doors and there was one man with only his buttocks and skinny legs showing from under a hood. A middle-aged thick chested man was sitting behind a worn wooden desk in the attached small office.

"I came about your ad. I'm an honest man and punctual. Name's Darren"

The man's heavy head rose slowly and dark brown eyes gave me the once over. "What do you know about cars?"

"I'm not a mechanic, but cars need greasing, oiling and washing. Their owners need respect, good work and on time delivery."

The man, obviously named Gulliver, leaned back in his seat and his eyes stretched opened. Three deep creases gradually appeared on his forehead. "I don't know about your work, but I like your philosophy. I suppose that would be a help in the broken car business." He began to run his lower lip across his upper front teeth. "Let's see your hands."

My hands again—I could not believe it. I put my hands on his desk face down and he picked at one of my nails. He turned my hands over, frowned and looked up at me. "No grease which is not a good sign. What's this? He poked at my calluses.

I started to tell him I was a gravedigger and then thought better of it. "I was brought up on a farm and my hands are not hands, they're tools."

"I don't know why, but I like you, Darren. I've had the ad for a month and in comes a greaseless philosopher." Gulliver drops his head and makes huffing noises, somewhere between a chuckle and a laugh. "Tools are what I need so, unless your hands are limited to milking cows, you've got a job. Seventy-five cents an hour, with a raise if you're still here in a month."

We shook hands and I went in and met "Jimmy." Gulliver was a mechanic too, but he sat in his office most of the time. Jimmy was the real thing. He knew everything about fixing a car. He was immune to electric shock and could touch both poles on a fully charged battery without feeling a thing. I tried it and Jimmy caught me before I collapsed on the concrete floor. My job wasn't complicated: I pressed the grease gun onto the nipples on the wheel bearings and squeezed the trigger; I put a bucket under the oil pan, took the plug off with a socket wrench, and got out of the way. Black oil came out and I got rid of it. Golden oil went back into the engine and I sometimes steam cleaned it. Every so often, the owner of a nearby pharmacy would drop his car off in the morning for washing. I took special pains with that one because I always got a half dollar tip.

It was not long before I had "garage–hands:" black under the fingernails and grease smudges everywhere. At night, I took a hot shower and scrubbed my hands with Lava soap and the coarsest brush I could find. Even so, only time would remove the last vestiges. I noticed my calluses were beginning to soften and I wondered what I could use for intimidation in the future. Another change I found disconcerting was the gray hair at both temples. My face was more lined and nobody would say I was thirty-nine. More like early fifties now and all of this in only four months. Was the stress that bad?

* * *

Lobo looked haggard. Snag noticed it first and said, "Who you sleeping with, boy? The bitch gonna wear you out. Like me to take over couple times a week?"

Lobo was too tired to slap him. "Can't sleep, Snag. That sum bitch, Tom, is driving me crazy. Hitman? No way he's a killer."

"He's got those hands and what about his piece and the knife?"

"Dress up, that's what! I'm gonna find him and skin him."

Lobo called the police in Boise the day after I left Spokane and told them I was heading for Seattle. The next day, the same sergeant told him there was no record of a Tom Hunter on any bus. Lobo lost it and cussed out the sergeant, who promptly hung up. An enraged Lobo drank four beers and that settled him down some. He thought I must have used a different name and Pinny was the only one who might know it. He headed over to Pinny's place.

"Hey, Pinny, got a question for you. Did that Tom fella change his name before he left?"

"I don't know. Why?"

"The police are looking for him and there's no record under Tom Hunter. Tell me what's going on and I'll keep the police out of your business."

"I don't know nothing."

Pinny's fat was jiggling and he was starting to sweat. Lobo took a well-used switchblade out of his pocket and snicked it open. "You made IDs for Tom. Maybe you made an extra one, eh?" Pinny sweated silently, but his eyes got bigger.

"Maybe you made a new name for him, a name with ten letters. One for each of your fingers." Lobo held up his right hand and spread his fingers. He moved the knife blade toward his thumb and pretended to cut it off. He folded his thumb into his palm and showed Pinny the back of his hand. Only four fingers left.

Pinny clenched both hands and put them in his lap. His eyes shifted around the room and then flicked back to Lobo's right hand and the knife blade. When Lobo was a foot away, he began reaching for Pinny's right fist.

"All right. All right. I made two IDs."

Lobo did not want to touch the fat pig. He had urinated and the spreading dark spot was already beyond where his hands scrunched into his lap. "Name, Pinny. Name."

"Darren Tubeeh." He spelled it twice so Lobo could write it in his notebook. After Lobo left, Pinny was unable to move for a long time.

Lobo told Big Boy his mother was sick and, with his father in prison, he had to go to Seattle to check things out. He'd be back in a week. He did not tell anyone Tom's new name, especially the police. He wanted to be the one to dispense justice.

Chapter Twelve

I'd been working for only four days and was bored silly and having no fun. At least I was getting paid for my dirty nails. What was I supposed to be doing in this encore life? I asked Jimmy, and an occasional customer, where an honest man might meet some friends. My eventual savior, a gray-headed pigtailed woman driving a Karmann Ghia, pulled up and wanted a wash. We chatted while she waited on a folding chair in the garage. She had red, yellow and purple on her fingers and told me about a local gallery opening that evening. It was walkable and, if nothing else, I'd bring art into my life. I missed it, somehow.

I trashed Jeff's well–used teenage clothes and bought several nice shirts, a corduroy jacket and two pairs of slacks. I filled my new Dopp kit with toothpaste, a hairbrush, after-shave and all the other stuff that made a man presentable. My biggest problem was my amnesia, which had wiped out history except for the last several months. I was scared of going to the police to get fingerprints that might give me a clue, as they would realize my IDs were fake. If anyone at the gallery opening asked, I'd have to confess I changed tires for a living. Maybe there was a woman out there who was into grease.

After walking fourteen blocks, I heard conversation and laughter before I got to the gallery. The place was packed; I'd guess a hundred patrons in one large room. There was an office, a storeroom and a kitchenette in the back. A big table in the corner held hors d'oeuvres, red and white wine and small Pollock-printed paper napkins. Most of the patrons were women, with some couples and a pleasant mixture of races.

I started to relax after my second glass of cheap Cabernet and several crackers and began to roam the room for sexy females. All of the artwork was abstract and several pieces were quite dramatic. One grouping had columns of colors alternating with shadowy shapes reminiscent of excited amoebas. After two walk-throughs, I dropped my bar down to the "semi-attractive" level. It seemed when nature— or God—gifted persons with talent, something else was taken away. It didn't help that among the women, makeup was nonexistent, clothing was eccentric and tattoos were rampant.

As it happened, I did not have to do the introduction. I didn't notice the tall woman next to me until I felt her slender shoulder pushing against mine. I'd been staring at a cloud form which contained ink figures, or buildings, or somethings, and had twisted my neck almost 90° to figure out what it all meant.

"Don't search analytically. Someone else's mind created this and put it down on paper. Much more important than trying to understand what it meant to the artist is feeling what it means to you."

"Ah, you make it simpler." We laughed together, her high-pitched twittering harmonizing beautifully with my deeper huh huh huhs. "You're absolutely right. It's what these things do to my emotions that are the point. Whether it's likable, is not the issue. If a painting has an emotional effect, I suppose that determines its worth."

"Not necessarily", said the woman. "A dreadful painting is worth a lot to a dreadful artist. The great names somehow, no matter what their style, affect the core of our sensibilities. It can be done with color, shape and subject matter, whether realistic or abstract."

"But I think most artists are trying to say something. Rothko was certainly expressing his philosophy in his blocks of color. He wrote about it."

"That's true, after the fact though. Before his son discovered the document, what did the color blocks floating in the background color mean? No one knew what Rothko was getting at so its importance and value depended solely on the viewer's reaction."

I said, "The color's power and slight variation in the shape and edging certainly caused big emotions in me. It turns out, at that time in art history, to be exactly what the painter wanted to have."

We were wandering about and I stopped dead, my eyes dilating and seeing nothing. My skin prickled as I wondered where on earth my opinions came from. Certainly not from Papi or Big Boy. What was art to me?

"Hey, are you okay? Was that an inspiration or a stroke?"

I laughed. "I'm fine, I was wondering where all my opinions came from. I can't remember that far back"

We had come to the table with the food and drink and we each ate a couple more hors d'oeuvres. I was about to ask for her name and telephone number when she said, "My name is Mimzy and I can only stand so much heavy stuff. If I like your name, I'm taking you home with me."

I couldn't believe my luck. She was female, had art smarts, and was obviously willing. "I'm Darren and you're the miracle that's happening at the best time for me."

Mimzy closed her eyes and whispered my name over and over, pronouncing it "Daring" which didn't offend me in the least. "With a name like that, tonight is going to be special." We held hands and she walked me to her tiny cottage, which was totally out of proportion to the queen–sized bed.

* * *

Lobo spent the time on the bus to Seattle thinking about how to find me. Slowly, he came to the conclusion he had no idea. He got off at the first stop, Bellevue, and, unfortunately for me, he had just enough in his skull to ask for help.

"Excuse me. Uh . . . could you tell me the best way to find a job in your city?"

The woman at the tourist booth in the terminal turned over her paperback and looked up. "What kind of work are you interested in?"

Lobo knew Darren had done farm work and not much else. "I been on a farm all my life and want to do somethin' different. I know 'bout animals, crops and tractors, but not much else."

The woman smiled and said, "Most of the animals in the city are dead ones that have been cut into pieces for your dining pleasure. If you know tractors, maybe something in the automotive business would be available. You can start out flipping burgers at Dick's Drive-in and work your way up to manager. Businesses and apartments usually have openings in janitorial work."

"What's the best way to find these jobs?"

"Word-of-mouth is the best, but if you don't know anyone, I'd start with the classifieds."

Lobo spotted a bookstore across the room that also carried the Seattle Times newspaper and he bought a copy and sat on a bench. There were hundreds of jobs and after a few minutes his eyes got fuzzy and he knew he had to pick some occupation before he went blind. He tried to remember what the tourist lady said and could only remember tractor and automotive. There was nothing under tractor, but two columns for cars and trucks. Car dealers? No. Car parts? No. Garages? Possible. Darren arrived in the city three days before and, in a rare moment of insight, Lobo asked the clerk if he had any back issues. Unsold papers piled up in the back and were picked up later in the week. He found the papers for the previous four days and started comparing the garage help wanted ads. Two of the ads were gone and he wrote the addresses of the two automotive businesses in his notebook. He'd check them out the next day.

Lobo went to a Ford rental agency, got their cheapest car, and drove to a motel. The car was a two-toned bright red and white Ford Fairlane. Lobo loved red; it was the color of blood. By now, it was early evening and he had not tasted a decent meal since breakfast. He felt like a new man after a hamburger, French fries and a piece of devil's food cake. Lobo was so excited he left the café without tipping the server. He drove back to the motel and took a hot shower. He sat on the bed and opened and closed his switchblade. He planned to cause Darren some discomfort before killing him. He checked his 38 caliber snub-nosed Smith & Wesson revolver. It was only a backup, as he didn't want noise to interfere with his fun.

Lobo watched TV and drank three beers before finally falling asleep on his bed, propped up with pillows. The last beer tipped out of his hand and soaked through to the mattress. Lobo didn't even notice it in the morning.

Chapter Thirteen

Mimzy was still asleep when I got out of bed the next day. My back and hips ached from the night's unaccustomed exercise and I took a long hot shower. I checked the tips of my fingers, remembering how they explored every hill and valley of her body. When I came out of the bathroom, Mimzy was beginning to move. The sheet shifted, now only covering her right leg and hip. I felt myself wanting her again, but I had to be at work in half an hour.

"Come back to bed, Daring. Last night was delicious." Mimzy's eyes lingered at my crotch. "I can tell you want me so stop staring and take your clothes off."

"You are virtually irresistible, but I need to go to work. Is there any possibility of seeing you again? By the way, it's Darren."

"I will never call you anything else but Daring. All my 'in and out' boyfriends have been young and I have never been with an older man. You take your time and make sure I'm happy. Oh yes, I absolutely want to see you again, feel you again and do you again and again."

I knew there was much more to life than "agains," but life was difficult for me since I climbed out of the river. I felt I deserved a break and this was a marvelous way to spend some time. Mimzy had no way of knowing the toll that multiple couplings with an ardent younger woman took on my body. I told her we could get together two days hence and Mimzy was kind enough to fling on some clothes and drive me to work. She had a beat up light green Chevrolet coupe that was years old, but ran well. Like me.

No matter what I was doing in the garage, I thought about my own life and tried to figure out who I was and what I used to be. Sometimes I had half an hour between cars and, reliving the gallery, got a pencil and paper from Gulliver and tried drawing. I was more a good Kandinsky than a bad Leonardo. It was obvious I appreciated the art form and had some natural talent. What else? Perhaps I'd been an architect or a scientist. I tried to think if I felt special joy in a bank, crossing a bridge or using a telephone. Nothing. I went down a whole list of things in my mind and nothing stood out.

The thought of spending the rest of my life searching for myself was depressing and frightening. There were times when I felt suicidal. I didn't have a good friend who could help me through my worst moods so I created an imaginary one named, "Henry."

"Tell me, Henry, what am I going to do with myself? Give me some hope."

"Man up, Darren, you're alive, you're educated and you've just had the best sex in your life. At least in your current life. The worst thing would be that you'd work your way up in some business and be highly respected. You'd have a wonderful live-in girlfriend and write books as a hobby. Incidentally, you'd do better at the moment if you moved a few states away so the sheriff can't reach you."

"That's not the worst thing at all. You are an optimist, Henry, and your sarcasm does not prepare me for troubles. I have to get a better job, guard against gonorrhea and watch for the sheriff. It's going to take me years to make enough money to get a car and a home. A live-in girlfriend depends on serendipity and as for the writing . . . well . . . actually, that sounds like fun. I could look for courses to take in the evening."

"See, Darren, I told you so. You're already making good decisions. Finish your writing courses and get a job on a newspaper or a magazine. Your future will blossom."

Henry could be difficult with his naïveté and optimism. Nevertheless, he always made me feel better. I went back to changing oil with a new attitude. Semi-optimism.

* * *

Lobo, looking at the automotive help wanted ads after breakfast, had two choices. The first one he checked out was a big service station on the main highway. It had a garage that was big enough to handle both cars and eighteen-wheelers. There was also a large attached store selling many products and Darren was smart enough to be a cashier. Lobo also knew I had only tinkered with tractors so it was more likely I would be one of the men who pumped gas and wiped windshields.

Lobo told the service station guy to check the oil and he pulled up his collar and pulled down the visor of his grubby baseball cap. He wandered through the store and the restaurant section, flicking his eyes left and right. He wandered into the garage, before he was chased out, and I was nowhere in sight. He inquired about a job, and the manager said he already hired a skilled diesel mechanic so Lobo knew he was in the wrong place.

In the afternoon, Lobo got totally lost trying to find Gulliver's garage and decided he'd get drunk and try again in the morning. He had a terrific hangover the next day and couldn't move until 10 o'clock. Lobo liked to get things done right away and this stalking business was maddening. He got a cup of coffee and a doughnut and drove to the nearest gas station where he bought a map. He irritated the manager by asking repeated questions about the location of Gulliver's garage and how best to get there. The manager finally told him to drive north for two exits and then ask somebody else. On the way back to his car, Lobo fingered his revolver and resolved to shoot the next person who annoyed him.

* * *

Mimzy could not stand it. Darren told her where he worked, but she had been in situations where a boy she really liked would lie to her and she'd never see him again. She couldn't let that happen now, not after she'd found the perfect match. She imagined what it might be like being married to a man like Daring. He was smart and it wouldn't be long before he'd have a really good job; money in his pocket. And the sex? Oh my! Babies would ruin it so she would make him wear condoms every time. Mimzy decided she'd check out Gulliver's garage and make sure he really worked there.

* * *

Lobo drove slowly down a street lined with occasional houses, but mostly small businesses and one-story warehouses. He saw Gulliver's in the distance and parked a block away. He was furious with himself for not getting binoculars and moved the car directly across the street from the garage. He couldn't see into the office and the bay doors were closed so he decided to wait. After an increasingly tortuous hour, a car pulled up and honked. A big chested man came out of the office and talked to the driver. The big guy was not Darren.

It began to sprinkle and the cold drops coalesced on the windows and then ran down in wavering rivulets, parceling Lobo's vision. The warm air inside the Fairlane misted the windows so Lobo turned the ignition switch one click and ran the windshield wipers and the defroster. The wetness on the paint made the red color undulate and sparkle and the hot exhaust gases looked like smoke.

Lobo, rubbing his hand on the window to clear the condensation, saw the garage doors rolling up and a skinny guy waving the driver inside. The other bay had a car up on a lift with another man working with something that looked like a large gun by a front wheel. The metal object and his arms obscured his face so, when the garage door descended, Lobo still didn't know if the man was Darren. He was beating on the wheel in frustration when another car pulled up. A tall woman jumped out and ran through the rain into the office. Through the window, he could see the large man get up and walk with her into the garage.

* * *

"Thank you, Mr. Gulliver," said Mimzy. "Daring's mother called me when she couldn't reach him and asked me to give him a message."

"Nothing serious, I hope."

"Quite the opposite. His dad is out of surgery and doing fine. I won't be long and I don't need to take any more of your time, sir."

Gulliver walked back to the office, but stood looking at her from the open door. Mimzy poked me as I was greasing a front wheel bearing. I'd been oblivious to her presence and jumped when I felt the sudden poke in my ribs. My head rebounded off the tire and smacked into the grease gun.

"What the hell, Mimzy, what are you doing here?"

"Sorry Daring, but after last night, I wanted to be sure you were real. I told Gulliver your father was doing fine after his operation to give me an excuse. How's your head?"

I made a big effort to stay calm. "My head is fine and we're going to get together tomorrow. Why don't you pick me up at the boarding house around 6 o'clock?"

"It's raining outside now so I'll come back a little past 5 o'clock today and drive you home."

"That's very nice, Mimzy, I appreciate it." I only hoped the woman didn't want to spend the night. We would wake up the entire neighborhood.

After a quick kiss, she left the office and headed to her car. She couldn't help noticing the bright red Ford across the street with the wipers going, smoke coming out of the tailpipe, and a man's face pressed to the window. She stared for a long moment and then got in her car and drove off.

Chapter Fourteen

Lobo waited another half hour and then his patience gave out. He decided to come back at closing time, presumably at 5 o'clock, and watch who came out of the garage. As he started the car to drive off, another automobile stopped and dropped a man off. Lobo kept his foot on the brake and watched as the man went into the office and then into the garage. The bay door began to open and Lobo figured out he was picking up his car, which was now off the lift. The new arrival shook hands with a man and backed his car out. The worker stood in the open bay and waved. It was Darren and Lobo reflexively reached for the Smith & Wesson.

"Not now, idiot. Get him on the way home," Lobo said to himself. If Darren lived nearby and walked, he would simply drive alongside and shoot him through the open window. If he had a car, that would take more planning. Anyway, the best news was he'd found him. The rest was easy. Lobo decided to celebrate for a couple of hours and went into a bar a few blocks from his motel. After his third whiskey, the bartender denied further service and asked him to leave. Lobo was too dizzy to shoot the bartender and was in no condition to confront Darren. He staggered back to his hotel and fell asleep. When he awoke, it was 5 o'clock in the morning and he had trouble figuring out where he was and why he was there. He never had dinner and, in a foul mood, remembered that Darren was the cause of his troubles. Two hours later, after pancakes and sausages in a nearby café, Lobo got in his car and drove to Gulliver's. It was still raining and he parked across the street in the same spot. The windshield wipers wiped and smoke continued to blossom out of the tailpipe. After two hours, boredom and anger got the best of him and he decided to return in the late afternoon. The waste time in the middle drove him crazy and he had two beers with his lunch sandwich and grew meaner every hour.

* * *

Lobo's meanness turned to rapture at 4:30 PM. The boss was not behind his desk. The blue car that was parked in the front was also gone and it wasn't hard to figure out the big guy left early. He saw the skinny guy leave exactly at 5 o'clock without locking the door. That meant Darren was alone. Lobo didn't want to shoot him in the garage as Gulliver and the skinny guy might have spotted his car. He'd pop him on the way home. A few minutes went by and Lobo didn't understand why he hadn't left yet.

At ten minutes past five, an old green Chevy drove up and stopped in front of the office. A tall woman got out, hesitated a moment and then got back into her car. Lobo remembered he'd seen her before. She was probably Darren's girlfriend and planned to drive him home. "Shit. That bitch is going to screw things up. I can't wait any longer, as soon as she goes into the garage, I'm going to off them both. He reached for his pistol, which was in the pocket of his jeans.

Mimzy saw the same red car the day before and again this morning when she drove Darren to work. It was sitting there with the windshield wipers going and some bozo watching the place. Could be the cops, but they would not be so obvious as to keep a red car running directly across the street. She stepped out of the car, went into the office, and locked the door from the inside.

"Daring, where are you?"

"I'm over here washing my hands. We can leave in half a minute."

"There's a red car across the street with a guy in it looking out the window at us. He was there yesterday. What's going on?."

"I saw him this morning and thought it might be a customer. Is he still there?"

"Yes, maybe it's the police."

I said, "No way. I'm going to have a look." I went into the office and peaked around the edge of the window. There was a man who seemed to be writhing around in the driver seat. Then he held something up and examined it.

* * *

Lobo had a heckuva time getting the revolver out of his tight blue jeans. He didn't want it to go off so he had to hold the hammer down with his thumb while he moved this way and that, trying to loosen up the fabric. He was sweating when he finally got it in his hand. Lobo brought the weapon up in front of him, flipped the cylinder out, and checked to be sure all six rounds were there. He flicked his wrist and the cylinder swung back and locked. Just holding the shiny blue weapon gave Lobo a rush. He looked both ways and opened the driver's door.

* * *

"It's Lobo and he's got a gun. He'll do us both. I know you locked the door, but he'll come through that like shit through a goose."

Shock paralyzed Mimzy. I shook her shoulder hard and told her to go out the back way, turn left, and run as fast as she could for a hundred yards and then hide. Still speechless, she raced for the back door. I heard traffic going by outside and figured I had thirty seconds to do something. I could not outrun a bullet so my life depended as much on luck as it did on my plan.

I grabbed the water hose used to fill radiators, and made a large puddle on the garage floor immediately in front of the remaining car inside the garage. Shaking, I let it run under the car itself. I opened the hood, clipped a set of jumper cables to the battery, and then gently dropped the hood. I touched the positive to the negative briefly and sparks flew. I put one alligator clip in the puddle and the other on the dry floor by the left front tire. Thudding on the outside office door had begun several seconds before and I stood up and took a couple of steps until I was on the edge of the puddle. I felt panic and hoped Lobo was not as shock resistant as Jimmy.

* * *

The traffic irritated Lobo and he had to let three cars pass before he sprinted across the road. He looked at the office door and smiled. "I can get through that with one shove." He was furious when it didn't happen and he had to kick it five times before the old wood gave way. He drew his pistol and fondled the blued metal, sniffing around the cylinder and hammer. The smell of gunpowder and oil always turned him on. When he stepped into the garage, he saw Darren standing in front of a car with his hands half raised, his palms toward Lobo.

"Who do you think you are, Darren, a superhero? You gonna shoot fireballs at me?" Lobo thought the scene was very funny and started a good belly laugh, which trickled down through snickers into a low growl.

"Please, Lobo. I didn't do anything to you or the guys. I'll come back with you and we can join up again."

"Where's the girl?"

"She's behind the boxes over there in the back. Leave her alone, she didn't do anything to you."

"You're no hitman, Darren. You're a fake who took advantage of us. Big Boy didn't see it, but I know. We don't tolerate snitches." He lifted the gun and walked slowly toward me.

I raised my hands and begged for mercy watching Lobo's grin spreading across his face. Knowing Lobo loved to draw out a kill, I put on a frightened face and backed up slowly, mumbling, "Please Lord, help me." I waited until both his feet were in the puddle and then I kicked the dry clip end into the water under the car.

Lobo stopped moving, rigid, staring past me into space with his mouth open. His trigger finger convulsively fired off one shot that went into the ceiling of the garage. I had a tire iron in my hand when I stood up. I ducked under the firing line of the pistol, in case it fired again, and raised the tire iron. I immediately thought better of it, grabbed the two cables, and pulled them out of the puddle. Lobo collapsed in a contorted heap and I wrenched the revolver out of his hand.

* * *

Mimzy, hiding behind a house two blocks away, heard the single shot and screamed. She began running again and at the fifth house, banged on the door yelling for help and for someone to call the police. An elderly couple appeared at the door and the woman went back inside and began dialing the police with a shaking hand.

* * *

Thoughts were running through my head so fast I had to pinch my thigh hard to settle down. I could probably give him a heart attack, but the resultant police investigation would hold me up for days, perhaps weeks. No one knew I was Tom Hunter so I was safe unless Lobo talked. I had to keep that from happening. The gunshot would get the police involved at any moment. Lobo began to move so I touched the positive and negative to the water for a few seconds and he froze again. I dragged his upper body out of the water, stuck both ends into his mouth, and touched them together. The sizzling sound and the smell were obscene, but I knew the damage would eventually heal. The sirens were outside and I quickly wiped the revolver down and put it into his right hand. I left the cable ends in the water and ran to the office door.

"He almost killed me. Thank God you're here." I raised my hands and two officers led me away. I told the sergeant I was working on a car battery when this guy with the gun came in looking for money. I said he was probably an addict because he went berserk when I told him I only worked there and the owner takes the cash home every night.

"He came at me with a gun, Sergeant, and I dropped the jumper cables and started to run away. I had filled the radiator and he was standing in a puddle when the positive and negative went into the water and got him electrocuted. God saved me."

* * *

Mimzy was devastated, but her curiosity was too much. She believed I was shot by the deranged killer, but could not resist going back to the garage. She couldn't believe it when she saw me outside, surrounded by officers. Maybe they could be together tonight, instead of tomorrow.

* * *

I flashed my ID at the sergeant and told him where I lived. The crime scene was exactly as I described and there was no reason to hold me after I gave my statement. I told him the current must have gone up a leg and through the fillings in his teeth before grounding out through the other leg. That seemed a logical explanation for the electrical burns in his mouth and on his tongue, which prevented him from speaking intelligibly. He'd be going into a hospital with a police guard and I knew I had to get out of the city before he could convince the officer that what I told the police was only half the truth. It could be a matter of hours. I got Mimzy to drive me to the rooming house and shakily told her we needed to wait until the next evening. She said she'd come and get me at 6 o'clock. I packed up after she left and called a taxi.

I hated to forgo another wild night with Mimzy, but it was too risky. Where to go now was the problem. If I went to Vancouver, my name might be on the border when I came back and that would be a disaster. Something zipped into my mind and told me to head south to California. On the train ride, I wondered why I never considered other alternatives.

Chapter Fifteen

When I got off the train, I could smell the city and knew I'd been here before. There was a newspaper kiosk on my way out and I glanced at a newspaper to keep myself oriented. It was late November, 1955. San Francisco has great food, exhausting hills and mind-expanding walks along the coast. It is also expensive and I needed to get work. I had aged into my fifties somehow and that was not good for a job hunter. I found a room rented by an elderly couple with access to their kitchen. I became a moderately good cook at the farm, under Mama's tutelage, and Lily Parsons was excited when I offered to help her prepare meals for all of us. Her husband, Charlie, was a retired geriatric nurse, who worked mostly with terminally ill cancer patients. He saw me looking at the classified section and offered to help.

"My former unit at the hospital is looking for people who can work with the dying. Most people, when they look at the terminally ill, find themselves staring at their own mortality. Living with that on a daily basis is not easy and it takes a special person to do it. I can give you a number."

Vanishing for eternity? Come on, dying is a scary thing for most people, faith notwithstanding. I had a strange vision of Stephen Hawkins, a very bright man, saying heaven is a "fairy story for people afraid of the dark." Is intellect worth more than faith? Not for believers. Then what is the comfort zone for the rational?

There was an idea wandering around in my head, but I could not put it into words at the moment. Charlie was staring at me so I turned my head and nodded.

"I believe I can do it."

"All right then," said Charlie. "I'll call first thing tomorrow."

Lily was starting dinner in the kitchen and I joined her. "Beginning tomorrow, I'd like to pay half your grocery bills while I'm living here. There's no charge for being your sous chef." I smiled and touched Lily's shoulder to make sure she knew I was serious. She put a cucumber, a tomato and a pepper out on a cutting board and handed me a chef's knife. I started chopping while she reheated the beef stew she'd made a couple of days before. I toasted three slices of sourdough bread which would be used as "pushers." The stew was delicious and the salad was my contribution. The conversation was wide-ranging.

Lying under the covers on the squeaky little bed in my rental room, I wondered what this sweet couple would think if they knew I was an amnesiac, wanted by the police for an alleged rape. Would they believe I escaped from a killer sociopath by the luckiest of circumstances? When I looked in the mirror I could see more gray in my hair and deeper lines in my face. I was aging more every month. Perhaps it was only Lobo's freaky presence in my life and I wondered if I should have given him a heart attack with the jumper cables. Time would tell.

The next day, the woman in charge of the Care and Comfort floor at the Wellstead hospital interviewed me. Ursula truly cared about what she was doing with the patients in the C&C unit, but she was obsessive/compulsive to an extreme. She ran the third floor unit as if she was a fanatical colonel looking for a shoulder star.

"Charlie called me and said you'd be an excellent addition to my staff. I'm always looking for orderlies who can assist in the management of my patients. What training have you had?"

I knew Charlie told her I had lost my memory, but I was able-bodied and felt I could handle the job. He said Ursula was desperate to find an additional person so I guessed the interrogation was her way of letting me know who was boss. "Since I lost my memory, I've been a farmer, a construction worker and a garage mechanic and I seem to have some medical knowledge. I turned down a very lucrative offer as a hitman."

"That's not funny. Our work here in Care and Comfort is very serious and infractions of our rules by anyone are dealt with harshly."

"As they should be. I am healthy and strong and I have been devoted to whatever I'm caring for, be it buildings, cars, animals or people. Why don't you follow my progress for three days and if I don't measure up, you can have the pleasure of firing me."

It was obvious that humorless Ursula had never met anyone like me. She sat silent behind a large desk, trying to figure out if I was putting her on or if I was truly a devotee of many things, including humans. Her needy situation finally tipped the scales and she hired me for a dollar an hour.

"Remember, Mr. Tubeeh, you are on probation here until I am satisfied you can meet our standards of care." She insisted on getting the last word.

My hours were 8 AM to 4 PM and I had to change from street clothes into a blue uniform similar to operating room "scrubs." At eight sharp, the other two orderlies stood (more or less at attention) in front of Ursula's desk and received eight patients each in our third floor unit. There were three wards holding eight beds each with RNs in charge. My eight patients ran the gamut: Alzheimer's, solid cancers, leukemia and even mental illness. Most of the cancer patients were receiving chemotherapy and the rest took various medications. The Japanese captured one of my veteran patients, Joey, during World War II in the Philippines and he somehow survived the Bataan death march. However, the merciless cruelty of his captors did something to his mind. A harassed Army physician, observing a flashback, made a diagnosis of schizophrenia. To my surprise, I knew this patient had severe "battle fatigue", not a psychosis. *How did I know that?* Three of the cancer patients were still on chemotherapy, although it was obvious the treatments weren't having any effect. Keeping them on ineffective drugs was actually harmful. A hopelessly senile patient, who could not even recognize his own children, was also placed here as there were no other alternatives.

I moved patients into wheelchairs, emptied bedpans, checked intravenous lines and doled out medications. It was important for me to get to know each one and I made time to sit at the bedside. Although it was not part of my duties, I also spent as much time as I could with visitors, be it family or friends. Many of the families were unhappy their loved ones, often in pain, received drugs that were wiping out their immune systems without stopping the spread of their cancer. Two of the patients prayed for death in loud voices, which upset the staff as well as other patients.

Ursula, like an Osprey, kept a sharp eye on us three orderlies swimming in her personal pond. I was her particular target and knew she was waiting for me to screw up so she could dive in, snatch me out of the water and drop me on a rock. Nevertheless, I was resolved to do something about the suffering I saw all around me. In quiet times, I was amazed at my determination and could not imagine where I got my confidence.

My sessions with the relatives of patients revealed that two families were keeping a parent alive out of guilt feelings. A ne'er-do-well son, who wasn't going to inherit a share of his mother's estate, insisted on maintaining chemotherapy as punishment. Some were being treated by their doctors from either ignorance of the "Do no harm" admonition in the Hippocratic Oath or apprehension because of the malpractice sword hanging over their heads.

Joey, the veteran with battle fatigue, joined the infantry in nineteen forty-one and was eighteen years old at that time. His future was hopeless with a diagnosis of schizophrenia and I was determined to get that corrected. His flashbacks and depression, misdiagnosed as hallucinations and social withdrawal, were tragic. Although schizophrenia is wide ranging, he had none of its usual signs. I was the only one who showed him any respect or interest in his condition. He certainly needed to get off his current medication, as a sedative only made his depression worse. Under the circumstances, I'd be depressed too.

Ursula felt her duty was to keep everyone safe, well fed and as happy as possible. In her view, all the patients were getting optimal care and she never questioned their care. I treated Ursula with the utmost respect, almost obsequious, as I thought it would help me change things. However, I found after ten days, she loved my fawning, but did not question the treatments. Going over her head was a serious risk, but I had to do it. I sent a written request to our third floor physician, with a copy to the Chief of Staff.

Once a week, we had a meeting with the physician in charge of the third floor (which included our unit) in the five-story hospital. The Chief of Staff was above him and had ultimate control of the entire hospital. I pretended to be a bright and eager nonprofessional with some self-taught medical knowledge. As I asked questions, I gave credit to Ursula and said she was an inspiration to all the orderlies. Before the meeting, I talked to my two peers and asked them not to take issue with that statement. There was much eye rolling, but they finally agreed. The psychiatric texts I brought with me to the meeting seemed out of date and I wondered if I'd been placed in a time machine.

My request was apparently provocative enough to the hospital administration that the Chief of Staff joined the physician floor manager at the meeting. Ursula was sitting in a corner and did not look happy. After a general patient care discussion, the third floor physician turned to me frowning. "I understand you have some issues with the diagnosis of schizophrenia in Joey's case."

"Yessir. The young man is a veteran and we owe him a proper diagnosis and treatment. I've brought current texts on battle fatigue, which is not a psychosis, and . . ."

The floor physician lurched forward and looked at the Chief. "I thoroughly examined Joey and I've talked to him regularly during the years he has been here. This orderly is new and I hope he has a change of attitude if he values his job. As a physician, my diagnosis is schizophrenia."

The chief was regarding me curiously throughout the discussion. He turned away and said, "Let Mr. Tubeeh continue. He's not exactly a babe or suckling, but we all know the proverb that starts, 'Out of the mouths of'. . ."

I tried to ignore the manager's nasty stare and continued, "I have carefully observed Joey's flashbacks as he relived some of his horrible experiences as a prisoner of war under the Japanese. His depression is an accurate diagnosis, but I think most of us in this room would be under the circumstances." I continued on, reading the symptoms of schizophrenia from the textbook and delicately suggesting he had none of them. "In between his flashbacks, Joey suffers from none of the signs or symptoms of schizophrenia. If we can concentrate on his depression and help him cope with his frightening visions from the war, we can give him a reasonable and independent life."

I arranged, prior to the meeting, to have my best friend among the orderlies wheel Joey into the room. There was an angry objection by the manager, which the Chief gently suppressed. He brought a chair over, sat next to Joey, and questioned him in a calm and reassuring tone. After I wheeled Joey out, the Chief physician resumed his seat at the head of the table. "I believe there is enough evidence to consider

Mr. Tubeeh's concerns." He turned to the red-faced manager and said, "Let's have him examined by the consulting psychiatrist and please apply that rule to any patient admitted with a psychiatric diagnosis."

I had now made enemies of both Ursula and the unit physician. However, if Joey's diagnosis was changed, I felt I could count on the Chief of Staff to support some of the other situations I had in mind.

Chapter Sixteen

Stanton Mulloy was one of the cancer patients who was receiving long term chemotherapy. Physical examination showed that the tumors were growing and new enlarged lymph nodes were popping up every week or so. The twice a week treatments were always followed by increased pain, severe nausea, vomiting, and loss of appetite. I could understand why doctors wouldn't want any patient to die on their watch, but I wondered what Hippocrates would say under these circumstances. Carrying such patients beyond their biological lifespans, and making them suffer because of it, seemed unnaturally cruel. I was again up against the unit's physician.

I learned, when dealing with Lobo, that it was a death sentence to go up against an armed man without some kind of safeguard, benign or otherwise. In this case, my protection was (I hoped) an oncologist, the hospital chaplain, and the patient's family. I again sent a request to the third floor physician with a copy to the Chief of Staff. I didn't want to ignore Ursula so I tried to discuss the pluses and minuses of chemotherapy in such patients with her. As expected, she shut me down quickly, but she could not say she wasn't in the loop.

It took several weeks of meetings before my concerns were on the agenda. I was sure the delay was due to stormy conversations between the Chief and the unit physician. I had the hospital's oncologist, the chaplain and three family members on standby and the oncologist was the first to join us in the conference room.

"I'm here at the Chief of Staff's request, but I'm confused about the purpose. Mr. Mulloy is seventy-eight years old and has widespread cancer, which I am treating with chemotherapy. I have never refused to treat a cancer patient. That's the same as killing him. Letting this man die goes against medical ethics."

The Chief, knowing an orderly would have no chance asking the questions, told me in confidence he was going to handle it. I seated myself in the back and, in spite of my frustration, tried to maintain a humble and demure expression. It was not hard for the Chief to bring out the fact Mr. Mulloy was terminally ill. Although he had received proper doses of every chemotherapy drug available, the current ineffective treatment was destroying whatever quality remained in his life. The oncologist sat speechless, as he had never thought about the ramifications of continuing a futile treatment.

The chaplain was next and there was nothing in his years of training that prepared him for this particular moment. "I'm not the one who should be saying 'yay' or 'nay' regarding chemotherapy for a dying patient. I have prayed on this and have not received God's word on the subject. As a devoted and God-fearing man, all I can do is give you my rational and honest opinion. I truly believe God should be the only one to take a life. Without chemotherapy, the patient probably would have died years ago. I believe the Lord has no objection to the extension of time given to patients like Mr. Mulloy. Nevertheless, when the treatment ceases to be effective, that is a sign it is time for the patient to pass through the gates. Letting a patient die a prescribed death is not the same thing as killing him."

The floor physician, obviously furious at allowing a mere chaplain to give medical advice, stood and opened his mouth. The Chief of Staff, nodding as if in sympathy, waved him down before he could speak. The chaplain left the room and three members of Mr. Mulloy's family entered: his wife, a son and a daughter.

Mrs. Mulloy was dressed in a dark brown skirt and a blouse of muted paisley colors. She had pulled back her hair from a narrow face and she had deep lines around her mouth and desolate eyes. Her tan purse had obviously been with her for a long time. "I have been married to my husband for fifty-four years. I cannot bear to see Bill suffer as he has for the last several months. He didn't want to upset our dear children, but he told me many times he didn't want to live like this. He said it was 'his time' and God had given him the key to the gates. Please don't hold him here anymore."

The Chief, along with the third floor physician, the oncologist and Ursula, left the room and talked with Bill Mulloy for several minutes. When they came back, their faces were tense and even Ursula looked downcast. The chief said nothing, simply looked over at the oncologist.

The specialist said, "I don't know what to say. I was doing my very best. I thought the medical profession was about saving people and that is what I've been trying to do all my professional life. Harm never entered my mind because I thought letting people die was an admission of failure." The doctor sat down at the table, his fingers supporting his head. Ursula began to weep, and blotted her eyes with a Kleenex.

The oncologist lifted his head. "Giving my patient an extra fourteen months was the victory. Extending it beyond that was fallacious, based on a combination of egotism and poor judgment. Common sense would've made the right call."

The Chief, seeing the grief and self-recrimination in his colleague's face said, "Placing blame does no one any good. We are all responsible."

The oncologist stood up and looked at Ursula. "Please brings me the charts of all my cancer patients. I've got work to do and some calls to make." On the way out, the doctor could not bear to say anything, but came over to me and shook my hand. The Chief didn't need to add anything and left the room biting his lower lip. Ursula, believing this was against everything she had always stood for, wondered why she was crying. I felt vindicated, and that was a good feeling, but I wasn't close to claiming victory as there was another patient who needed immediate help.

Billy Joe was only forty-seven years old and close enough to my age to make it doubly hard. It was not possible to remove the large tumor in his abdomen so radiation followed. However, the high-energy waves had the opposite effect. The malignancy spread throughout his abdomen and burrowed into the nerves in his spine. His surgeon placed a feeding tube into his stomach and chemotherapy started. It had no effect. Billy Joe was in constant severe pain and vomited everything that went into his stomach.

"Dr. Darren, stop all my treatments and let me go. I can't stand the pain."

I squeezed his hand, telling him I cared and was listening. It was not easy with the odor of puke fouling the air in his room. "I'm not a physician, just an orderly, and I can't legally do anything like that. I'll increase the morphine." I fought not to lose control.

"It's not working. It helped when they started, but not anymore. Look how thin I am. The damn doctors are feeding my stomach and all I do is throw it up. Stop the chemotherapy and feedings so I can die comfortably."

Billy Joe had no medical training, but he was making more sense than his physicians. "I'm going to talk to both your doctors today, Billy Joe. I think you're absolutely right."

Ironically, Billy Joe's father was a lawyer and he begged me to help his son. I didn't trust him at first, but found out he was a highly respected corporate litigator, known for his integrity. His mother, after her first visit, was devastated to see her son writhing in pain and vomiting green bilious stuff every few hours. When his wife and children came every Sunday, I made sure he was comfortable by emptying his stomach and turning up the morphine drip.

My conversations with Ursula met with sympathy, but her hands were tied. I couldn't blame her as she had a family to help support. I talked with the third floor physician manager who angrily told me to get the hell out of his office. The oncologist, after talking to Billy Joe, stopped the treatments. The patient was very grateful, but starving to death would take weeks of torture. Seeing him in constant agony finally ate away my reluctance to help.

I talked to Billy Joe and his father at length about what he and his son really wanted the doctors to do and, on that basis, made a decision on my own. I had the odd feeling that, sometime in the future, physicians, lawyers and legislators would get together and allow Billy Joe to die in more peaceful circumstances.

That evening, I talked to Lily and Charlie and they both agreed with me that Billy Joe wanted, and deserved, something more definitive. However, they strongly advised me not to get involved and jeopardize my job and reputation. What I was going to do that evening would jeopardize both, but I wanted to be sure they knew my reason. I put enough money in an envelope to cover my room and board for the next month. Later, when I left their home at midnight with my suitcase, I left the money on the kitchen table.

Everyone in the hospital knew me and I answered questions by saying that the night orderly was not feeling well and I was going to help out. I hid my suitcase in an empty classroom and took the stairs to the third floor. There was one orderly covering the entire floor and most of his time involved making rounds in the other sections. As soon as he left C & C, I slipped in and went to Billy Joe's bed. He had dozed off and I decided not to wake him. I reached up to the morphine bottle and opened the valve all the way. In addition, I raised the arm of the IV stand so it was a foot and a half higher and that increased the outflow even more. I found a towel and wiped the glass bottle and the valve free of my fingerprints. The nearly full bottle was no longer dripping; there was a steady flow into Billy Joe's vein. I knew he would never wake up.

He would die peacefully during the night and the open IV valve would charge someone with murder. The other orderlies would say the patient himself threatened to do it. Proving murder would be difficult, but I had a history of being an activist, outspoken about patients' suffering and offering solutions. I picked up my suitcase and headed for the bus station once again. The police might not be far behind.

Chapter Seventeen

Lobo was one thing, but the police was an immediate concern. They could communicate everywhere and could follow a person in many ways. I didn't have a credit card and paid cash everywhere I went. However, the name Darren Tubeeh would be out on an APB as soon as they found Billy Joe's empty morphine bottle. In retrospect, I should have had Pinny make a half-dozen IDs for me. I bought a bus ticket in Darren's name south to San Diego, but never got on the bus. Instead, I went to the train station and ticketed to Los Angeles under a different name. It was a well-known city with a significant percentage of Mexican immigrants. Hispanics were all over the West Coast and my impression was they were honest, hard working and family oriented. The children were learning English in school, but older generations only spoke their native language. There was a significant need for bilingual teachers.

I had no idea where it came from, but I had a smattering of Italian and French in my head. French was useless, but since Italian was similar to Spanish, I figured with the aid of a Spanish/English dictionary, I could earn a living giving private lessons. To do it right, I would choose the students carefully and pick only the ones who had a modicum of English. I hoped being available at night and on weekends would increase my desirability.

I again found an older couple with a room to rent inside the city limits, and made a serious effort to show them I was a decent human being who was educated and honest. I used the name Tom Hunter again, figuring my hosts, Pam and Jerry Hillbrook, would have no access to police bulletins. Before I started my tutoring efforts, I went into the editor's office of the Los Angeles Times. I said I was a healthcare worker who was compiling statistics on abuse of retarded people. The editor's secretary shifted me off to a reporter.

I had to give the reporter all kinds of made-up statistics and the name of the abused to get what I wanted. He found out, through the Society for the Prevention of Cruelty to Children, of Chinny's abuse by her father and wrote an article about it. Papi was arrested, but his trial was still months away. Jeff, as well as Chinny herself, cleared my name and there was no longer a warrant out for my arrest. It was safe for me to use Tom Hunter's ID again, and you can imagine my relief.

There was a program called Learn to Read that was popular, not only with second-language immigrants, but also with youngsters who had skipped school too often and were now, as adults, anxious to get a better job than stocking shelves. Even with volunteers, the program was chronically understaffed and this was good news for me. I placed ads for my services in local newspapers and posted some around town. I figured seventy-five cents an hour would attract enough of the students to cover my expenses. I totally misjudged the demand and had to cut off applicants when I got to twenty. I worked four to six hours each weekday plus three hours in the evenings and some on weekends. It was the Mexicans, not the Caucasians, who worked the hardest and stuck with it the longest. Most of my students got at least to the sixth grade level and that enabled them to read signs, write letters, and get the gist of news reports. I hadn't felt so safe and satisfied in a long time.

A bus line gave me easy access to beaches and I had a marvelous time walking on the sand. Unfortunately, it was too cold to swim in the winter, but I met all kinds of people and being among healthy folks was a delightful change. The prickling memory of climbing out of the river naked with a hole in my arm began to fade a little.

Los Angeles, with its Hollywood reputation, was a pulsing town. The restaurants, bars and music were the throbbing rhythm of the city. The foot traffic, both tourists and locals, was constant and raised my hopes I'd find an attractive and intelligent woman. Ten days after my arrival, that's what I thought happened. I finished my tutoring at 3 o'clock on a Friday afternoon and by 5 o'clock, I was walking through a lively section of town. Fridays and Saturdays were frenetic and even walking on the sidewalks was bumpity bump with others.

The jazz music drew me to this particular restaurant. Its name, Pungent, suggested that the food tasted good and had excellent aroma. I was hoping some of the clientele had the same qualifications. The band consisted of three middle-aged men with a piano, a bass and a saxophone. This time, there was no Mimzy cuddling up beside me so I had to do a little stalking on my own.

Pungent began to fill up over the next hour and I was reluctant to leave my chair to check out the place. Half of the space was a restaurant and the other half was a lounge with a bar and seating. The band was on a raised platform at one end of the lounge. My seat was in the back of the lounge at a table for two. I likened my situation to fishing; I was the hook and the chair was the bait. Sure enough, along came an overly nourished grouper with stringy hair. She smiled at me with uneven teeth and gestured at the seat.

"I'm sorry, my dear, but my date is in the bathroom and if I don't save her seat, I'm going to be miserable for weeks." The grouper's mouth settled into a pout and when she walked off, I could hear her thighs scuffing together. As I watched her retreating figure, two women stepped out of her way and headed in my direction. They were talking animatedly to each other while at the same time looking around the room. I didn't know whether they were meeting somebody or not, but I decided to cast my line in their direction.

They both appeared to be in their early forties and were nicely dressed. The trout wore navy slacks and a white shirt with subtle designs. The pike wore tight jeans and a ruffled blouse that was unbuttoned enough to make out half of each breast. As they started to pass my table—I was still staring at them—the trout slowed down, looked at the chair, and then at me.

"Ladies, you're welcome to sit here if I can find another chair."

Pike looked at her friend and said, "It's a miracle, Neeva. I thought we would have to find some other place. Now, all of a sudden, here's an empty chair and a nice looking gentleman."

I got up slowly so as not to appear too anxious. "There's a table for four over there with only three guys. I'll have a go." I got lucky and carried the chair high in the air back to my little table. Trout had not said a thing so I stuck my hand out and introduced myself to both of them. "I'm glad you both came by because I was about to run out of excuses."

Pike giggled, but Neeva smiled at me and I liked her low-throated chuckle. We chatted aimlessly about one thing and another and I ordered a second round of drinks for all of us. The women were assistant managers in a local department store. They said they were both divorced and this was the week their children were with their father. I didn't see a way to get them separated and a threesome never entered my mind.

Pike said, "What do you do during the week, Tom?"

"I'm teaching English to people from other countries and Americans who neglected their studies in school. When you can't read, it has a way of limiting your future."

My companions looked at each other, nodding their heads and then Pike began looking around the room, as she'd been doing ever since she sat down. Neeva moved closer to me. "Have you ever been married?"

"Not that I remember." The sentence popped out of my mind as it was the only true statement I could make. Neeva, of course, thought I was making a joke and grabbed my hand, giving me that low chuckle again.

"Why not?" She said, gazing at me with a puzzled look.

The question remained in the air because, at that moment, Pike slid her chair back and jumped to her feet. She turned to Neeva and said, "He's here. You two have a super night." Pike made her way through the crowd, zigzagging and bumping people until she found her target. The man was her height, but obviously a decade younger. I was startled to see him grab Pike around the waist and, with one hand on her butt, pull her vigorously towards him. They kissed sloppily in the middle of the room before heading towards the bar.

Neeva had observed the whole thing too, and I looked at her and raised my eyebrows.

"Dora met him a month ago and he comes here often. They've had a really good time together and she hoped tonight would be another one."

The relationship was undoubtedly a series of one-night stands. Where this left me was unclear, although Dora's departing remark seemed implicative. She could have said, "Have a nice time" or "enjoy yourselves," instead of "have a super night."

I'd already established they were both high school graduates and were brought up within fifty miles of Los Angeles. It seemed they were out only for fun, which was ideal. "Do you want another drink, Neeva, or would you like to walk around and find another place?"

"Yeah, let's get out of here. Dora hates me to stick around when she's with a guy. She says it's embarrassing. One more good band is fine by me, then maybe something a little cozier."

Bingo!

I had no idea it might cost me my life.

Chapter Eighteen

Big Boy was pissed. Lobo called him eight times to bail him out of jail. He was arrested on a weapons charge, but the docket was crowded and it would be twelve days before a preliminary hearing. As luck would have it, the pro bono lawyer assigned to Lobo was good. His firm was well-known and expert in criminal defense. Lobo was foxy and, aside from petty theft several years before, had no arrests for a serious crime. Other members of Big Boys gang were not so lucky. Three were still in prison and the ones who finished their sentences had to go elsewhere.

The problem the prosecution had was determining Lobo's motive. The owner of the garage and his mechanic, Jimmy, were not anywhere near their place of work and had airtight alibis. They both vouched for me as an honest and hard worker. Lobo had never been a customer and had no reason to be angry with Gulliver or any of us. Lobo told the police a known criminal, namely me, had attacked him. However, Tom Hunter's warrant no longer existed and I had no active record, criminal or otherwise, in their databases. Lobo said there was a girl involved, but no evidence existed. The police found jumper cables attached to a battery lying on the garage floor, but the story about Tom trying to electrocute him was a strange tale. Lobo was in a puddle of water, but it looked like an accident. Water was often on the floor in a garage and was difficult to see in the late afternoon. The mechanic probably dropped the cables when he saw an armed man breaking the door down. The tongue burns remained a mystery. Lobo said he had no memory of it and the police thought, based on his lack of education, he probably tested the cables with his tongue to see if it was "hot." Much laughter followed.

Since Lobo kicked the garage door open, it seemed he was there to rob the place. Although was carrying an unlicensed handgun, the cash register was not touched. Since a robbery had not occurred, all they could get him for was carrying the pistol and "breaking and entering." Lobo's lawyer said his client saw a kicked-in door and went into the garage to check it out. Lobo had used his shoulder and a shoe so there were no fingerprints to prove otherwise.

Over the course of several hours, Lobo told the police two different stories. He first said someone named Darren had tried to electrocute him and then said he was walking by and went in to see if someone was robbing the place. Did not make sense. Lobo was not a felon and his lawyer got the judge to confiscate his gun, give him a misdemeanor, a five hundred dollar fine and a year's probation. Big Boy deliberately did not bail him out right away to teach him a lesson. Lobo was the best enforcer his gang ever had and he didn't want to lose him. Big Boy eventually paid the fine and took the cost off Lobo's payout from the gang's prostitution and extortion profits.

The burns on Lobo's tongue took over two months to heal and he still could not pronounce some words properly. I was still alive and this festered in Lobo's soul like a cancer, spreading bit by bit, into every part of his being.

* * *

Neeva and I didn't stay long in the next club listening to another band. It was obvious, as I licked the salt off my third margarita, the woman was more than anxious to get "cozier." She sat close to me and, using any excuse, put her hand on my arm, and even my thigh. It was what I wanted, of course, but there was something pushy, something urgent about it that did not sit quite right. My little head was not listening.

"I'm staying, for the moment, in a room I rented from a nice older couple. I love Los Angeles and would like to start roots growing here, but a better place is going to have to wait for a while."

"No problem, Tom. I'm only fifteen minutes away and I think you'll find my place has everything you like. Everything."

After saying that, she stuck her tongue in my right ear. I guess she thought it was erotic, or at least naughty, but I've never thought a wet ear was particularly seductive. She made it worse by blowing into my ear canal with the effect the evaporation of her saliva turned that sensitive area frigid. It was not a turn on and I must have jerked away because Neeva look distressed.

"I'm so sorry, Tom. Most people like that. Do you have a sore ear?"

Not wanting to spoil the evening, I said, "My ears have always been sensitive. My mother used a Q-tip from time to time and it hurt like hell. It's nothing to do with you. It's my weakness so don't worry about it."

We drove about ten miles to an area with small houses and flat roofs. There was a two-car garage and I thought for sure she would put her car inside, to cover my exit if nothing else. Instead, she stopped the car in the front of the house and got out. I followed her to the front door and we went inside.

"Don't you want to put your car into the garage? It's cold outside."

Neeva turned toward me, blinking furiously. "I'm using the garage to store a lot of stuff for my mother." She hesitated, trying to think. "I'm going to drive you back to the bus station and it'll save time this way."

I figured she'd at least ask me if I wanted a drink—which I didn't—but she grabbed my wrist and pulled me upstairs. It was a two-bedroom house and we bypassed the master and went along a corridor to a second room. As soon as she closed the door, she unbuttoned my jacket and lifted it off my shoulders. Then she started on my shirt while I stood there amazed at this woman's urgency.

I had a reason for wanting to do my own slacks so, after she undid my belt, I rather roughly took over and pushed my slacks down below my knees. From the outside, I managed to unfasten the strap from around my right calf so my diver's knife and sheath slipped out with the slacks. In my briefs, I held her shoulders and said, "Hold on, sweetheart. Now it's my turn." I unbuttoned her blouse, turned her around, and undid her bra. She turned back and, without looking at her breasts, I undid her slacks, push them over her hips, and she stepped out of them as they slid to the floor. As I brought my hands back up, I brushed her breasts as if by accident, and ended up with her face in my hands and my lips on hers. She was shaking and breathing hard when I finished kissing her and she tore off her panties and scrambled on top of the bed.

I took my time with my briefs, teasing her. There was much thrashing about in the next few minutes before we separated. I didn't know if this was a one night stand for her so I swung her on top of me for another bout before I decided enough was enough. We took turns in the bathroom and then got dressed. Leaving the bedroom, I glanced over at a hall closet and noticed the padlock.

"Is that where you keep all your jewelry?"

Neeva stopped dead, looking startled, even a little scared. She looked at me and then stared at the closet, apparently thinking again. "My mother's stuff is in there. She has some expensive clothes and other things and she asked me to lock it up."

"Does your mother live close by? It's nice to be able to get together with her from time to time."

"She has a tiny apartment and doesn't have room for much."

I could see the conversation bothered her so I didn't persist. We walked down the stairs, out the front door, and got into her car. There was not much conversation as we drove to the station except as I began to open my door.

"When're you coming back to the city, Tom?"

"Any time I can get a break from my teaching. I've got a waiting list for new students, which is nice, but I need time for myself."

"I'd like to see you again. How about two weeks from now? You made me feel very cozy."

"How about next week?"

"Um, my boss has me doing inventory next week so I'm stuck. Give me your phone number."

"Sorry about that. Inventories are a pain in the ass. Two weeks it is." I gave her my phone number and asked for hers. Neeva didn't refuse outright, but simply said she'd rather call me.

I caught the last bus and, on the way back, had plenty of time to wonder why Neeva never looked me in the eye when she struggled to answer my questions and didn't want to give me her phone number. It was a matter of trust, I suppose, as I was a relative stranger in her life and we were only in it for kicks.

I learned the hard way that it is foolish to ignore a red flag.

Chapter Nineteen

My current job was one of the best since I climbed out of the river. It was not always easy, depending on the attitude of the student. The foreign-born were the most eager to learn the English language and never missed a day of homework. Their passion was due to many things, especially because they were now in the United States. They left their homeland because of wars, religious prejudice, lack of work opportunities or because they were joining members of their family who had already immigrated to this country. Future happiness depended on learning the language and their determination made me equally determined to provide that for them.

The American born students, mostly young, had goofed off in their teenage years and were now paying the price. There were no wars or lack of opportunities to make it impossible for them to learn to read. A touch of entitlement tempered their diligence and the indolence that caused the problem was not easy to overcome. Like an alcoholic, the craving for a successful life without travail was constantly present. Their homework was occasionally inconsistent and they sometimes missed appointments.

Regardless, my tutelage was extremely rewarding. Spending your precious time in making someone else's life better, and seeing it happen right in front of you, was much more than an ego trip. My lessons affected generations to come so the difference you were making was not limited to one life. The value grew exponentially. The mutual respect that developed between a tutor and a student, even if the relationship was initially hostile, could be a life changer.

One of my assignments was a fatherless eleven-year-old boy, sent to me twice weekly from a juvenile rehab facility. A wise judge included tutoring for the length of his incarceration. His release date depended on a number of obvious things such as behavior, but also progress in learning to read. His first and middle names were Jason and Victor, but everyone called him JayVee. His crimes were not violent and he never carried a weapon, although he sometimes used force to release himself from someone's grip. His string of shoplifting, robberies and home invasion arrests was long. He felt owed and wanted the same lifestyle as working stiffs and he doubted that most young men with cars acquired them by honest effort.

JayVee never knew which of the men who came in and out of his mother's life was his biological father. His mother was on welfare and the cigarette smoke that eddied through the house smelled like they lived next to a smoldering trash dump. He was a truant, perhaps because of his mother's indifferent efforts to keep him in school. Her motive was not so much her son's education, but the fact she could make more money when he was gone.

JayVee had no respect for anyone in his life and didn't even know what that meant. I learned JayVee's last name was Shakkar and that's what I called him throughout our relationship.

"Please have a seat, Mr. Shakkar. My name is Tom and I am going to be working for you. I can read English perfectly and will teach you that skill. The State of California, where we live, is going to be checking up on me to be sure I'm doing right by you."

Nobody in JayVee's life had ever called him Mr. Shakkar. The fact he could call me by my first name and I would be "working *for* him" left him stupefied.

I said, "You look tough and smart so I don't think you're going to have a problem with this. Work is necessary in whatever we do, whether it's stealing stuff from a store or learning to read, so you and I are both used to making an effort. I have to work hard because each new person I teach is different. For you, reading is simply going to be a different kind of challenge.

"I think of this as a partnership, even though you are going to be the boss. Let me explain: if you have a problem, I am going to fix it for you; if you have questions about the work, I'm going to explain it for you. There will be times when you will be irritated with me, but the best bosses are kind and listen to the people working for them. There will be times when I'll be irritated with you, but there will always be respect between us. Working together, we are going to win and I will get satisfaction and you will be able to live a free, prosperous and happy life."

"Satisfaction?"

"Yes, it's a prize, an award, an honor. Like any success, it makes a person proud and happy. Accomplishments create a good feeling and it's why I do this work."

The concept that JayVee could acquire a "free and happy life" by honest work was completely foreign to the boy. He had not thought of the stress and effort of a robbery as being comparable to honest work. He wrote off his multiple detentions as the cost of doing business and never factored that into his life. I knew it would take weeks for him to appreciate a different kind of existence and, in the meantime, we had work of our own to do.

I knew it would take some time for JayVee to become accustomed to our role reversal. He probably believed the respect I was according him was BS and would not last long. I was sure he would challenge me soon. On the first day, I tested him to see the level of his reading and comprehension. He read at the fourth grade level but, surprisingly, his comprehension was two grades higher. Getting him to complete those two tests was a struggle as embarrassment was a factor throughout. I gently reminded him his freedom was dependent on his cooperation. At the end of that first day, I gave him a children's book to read at home and an appointment three days hence.

When JayVee slouched into our small room, he was carrying the storybook, but it looked a lot more beat up than when I gave it to him.

"Did you like the story, Mr. Shakkar? Your book doesn't look very happy."

"I got mad."

"Why?"

"Some of the words didn't make sense."

"You forgot you have somebody who is working for you and can help you. Please do not get mad at the book because it can fly up in the air and come down on your head. That doesn't help. My job is to explain words that don't make any sense to you. Take a pencil and put a line under words that are a problem and keep reading. Ask me about them when we get together."

JayVee stared at me and then down at the book. His life had never included the conversation like the one we just had. "Why do you call me Mr. Shakkar?"

"As I told you, I am working for you. It would be rude to call a boss by his first name, but you can call me, Tom. Maybe if I do a good job and you like me, you can give me permission to call you JayVee. That depends on how well we do together."

JayVee could not believe what was happening. He was suddenly the one with the power, but a part of him also realized he had to work to keep it. He showed up mostly on time and kept his temper in check except for two times in the first couple of weeks. When he got so frustrated and angry that I knew my voice couldn't settle him down, I told him to put the book down and walk with me. We went outside where the air was clear.

"I get pissed too, Mr. Shakkar, and I found the best thing to do is take a break and do something I liked. Then my anger goes away." I took the boy three blocks away to an ice cream store. "There's nothing like a chocolate ice cream cone to make me feel better. Now I can do anything. Nothing can beat me."

JayVee liked chocolate too and we walked back to the reading center and finished our cones, smiling, with our feet up on a chair. I taught him to take a deep breath, high five each other, and start again. It worked and I actually began to like the kid. This was not a good thing for a teacher because I had to fight the tendency to give him credit for things he did not do. He occasionally tried to manipulate me with fake fits of anger so he could get ice cream.

"Mr. Shakkar, you are a very smart young man. However, teachers have a special gift and they are able to tell when you are really mad and when you just want an ice cream cone. I was going to take you out to the store today when you weren't angry at all because you're doing good work. Now, you made me sad because neither of us is going to get any chocolate." I put on a sorrowful face and turned the page in our workbook.

JayVee got it. He never apologized or said he was sorry, but he worked hard and in the middle of our next appointment, out we went for chocolate ice cream cones. My reward came in his last week with me. He said I could call him, JayVee.

Chapter Twenty

Neeva seemed to have a very busy and disorganized life. Two days before we were supposed to get together again, she called me midmorning to say she would have to postpone our rendezvous for another week.

"What's the problem this time, Neeva? I hope your inventory is over by now."

"Yes, that's finished, but an inventory means you have to neglect all the other business you are responsible for. Now I have to catch up."

"How's your friend? She must be in the same situation, too."

"Exactly the same."

Our mundane conversation went on for another minute before we confirmed our date in nine days' time. I wasn't too bummed as I knew this was an appointment solely for sex. Nevertheless, it did make me miss a more loving relationship. One of the most important things about loving someone is the element of trust. Neeva put me on edge. I saw no evidence of another person in the house, but she could have cleansed each room of telltale signs. My libido was off the charts and I decided not to question her before we met as it might make her mad enough to cancel.

Meanwhile, my tutoring was going well and, with a modest salary increase, I was making reasonable money. Pam and Jerry were delightful landlords and I enjoyed our conversations. I helped around the house and in the kitchen as opportunities presented themselves. Los Angeles was a delightful place to live and I began to think seriously about starting my middle-aged life there. However, a serious hiccup came up three weeks after I arrived. I was there long enough for Pam to notice something odd about my appearance. Women have a way of noticing these things long before it becomes obvious for a man. The three of us finished dinner and were sitting in the living room enjoying a bottle of sipping tequila. I wanted to show both of them how much I enjoyed their company and gave them the bottle of the expensive liquor.

Pam said, "This is really tasty. I was born in California, but never realized how exquisite Tequila could be." Jerry echoed her words and patted me on the shoulder. Then she continued, "This is a very personal question, Tom, and you don't have to answer it if you don't want to. I was just thinking about the change."

Jerry, obviously embarrassed and surprised at his wife's nerve, gave her a "look."

"Ask away, Pam. I didn't realize something was changing."

"Your hair was not so white when you came here. Were you dyeing it?"

I decided to lie. I was concerned about my accelerated aging process for a while, but chose to ignore the signs. I knew my life would be over at some point, but obsessing about it in the time remaining didn't seem constructive.

"I had a troubled middle age and wanted to go back a few years and start over. One of the ways I decided to do that was to dye my hair. Recently, I decided it was foolish and immature and thus I am aging again before your very eyes." I laughed and hoped neither of them noticed the false notes.

Jerry settled down and Pam gave me a big smile and said, "We are much older than you are, Tom, and you can see how happy we are. Birthdays are only numbers and should have no bearing on how we feel about ourselves and how we live our lives. Obviously, some people are more fortunate than others and we all have to play the hand we're dealt. Jerry and I look at it this way: life is like a mountain. If you're lucky, you get a high one and it's a long road to the top. As you age, you have to take smaller steps, but never stop climbing."

The Hillbrook's simple philosophy entranced me. I put my head back and tried to see through the ceiling, to get a glimpse of my own mountain, to get some idea of how long my trail was going to be. Of course, no one ever saw their own top. The point was to keep climbing, no matter how small the steps you need to take.

"Thank you both for that. I'm still stepping and have no intention of looking down."

The three of us sat silent for a moment and then drained our tiny glasses. Tasting was only one of the pleasures life still had for us. Jerry shook my hand and Pam gave me a hug before we went off to bed.

* * *

Big Boy thought Lobo had lost his mind. His fearless enforcer began reading the LA Times newspaper when things were slow. If he missed a day or two, he would go to the library and peruse the sections that contained local West Coast news. Darren, or Tom if he had gone back to his old name, was a troublemaker and he knew that eventually, the man was going to be involved in something seriously bad. Reporters loved that kind of stuff and sooner or later it would be written about. When that happened, he'd ask Big Boy for more time off.

Lobo put a finger in his mouth and felt the scar tissue on his tongue. He tried to say "hallelujah" and it came out "*hah yoo yeah ya*." It didn't matter, because a gun was too good for little Tommy. He'd shout the word over and over as he carved the bastard's heart out with his new switchblade.

* * *

Neeva finally had the opportunity she wanted to spend the night with Tom. She could not wait. It was weeks since she had an orgasm and she hoped Tom would be up for more than one. The bruise on the side of her face went from blue to green to yellow and was now, with a little makeup, invisible. Her right arm wasn't sore anymore either and in the dark, Tom would never notice the marks.

Neeva's mind slipped back to their last time together. She remembered what she saw when he was taking off his pants. This gave her the idea she was going to discuss with him after she gave him the best night of his life. He'd agree to anything after that.

Wait a minute. What was he doing with that big knife? It was strapped to his right leg. Maybe some of his students were gang members and threatened him. Perhaps there was a contract out on him and a hitman was trying to find him. Maybe Tom was a liar, maybe he wasn't a teacher, after all. If he had a knife, he probably had a gun. Regardless, the knife meant he was a violent man and capable of anything. It was a lucky break and she was going to make the most of it. There would be no more bruises.

* * *

I was getting dressed for the evening. Neeva was impressed with clothes and I wanted her aroused when we went to bed. I'd worn a sweater the last time as the evening was chilly, but now I had a yen for "California cool." I had a deep blue corduroy jacket with leather elbow patches that I thought would get her going. My slacks didn't mean as much, but I had some pressed tan ones that fit perfectly. My diver's knife would be a nuisance and I knew Neeva wasn't going to do me any harm. I'd worn it every day as a matter of safety, but in the end, I flipped a coin and let the fates decide.

Chapter Twenty-one

As I brushed my hair, I could see the gray was giving way to white. Pam, seeing me every day, noticed the change so Neeva should be able to spot it immediately. I thought about doing a "reverse lie", telling her I was dying it white. Thinking about that on the bus to L.A., I chuckled loudly enough so the guy next to me turned around.

"What's that all about, partner? If it's a good joke, tell me about it 'cause I've had three committee meetings today that were a complete waste of time."

"I'm not sure this is going to cope with three meetings, but it may get you over the first." I was laughing because I decided to tell opposite lies about the same thing to get me out of trouble in two separate situations.

My bus-mate frowned and stared at me with such curiosity, I had to say something. "I told my landlord I was dying my hair gray and told my girlfriend I was dying it white." I gave him a moment to digest the un-digestible and added, "If you knew the circumstances, you would not think I'd gone crazy. That's all I can say."

My new amigo was grinning. "Being a little crazy, in this crazy world, is a good thing. It helps us to cope with the tragic, the comic and the bizarre."

"Thanks. I'd be disappointed if you jumped up and ran into the next car."

A good conversation followed which shortened the time between my rented room and my date with Neeva. We shook hands after leaving the train and I gazed around the terminal for my quixotic date. She was ten minutes late which I hoped was not a red flag for the evening. I tossed my small duffel into the back seat and slipped in beside her. She leaned over, gave me her tongue for a few seconds, and then drove into the city traffic.

We headed to a bar and restaurant area and found a parking space without too much trouble. Neeva said she'd find the right bar which, of course, was the wrong place for me.. Neeva liked weird notes seriously loud. I drank two margaritas and still grimaced. I like rock music because it took me back to a place I vaguely remember.

"You're not gettin' with the program, Tom. I hope you're not going to be like this in bed."

"Only if you're bringing that band along with you. I don't mind if you holler a little, but I'm going to be deaf in another couple of minutes."

Neeva kissed the side of my mouth. "All right. Pay the bill and let's find something else."

We walked several blocks before I found something reminiscent enough to feel romantic. The songs were a mixture of Bill Haley, Chuck Berry and Little Richard. I remembered about half of the words, which amazed Neeva. She said, "I don't know how I got through high school. I can hardly remember anything."

That was not a turn on for me and I promised myself I would try to do better in the weeks ahead. Out of habit, I checked my right ankle and momentarily froze. Then I recalled flipping a coin and the fates decided against my diving knife. At least I wouldn't have to answer questions when I undressed. We ordered burgers, fries and small salads and by the time we finished, it was time for some real action.

We'd been drinking and I noticed Neeva was driving back to her house very slowly. I told her cops watched for that, as well as speeding, and offered to drive. She turned me down and I was relieved when we pulled into her little driveway. Once again, she didn't open the garage door. I decided not to aggravate her with more questions and we headed upstairs to the guest bedroom. Neeva was tipsy and she was not quite as responsive as she was previously. Nevertheless, we had a great time.

I was determined to get up in the middle of the night and check the garage, but after our third "bout" (with Neeva stuporous by that time), I was exhausted and didn't wake up until 6 AM. I dressed, left her asleep in an odd position and went down to the kitchen to make coffee. The fridge had some orange juice and the acid helped clear my head. I reluctantly came to the conclusion that Neeva and I needed to part ways. I paced the kitchen trying to figure out how I could get the Hillbrook's telephone number away from Neeva. She wasn't that smart so she had to have an address book somewhere.

I walked around the kitchen several times, lost in thought, so I was surprised when I realized the door into the garage was right in front of me. I walked to the bottom of the stairs and listened for noises above. Silence. I tiptoed back into the kitchen, opened the garage door and flipped on the light. Beyond the empty space in front of me, I saw a dark green pickup truck, with a white star on the door. I walked over and realized it was a Dodge military vehicle, probably post-World War II. There was no way this belonged to Neeva. She was married, or at least had a live-in boyfriend.

On the way back into the kitchen, walking fast, I noticed a board with keys hanging on hooks. I took the one key that looked like it belonged to a padlock and bounded up the stairs and down the hall. I unlocked the padlock and inside the closet were all kinds of sports things: footballs, baseball stuff and two rifles against the wall. A handgun was hanging upside down from a hook through the trigger guard. Rifle and pistol ammunition was stacked on a shelf.

I had to find Neeva's address book, erase my telephone number, and get the hell out of the neighborhood. I found the book in her bedside table and scratched out my number. Her man, if he was not a veteran, was probably a military nut and he'd kill me and bury the corpse in the yard. I took a baseball bat, just in case, and decided to drop the padlock key on the garage floor, as if it had fallen off the hook. When I left, I'd leave the bat in the garage. As I was locking the padlock, I heard the crunch of gravel in front of the house.

Then there were two male voices, one laughing and the other trying to talk over it.

Neeva, screaming, came running out of her room. "Get the hell out of here. I have to cover the bed and clean myself up. He's right outside."

As angry and scared as I was, I could not help saying, "This is what you get for lying to me."

"Fuck you. Get out of the house."

One guy said, "So long Buddy," and I heard footsteps receding.

I shoved everything into my duffel and ran my eyes over the room. Neeva, naked, was audibly freaking out and, after tucking in the sheets, was reaching for the bedspread. I raced down the stairs, two at a time, and headed for the back door into the rear yard. Halfway there, I could hear a key clicking into the front lock and the deadbolt being thrown. It sounded like Marines loading a howitzer. I knew I'd never make it so I slipped through a door to my right. It was a the utility room with a washer and dryer, shelves of powdered detergent and an upright ironing board clipped against the wall.

"Hey Neeva, whatcha doin', baby?" resounded through the house. The bass voice caused a slight rattle in the loose doorknob in front of me.

Chapter Twenty-two

It was dark in the utility room with the door closed, but I knew where the detergent was. I felt around until I located the box and pulled out two of the individual paper packets. I had the baseball bat, but against a trained opponent, it would be virtually useless. My only hope was that Neeva could straighten things up and get in the shower. The husband, or whatever he was, might get turned on enough to give me a chance to get out of the house. That hope was short-lived as I could hear shouts from the second floor.

"You bitch; you've been at it again. It smells like a whorehouse up here. Where's the bastard hiding?"

"No Chesty, the son of a bitch broke into the house two hours ago and raped me, swear to God!"

"Where is he? I'll tend to him first and then we'll have a little talk."

"I dunno. As soon as he heard the car, he ran down the hall."

I heard heavy steps in the upstairs hall and they suddenly stopped. I knew what he was doing, trying to get into the closet where his weapons were. I had the key, but maybe he carried one with him.

"Why the hell did you put a padlock on here, Neeva? What good is my gun if I can't get to it when someone breaks into the house?"

I knew he'd be coming down the stairs at any moment and I didn't want him to find me in this little room. In close quarters, I was

The Awakening of Thomas Hunter

a goner. I opened the door, slipped out and headed for the back door to the yard. I was halfway through when I heard a rush of steps on the stairs. There was a five-foot high wooden fence around the yard and if I could get over it, I could crouch down and Chesty would see an empty yard. With any luck, he wouldn't run around peering over it. However, in my rush to get out of the house, I had left the outside door open and Chesty never broke stride. He burst into the yard when I was halfway to the fence. My only choice was to fight him.

"There you are, you fucker. Nobody messes with my wife and gets away with it."

I turned and raised the bat, still backing toward the fence. That gave Chesty pause and he stopped about ten feet from me. He was younger and about my height, but weighed at least forty pounds more. His neck and arms were thick with muscle and his shaved head glistened in the sun. He had a handlebar mustache and, when he began smiling, even a dentist would be appalled.

"The bat ain't going to do you no good, punk. I'm going to use it to make your face look different. And when I finish with your legs, you're not going to walk for a long time."

The thought came to me, as I continued to move backwards, that if I hurt him, he would do twice as much damage to me. But what other choice did I have? I took a quick look around, hoping there was a neighbor who would call the police if I yelled loud enough. No such luck.

Chesty came at me in a rush and he would've been on me before I could swing the bat. I moved the bat in a straight line to his body and when he was about three feet away, I shoved it forward with all my strength. I aimed for his solar plexus, knowing if I tried for his face, he would have a much easier time avoiding it. He managed to move his right arm just enough to move the bat down so it hit him in his belly button. The combination of his speed and my force must've hurt like hell. Chesty fell to his knees and put his left arm out to keep himself from falling on his face, which was twisting in agony. I could've swung the bat and hit him on the side of the head, but I was afraid it would kill him. I'd spend the next thirty years in prison. I flung the bat away and headed for the fence, not looking behind me. I tried to vault over it by putting my hands on top and swinging my legs up and over, but that was a mistake. I forgot how old I had become. My right knee went over, but the left hit the fence and I was hanging there, painfully straddling the damn thing. I got my left leg over at the same time Chesty arrived and grabbed my left wrist and the collar of my shirt.

He'd hold me in that powerful grip until he could get himself over the fence. No punches of mine would stop the enraged man. My right hand was free and I reached in my pants pocket and took out one of the paper packets of detergent powder. Chesty had his right leg over the fence with both hands gripping me. I tore the packet open with my teeth and shoved it into his face. The man screamed and let go, rubbing his eyes frantically. Rubbing made it worse and I knew he'd be blind for a while. I ran up the alley and headed to the right. I ran past six houses until I saw a woman working on roses in the front of her house. I slowed to a fast walk so I wouldn't alarm her.

"Excuse me, ma'am. My car won't start and I'm supposed to be at the airport in forty-five minutes. Could you call a taxi for me? My son in San Francisco fell off a ladder and hit his head. He's in an ambulance on the way to the hospital. It's an emergency."

"Oh my goodness, the poor boy. You wait here and I'll call right away."

The nice lady hustled into her house and closed the door. I knew she was smart because I heard the snap of the bolt. I was careful to stay well away from the house and visible from all the front windows. I was out of breath, and had some of the detergent powder scattered on my arms and chest. I gripped my duffel, which I'd thrown over the fence before my unsuccessful leap. If she called the police, I would have a difficult time explaining what I was doing there. I knew it would not be long before Neeva called them to report a rape. It's the only way she could keep on her husband's good side. If he had a good side.

There was a large tree next to the road and I stood so anyone following wouldn't be able to see me. I was still in view from the house and it wasn't long before the lady opened her door and told me a taxi was on the way. She said, "Good luck. I'll pray for your son." I waved a "Thank you" before she shut and locked the door again. A half hour later, I stood in front of American Airlines. As soon as the taxi was out of sight, I got another one and headed to the bus terminal. There was a Greyhound bound for Tijuana at 2 o'clock, which would mean a three hour wait. That was too long; if the police were looking for a rapist, they would have all the exits from the city closed down quickly. I hoped Chesty's eyes would be a priority and a visit to the emergency room should hold him up for a while. I had enough time to call the Hillbrooks and I told Jerry I was off to Mexico.

I took a cab back to the airport and checked outgoing flights. American Airlines had a flight to Dallas leaving in thirty-five minutes. I bought a one-way ticket using my Tom Hunter ID. The only people who knew both names were dangerous, but I was far enough away from Spokane not to worry.

* * *

Even Big Boy's cursing and the rest of the gangs teasing didn't deter Lobo. Two days after I left San Diego, an item appeared in the local newspaper detailing a home invasion and rape in Neeva's subdivision. The emergency room visit of the victim's husband was reported as corneal damage, which if it did not heal satisfactorily, would necessitate corneal transplants. The rape of an innocent wife and the near blinding of her salesman husband with laundry detergent was just the sort of news crime reporters salivated for and the story spread to other papers along the coast. The name Tom Hunter jumped off the page and hit Lobo hard. He rubbed the black ink letters with such vigor he had trouble cleaning the newsprint off his fingers. He showed the article to Big Boy and the rest of the crew, but they all had trouble reading the gray smear that was Tom's name. Lobo tore the article out and put it in his pocket, mumbling, "*Hah yoo yeah ya*," over and over.

Chapter Twenty-three

I was confused when I landed at Love Field. I looked around the airport and it did not seem familiar, although I sensed I'd been in Texas before. Past knowledge was so foggy I could only conclude I'd floated down the river Styx and was now in the Underworld. If so, I was supposed to be dead. My presence would certainly upset Hades, the fellow who ran the show down here. No wonder he set Lobo after me, it would solve his dilemma.

What nonsense. I'd be crazy thinking a Greek myth had come to life. I needed a place to stay and a job and I'd pay extra to start off in a more upscale way. I didn't need any more Neevas or Chestys in my life. I checked the classifieds in a paper I bought at Love Field and there were a couple of rooms for rent around University Park. I selected the one owned by a widower, as I did not want to risk any female involvement. It was a ground-floor apartment with my own entrance, which was another advantage. My landlord, Denton Milforth, was a successful stockbroker in his seventies. Ostensibly, he was retired, but couldn't resist the game and worked on his own (with a few of his friends) almost daily. He lost his wife two years before and the work was helpful in moderating his grief.

Mr. Milforth insisted I call him by his first name, although it was awkward for me. I had a gut feeling my father was from the South and a stickler for protocol. Even in my mid-fifties, I called older men, "Sir", and never by their first names. I was supposed to treat women with the utmost respect and caught myself tipping my hat when I passed one on the street. I did this for a short time until I realized no one else was doing it. Anyway, only farmers wore hats anymore.

The first thing I did was to ask Denton if he knew of any jobs in the city. He perked up instantly and we sat down in the living room.

"Well, Tom, you're coming here is a nice coincidence. I'm on the Board of a Museum here in the city. There's a gallery attached and we've had trouble finding enough staff for maintenance and exhibition setups. From what you told me, you are a jack-of-all-trades and this would be ideal. You're not going to get rich, but there's plenty of excitement in museum work."

"Is it close by I don't have a car."

"Not very close, but public transportation will get you right in front."

My interview at the museum was very short. I suspect Denton put the word in, probably because he wanted to be sure I'd pay the rent. Not being born in the State was a definite disadvantage in Texas, but at least I wasn't from New York.

I did have to learn a new language, which was kind of fun. Texans have funny expressions like, "out-of-pocket," "I'm fixing to," and "pick-em-up" truck. I heard a unique one standing in the cashier line in a grocery store. The man ahead of me was deeply tanned and middle-aged. He was wearing bib overalls with galluses ("suspenders" in the rest of the country) over his shoulders. He kept rubbing his left knee and I said, "That looks like it hurts."

"Yeah, I had it cut on yesterday."

"What was it?"

"I had a risin' in my leaders."

"Oh, hope it feels better soon."

I had no idea what he was talking about. That evening, I asked Denton to translate.

"He was probably a rancher or farmer with horses. A 'rising' is a swelling and the tendons of a horse are called 'leaders.' He was telling you he had a boil behind his left knee lanced yesterday."

"Ah, now I get it."

Museum maintenance included keeping the floors clean, which was not easy considering the number of visitors who dropped stuff. The walls were painted different colors depending on the content of new exhibits. We hung paintings, placed sculptures and set up installations. I could not figure out why I felt so comfortable in this environment. When time allowed, I found myself sitting in on painting classes that the museum put on several times a week. I even bought a sketchpad, brushes and acrylic paints. Denton put a large lamp with a "sunlight" bulb in my room and lent me an old easel.

My social life was more of a struggle since I was considerably older than the demographic in the bars and music places around town. I rarely went to church, although I had a feeling I went regularly in my youth. These "alternative existence" recollections were fascinating, but also an irritant. They tended to put me into some kind of past existence without ever giving me the relief of understanding why.

I attended lectures on various subjects throughout the city and began to take small group painting lessons given by accomplished artists. Most amateur painters were either beginners or elderly folks who took lessons to avoid boredom. The teachers told me I was way ahead of the crowd. I eventually joined a large group of advanced amateurs who put on monthly shows to attract attention and occasionally sell a painting. I worked in my room most evenings, applying acrylic colors to art paper taped to a board on my easel. I did this, not only with brushes, but also with a variety of spatulas. Although I was meticulous by nature, I decided not to do things like blocks of color, geometric designs or reality paintings, but let my imagination choose the form. From somewhere, I knew about color and which ones to mix together to create whatever I wanted.

Debra, an attractive middle-aged woman was in my advanced painting class. I didn't notice her at first as she was sitting off to one side, but she noticed me. We were the only ones who didn't have a Texas accent. I said, "You did well" instead of, "You done good." I must have been very preoccupied after the lesson because she had gorgeous natural auburn hair. She made a point of sitting next to me at the next session and we had a drink afterwards at a local bar.

"This is quite a coincidence. I'm from Connecticut and you're from California, and here we are exactly in the middle of the country."

I said, "The fates at work." My mention of 'fates' reminded me of Neeva and I was not about to get involved with a married woman. "I want to be completely honest with you. I am not married and do not have a girlfriend. I think I was happily married at one time."

Debra laughed. "That's a relief. I'm glad you like women and don't have a wife. I was unhappily married at one time. It's been a while and I'm very particular."

"I think it's important to be with people when they're not on their best behavior. It's not only the youngsters who often present themselves as something they're not."

Debra suddenly looked seriously at me. "That's good. Only time will tell." She smiled to reassure me.

"I'll try to live up to that. In the meantime, would you give me a brief autobiography?" Debra was working at a prominent law firm. Her father was a lawyer and urged her to follow in the profession. She graduated in the upper half of her law school class and was in charge of guiding other lawyers in her firm on regulatory and compliance matters. She was apparently very good and could choose much of what she worked on.

As we got to know each other, trust developed and I told her about my eight months long amnesic past. I started with my rebirth in the river and gave edited versions of Papi's farm, Lobo, building a school, my life as a hospital orderly and finally as an English language tutor. Now I was a museum maintenance guy and amateur painter. It was a good life, especially since I met Debra. We got together several times a week and eventually, instead of restaurants all the time, she began cooking savory dinners in the house she owned.

The winter days in Texas could be icy and windy, but that was a small disadvantage compared to having a good job. I was liked and respected at the museum and had the company of an intelligent, attractive woman. Debra's sensitivity, humor and optimism was my winter overcoat and I thought it would last forever.

Chapter Twenty-four

Lobo was in Los Angles for three days and Tom Hunter had vanished. When he got off the train, he went straight to the Times and was finally able to talk to the reporter who wrote the article about the "alleged" rapist who had blinded the husband of his victim. The reporter knew my last location in the city and Lobo gave him what he knew about Tom. Lobo did not disclose my alias as he didn't want me in jail, he wanted me alone in a remote spot. Even the police didn't know where Tom had gone.

Lobo was so infuriated he bought a bottle of whiskey and spent the evening getting even angrier. Eventually, he put his fist through the drywall several times. Some of Lobo's fingertips were bloody and the knuckles on his right hand were raw. He thought the Hillbrooks might know my secret whereabouts and, the next day, chose "nice" rather than "scary" to approach them.

"Thanks to you, Mr. and Mrs. Hillbrook, for letting me talk with you. I know the police already been here, but I got questions. I work for . . . ah . . . an insurance company tracking stolen money. I need to talk to Mr. Hunter up close so I'd be appreciated to know where he went."

Pam and Jerry looked at each other and then back at Lobo, whose spider web neck tattoo was visible above his right collar. Jerry said, "Tom rented a room here for a while and kept to himself. His apartment has its own entrance so he came and went as he pleased.

We found his rent money in an envelope on the kitchen table when he left. He said he had a better job offer somewhere else, but didn't say where." Jerry opened his eyes wide and started his right hand trembling.

Lobo could tell the old folks were scared and they probably knew a lot more than they were telling. Time for Plan B. He took off his baseball cap to show them his shaved head. He unbuttoned his shirt halfway down and they could see a huge tarantula on his chest web. He balled up his right fist and moved it slowly, toward Pam and Jerry's face. The word tattooed on his fingers, below the knuckles, read "pain."

Pam was under control, but couldn't help a sharp intake of breath. The rest was pure Hollywood. "Please don't kill us, sir. Jerry was not here when Tom told me on the way out he was going to Mexico. I don't speak Mexican, but it sounded like, *Tee ah wanna.*" She grabbed her husband's upper arm and started to cry, shaking and breathing irregularly.

"Mexico?" thought Lobo. "I'll never find him down there."

Jerry said, "Tom didn't speak Mexican so I think he'll be back sooner or later." He put his arm around his wife and whispered loud enough so Lobo could hear, "I think this guy is an undercover cop and if Tom's done something wrong, the Mexicans will send him back."

Undercover cop? Lobo looked at the couple, frightened out of their minds, and knew they had nothing more to offer. Cutting their fingers off for fun would get the local police pissed off and he didn't want that.

"Thanks for your help. If he comes back, let me know right away. There's a reward. A big one." Lobo handed them a torn piece of paper with a phone number on it. "I'll call the cops before I come down and make sure he's the right one." As soon as Lobo got in his rental car, he slapped the side of his head thinking, "They thought I was an undercover cop. What a kick. Big Boy and the guys will love it."

Jerry double locked the door, hugged his wife, and dialed the police. Pam said, "That guy was a real low life. Funny way of talking too . . . something wrong with his mouth."

Unhappily, the police never got to chat with Lobo. By the time they decided it was worth a follow-up, he had turned in his rental car and was already on a train heading north. Chesty beat Neeva badly after his treatment at the hospital. She had a long history of emergency room visits and the detectives decided he made up the story to hide domestic abuse and it was Neeva who blinded him. There was no warrant issued for Tom Hunter.

I, of course, knew nothing about Lobo's visit to L.A. and thought he had given up long ago. You have to be insane to continue to pursue someone who had never hurt you without provocation. That was the problem of course; he was psychotic.

* * *

As Debra and I moved closer emotionally and intellectually, I began to get more and more concerned about my past life. If I had a wife, was I still married? What about children? I knew I was in some kind of time warp, as I had frequent intimations of the future too. For instance, when I was walking on the street and wanted to make a phone call, I instinctively put my hand in my pocket when there was a phone booth right on the corner. Dick Tracy had a wrist phone so people in the future must have something similar.

Debra was intrigued, even excited, about my history. The thought of having a boyfriend from another time was so incredible she wanted to retrace my journey back to the river so she could write a book about it. I told her Lobo would be the only one happy about seeing me again. The other part of my new life was the aging process.

After only ten days, Debra put her hand on my face, lifted the skin on my forehead and stared at me from a different angle.

"Are you using the cream I gave you, Tom? People can get really old, really fast, if they don't keep their skin from drying out."

"I use it every day, but I think I need to try a new brand. It's giving me wrinkles." I walked out of her living room into the bathroom and stared at myself. My hair was now almost totally white and the laugh lines around my eyes had deepened. There were tiny furrows and looseness under my upper arms that weren't there a month ago. I was losing muscle mass and shrinking inside my own skin. None of this was a laughing matter. In less than five more months, I'd be out of the river for a year and I was approaching sixty. At this rate, I'd look over eighty on my first anniversary. Was the length of my second life predestined?

I decided the best way to get through the time ahead was to live life to the fullest. I wanted to make every day count for myself, my friends and especially for Debra.

"I don't know how much time I have left in this life, my dear. I'd like to spend it here working, painting and being close to you."

Debra looked at me strangely, a mixture of sorrow, caring and fear. We were sitting in her living room after dinner, sipping Madeira. I was truly happy and relaxed and wanted to do this as often as possible to the end of my days. Debra rose, crossed the living room to the bay window, and stood for a time, looking out over the city. I started to get up and join her, but she turned and motioned me back down. I felt the life flowing out of my being at the thought of this extraordinary woman disappearing from my life. I couldn't blame her. What would I do if the situation was reversed? What if she was the loved person who was dying? It would be difficult for me to touch her.

I heard Debra sigh and I looked up and glimpsed her reflection in the bay window. All color had vanished in the black and white image on the glass. She became an old-time photograph, something her great-grandchildren would look at for a moment before turning away. It takes yearning, determination and imagination to color such an old photograph and bring it to life in your mind. Debra turned, brought herself to life, and looked at me for almost a minute.

I was paralyzed with fear and longing. I don't know whether she read the love in my eyes, or decided on her own to treasure the time we had together and whatever was to come. I watched her face for a sign as she walked towards me. Her smile was so faint her lips moved up only at the corners, leaving my questions unanswered. When she stood in front of me, she blurred as my tears distorted her presence. I never saw Debra move a hand to mine, but felt it slide into my palm and lift me out of my seat. It was done with such gentleness I thought it might be my imagination. I slipped into a past-remembered journey as she drew me behind her down the hallway.

Debra undressed me slowly and when I was naked, she put her arms around me and drew me to her clothed self. When she released me, I lifted my hands to unbutton her, but she drew back and gestured to the bed. I sat on the edge gazing at her, following the strangely familiar motion of her hands on her blouse. When she was nude, she stood for a while, watching me caress her skin with my eyes.

When she started towards me, I moved over and lay on my left side waiting. Debra came and lay on her right with her left leg on top of me. She shivered slightly and slid closer until there was no space between us. Our eyes were open, studying each other. We kissed, our lips moving and searching, before our tongues reached out to each other. I could feel her leg's increasing pressure and the firmness of her breasts against my chest. We drew back and took deep breaths. In that narrow window, Debra moved away from me onto her back. Her arms spread out on the sheets and she bent her knees and slowly opened herself, inviting me to share her life.

Not a single word had passed between us since she left the sofa and lost her color in the window glass.

Chapter Twenty-five

I was very busy when the museum put on a new exhibit, gave classes to fifth-graders or scheduled a lecture. I got requests from all parts of the building to, "do this" and "do that." "Thank you, Toms" rained down on me some days, and occasionally they poured. I reveled in my work and the pleasure it gave everyone to see their ideas and plans come alive with my arrangements and lighting. Often it was the meticulous placement of objects that made a 3-D exhibit sing. It was a surreal world in there, different from life outside the museum and I identified with it. Now my life was a dimension away from the one wiped from my memory.

All that effort was for others, but painting was for myself. I had my first hint of an artistic gift when I went to the gallery with Mimzy in Seattle, but I think my own art would have happened sooner if I'd been with Debra. I treasured the break when the museum closed on Sundays and Mondays. I disappeared into the red sable, badger and hog bristle hair in my brushes. The color wheel from long ago still lingered in my mind and allowed me to mix primary and secondary colors almost without thinking. Acrylic hues, some warm and some cool, surged onto the paper in forms and designs I had no control over, but meant something to me. Some came from a previous existence, but most from my emergent life after the river. When I first started this, I feared Lobo's darkness would infect my work. That did not happen because of Debra. Her love and enthusiasm cast a hopeful mood over almost everything I painted.

I couldn't imagine what others might think, but looking at my vision of childlike Chinny on the paper affected me. It was not a portrait. It was the shape and color that made me feel her resiliency and her desire to experience what life can bring to all of us, regardless of shortcomings. I did several on Mama's cooking and a funny one about Dicker and the fiery whorehouse.

Sunlight doesn't shine every day and I'd mislead you if I ignored the rain. The end of Billy Joe's life affected me deeply and I painted his terror, his acceptance and the peace I experienced with him at the end. I included his strength, his faith and his father. I felt it all as it flowed from my brushes. Sometimes I wept in the middle of a stroke and I left the tears where they lay. I never used black paint. Any darkness in my work came from mixing wrong colors together on purpose.

The spatula was elevating; I could spread the colors on wildly or sensibly. Joy and anger were as different on the paper as valleys and mountains. Acrylic dries quickly and I often added more thickness and variant colors later. I sometimes scattered whatever came to mind onto the acrylic before it dried. I used salt, pine needles, sand and metal filings as the spirit moved me. It was folk songs and opera, jitterbug and waltz. Painting took me out of myself and gave me a taste of eternity.

When I finished a painting, or took a break, I had difficulty coming back through the wormhole. I'd pace around the room, occasionally bumping into the furniture. I tripped over my boots once and ended up lying on my back, laughing at the pranks astrals could play on you.

Making love can also offer a taste of eternity. Just a taste, though. The French call orgasm, "La Petite Mort" (the little death), and refers to that brief period of transcendence when one is no longer in the material world. I can tell you, though, it lasts a lot longer when you paint.

Debra and I became deeply involved, emotionally, spiritually and intellectually. She knew I respected and loved her and complete trust developed progressively. She had two children from a previous marriage and they knew we were special friends. They were both in their late twenties and after they knew me, were happy their mother had a companion who would never take advantage of her. I'm sure they wondered about our future relationship, but I was determined to keep it on an informal basis. I did this because I knew I was aging much faster than usual. It was hard because I could see Debra yearned for futurity and loved me as much as I loved her.

I saw her often and she had no idea of my advancing senescence until weeks went by. I finished my shower and was standing in front of the mirror with a towel around my waist. Debra came over to pick me up before we went out to dinner and happened to see me in that reflected light. I could see surprise and worry washing over her face as she stood behind me, staring over my shoulder into the mirror. I knew she would never say anything.

"I'll tell you all about it, Debra, after I get dressed. Make yourself a drink and one for me if you don't mind. Let's talk before we go out." There was a small sitting room next to my bedroom and when I was dressed, I was relieved to see Debra there. I wasn't sure, in the bathroom, whether she would leave and end it. It was a bad sign there were no drinks on the coffee table and her eyes had darkened perceptively.

"It's been five months since I came out of the river and I guessed my age at that time to be about forty. I'm now at least in my late fifties. It was not easy for me to come to terms with this, but I've done it. I love you too much to inflict my limited future on you. That's the sole reason we've been living day to day, without talking about anything more."

Debra wasn't looking at me and gravity took over her features. I knew she was in shock and it would be a few minutes before the muddle in her brain settled down. I sat in a chair away from her as I knew a touch would make it worse. I could have told her about my aging when we talked about my life after the river, but I'd put it in the back of my head long before. Keeping it in a lockbox allowed me the freedom to live fully in the time I had left. It was a good plan and worked well until now. Finding someone like Debra was a dream I thought would never happen. When the dragon poked its head out of the cave, I was too scared to do anything but run. Now I was going to get burnt.

I sat absolutely still with my eyes averted so I was not looking at Debra, but could still see her in my peripheral vision. I tried to work out whether it would be best for me to keep talking or to let her say what she needed to. I gave up the struggle and closed down. It seemed like hours before the motion of her head alerted me. I turned towards her and we looked at each other.

"It never occurred to me. I never expected this, Tom. You must be an alien or something. It's not normal."

"I never expected to meet you, Debra. I'm in love with an earthling and the astrals may not be happy with me."

"The what?!"

"I made the second part up. The first part is true. I don't know how I came to have a second existence. It makes no sense to me and the divine wind, or whatever governs the universe, has not thought to give me an answer. Not even a hint."

"How can you deal with this?"

"It is what it is. I've been dealt a hand with cards that make no sense. I had two options: live it or end it. As long as I've still got the cards, I'm going to play the game."

"What about us?"

That, of course, was the sixty-four dollar question. I'd been playing my cards since I roused in the river and had both losses and wins. Debra was the best win by far. Nevertheless, I'd give her up in a heartbeat to keep from hurting her. "Let's take a break and talk about it in two days. Write your decision down on a piece of paper and I'll do the same. When we get together—over a stiff drink—we'll trade notes and find out the answer."

I thought my plan was a good one, but Debra seemed too stunned to think straight. She nodded uneasily and walked toward the door. I didn't want to touch or hug her because I needed this to be entirely rational. That is the only way the answer would be right. At the door, she turned around and stared at me so intensely it frightened me. She probed my very soul. Then she gave me a slight smile, shook her head despairingly, and left.

I went back into the bathroom and washed my hands. I didn't know what it meant, but it occurred to me I might be doing the Pontius Pilate thing, washing my hands of this precious relationship. I hoped for some miracle because, without Debra, my life would be like the window reflection, a black and white negative completely devoid of color.

Chapter Twenty-six

Debra, when she got home, had no memory of how she got there. She lay on her bed grasping at images and conversation bits. "It has to be some elaborate hoax. Tom says he woke up with amnesia in some river in Idaho and then went from place to place, aging a year every week or so. He showed me newspaper articles and proofs of jobs he had, but that doesn't mean he isn't a traveling psychotic. What possible motive would he have?

"And what about Tom's artwork? Those paintings make me think, make me happy and make me cry. I want one in my home so I can sit in front of it and feel, really feel." There was a gallery attached to the museum and Debra decided to get a couple of his paintings and enter them in an upcoming competition. The best forty submitted would hang for a month and the public could come, see and buy. Tom would object, but she would sneak them out of his studio.

Debra thought about their relationship and questioned whether his love was real. She was not a wealthy woman and it didn't make sense to say he loved her, just for the thrill of thieving. More often than not, he paid when they went out to eat and he had never asked her for a loan. She fastened on his face and his eyes when they were together. She felt his fingers on her skin and his lips on her body. He was totally unselfish, not the actions of a Lothario.

"What if it's true, his whole story and what's happening to him? Has there ever been a time warp before and nobody thought to question it? Over millennia, there were 'miracles' that allegedly happened. Could it be that mere coincidences defied logic? If there is a God, is He doing this to Tom for a reason or is He just having fun? Can the cosmos itself, with its black holes and space-time ripples, leak enough quark fragments to confound rationality? " None of this made any sense to Debra and asking questions that had no answers only served to frustrate and upset her. She needed to confront the immediate concern and decide in the next two days what to do about Tom.

* * *

I knew in my heart Debra was right. I was an anomaly and had no right to get upset at her for leaving me. It would be easier for her to put up with an alien from a distant planet than a real human who had a brief second opportunity at life. I had no idea what I would write on my note to Debra when next I saw her. I needed to have a better idea why my remains came alive in the river last September.

I didn't believe I was put in the river at the place where I woke up. If there was someone who wanted to get rid of my body by throwing it into a fast-moving river, they wouldn't put it where something could halt its downstream progress. As a matter of fact, I didn't think my body was thrown into the river all, at least my body in its present form. The clue was in the large chunk of tissue that was missing from my left forearm when I first examined my naked body. The whirlpool close above me had silt, leaves, gray flecks and twigs whirling around in it and that arm went through its center before I got to a low place on the bank. At the farm, I noticed my arm had largely healed, leaving minimal scar tissue. I was too frightened and cold to question anything rationally at the time. The answer came to me in jigsaw fragments when I happened to wake up in the middle of the night and I only recently put the pieces together.

The wound in my arm was strange in that there was no bleeding and no fresh tissue. Nothing traumatic happened during my long trip down the river. My left arm healed when it wound up in the vortex of the whirlpool as I struggled upstream. The gray flecks among the circling debris were ashes, the few that had not reconstituted. I died, was cremated, and someone put my ashes into the river. They flowed downstream and, by luck or perhaps design, they went to the left of the big boulder, and into the whirlpool above the fallen tree. Obviously, not all of the ashes coalesced the first time around and it wasn't until my arm was sucked back into the whirlpool that the last remaining flecks joined the rest of their brethren. What I don't understand is how, or why, the ashes resurrected themselves into a middle-aged me.

I was aware of the Bible, and the resurrection of Jesus. However, I was no saint, much less a God. The Book says His intervention raised Lazarus' body from the dead so it's possible mine was a heavenly blessing. The resurrection of mere ashes, however, put this in a whole different category. Even without a memory, my gut told me there was no precedent for my experience. The reason "why" it happened is the real conundrum. I had no idea what I did during my initial lifetime. My experiences so far seemed to indicate I was a jack-of-all-trades, and a king of none. I didn't feel at all pious as I passed churches and remembered the singing, wafers and vestments. There is purity about religions in spite of the corruption, the scandals, the wars and the greed. None of the faiths were immune and it could all be make-believe.

Even thinking about the science of a rebirth, it did not seem possible a stream of ashes could reconstitute itself into a man. I thought of the notion that a monkey, given a billion years and a box of paints, could produce a Monet. That was penny-ante compared to my situation. Could there be stem cells still extant in ashes? I don't think so. Understanding any part of my presence is totally beyond human intelligence. A miracle is supposed to be both amazing and wonderful. In my case, it certainly is the former, but the jury is still out on the latter.

Thoughts of Debra obsessed me over the two days before our meeting. I went about my museum duties in a fog and the addition of the upcoming juried show in the gallery added several hours to my day. There was only room to hang forty paintings and set up a half-dozen sculptures. We had three hundred and fifty-two submissions to judge and then hang or place the ones chosen in suitable areas. There was a three-person panel of well-known experienced judges with different ideas. Gallery employees brought works in, got the word from the jury, and carried them out to storage or place them properly in a room. I was astonished and irritated when I found two of my paintings on easels in front of the jurors. I knew instantly that Debra was responsible for the fiasco. All the employees would hear about this and I'd be the butt of jokes for weeks.

I watched the jury of a woman and two men scrutinize my paintings. One of them stood up and came around behind the others, pointing at something. Another took a painting, walked about six feet in front of their table, and held it up. One laughed and another smiled. I was devastated. I went over and stood close to my colleague.

"What the hell are you doing with my paintings? How did you get them, anyway?"

"Debra gave them to me and I had to promise not to tell you about it and to sneak them to the judges. She knew you'd object."

"It's not your fault, but I didn't give her permission to do this. She'll hear about it."

"I think they're very strong, Tom. She's trying to make you famous."

"I'll be famous all right. If you tease me about this, I will not be happy."

The judges finished with my paintings and my co-worker went to get them. I hustled off in the opposite direction to get a sculpture. The crazy looking bronze thing was heavy and by the time I got to the judges' table, I was furious. I couldn't wait to give Debra a piece of my mind. I reminded myself to stop in storage at the end of the day and bring the paintings back to my room.

Chapter Twenty-seven

Big Boy was torn. Lobo was the best enforcer he'd ever had, but he was not the same man he was months ago. He was probably right that Tom Hunter was not the hit man he said he was. Regardless, Tom didn't do any harm to the pack of wolves and the best thing would be to let him go. Big Boy knew he should have stopped Lobo from going after him, but had no idea he was so obsessed. Now Lobo had a messed up mouth and no idea where to find his quarry.

Lobo's festering rage was interfering with business. Recently, Big Boy had several encounters with neighboring gangs who were encroaching on his turf. It was a constant annoyance and Lobo was sent to smack some people around. That would usually settle things down for a while and the police were happy to have the gangs discipline themselves. However, Lobo started venting his fury over Tom by using his knife to cut rivals into pieces. He broke the rules.

Lobo's new persona was nasty and the citizens of Spokane were up in arms about it. The newspapers couldn't get enough so the police were being forced into action. SWAT teams made two raids and several arrests so the gang of wolves was now short of personnel. It's a matter of time before they discover Pinny. That would be a major blow to Big Boy's fake ID business. Besides, Pinny knows many things Big Boy wanted to keep secret. The boss debated whether to move the fat forger out of the city or to send Lobo in to terminate him. As an alternative, Big Boy began thinking of a way to eliminate Lobo and make it look like a rival gang did it. He was sick and tired of having his personal domain look like a forest fire.

* * *

At the end of the juried show in the gallery, I went down to storage to pick up my paintings. When they weren't there, I ran up the stairs looking for my co-worker. The lights were shutting off and I heard he had already left. My helper was a museum employee and I only saw him at work and had no idea where the fellow lived.

Back in my room, I picked up the phone to call Debra and then decided, in my present state of mind, it would not be a good idea. There was a barbecue place several blocks away and the effect of a craft beer and baby back ribs was magic. A happy stomach digests away troubles. I decided Debra's motive was rather sweet, but I wouldn't let that influence me when I wrote my note about staying together. We were going to meet at an Italian restaurant at 7 PM the following evening so I had a full day to make a decision.

The next morning I found my helper and asked him where he'd put my paintings.

"I put them where the judges told me to, in the gallery. I told you they were good. You have a break now since no new exhibits are scheduled and the show won't be taken down for a month. Go over there and take a look."

I was stunned. My paintings were for me and I had mixed feelings about showing them off. I walked into the packed gallery building and struggled through the crowd. Three large rooms were painted different colors and chosen paintings lined the walls. I walked slowly, looking at each painting and seeing how truly special they were. I tried to decide, if I had a home and money, which ones would be nice on my walls. I picked very few because the subject matter, the colors and the skills were all so different. I saw both of my paintings in the third room and even from a distance, the scene stunned me. There was quite a crowd in front of them and it took a little while for me to wiggle to the front. One was the painting I did remembering Billy Joe's agony and the morphine I used to give him eternal peace. Even now, it brought tears to my eyes. There was a gold ribbon attached to it with a medallion that said, "Best in Show." My other painting was next to it and had a white ribbon which said, "Honorable Mention."

* * *

Savanna Golden owned a large gallery in Dallas, which dealt not only with the classics, but also with the best up-and-coming contemporary artists. She had a keen eye for those who, in a few years' time, would be the most sought after. She went to all the openings in an unpretentious way and amassed a fortune with her talent for recognizing a masterpiece. Savanna always drove to these showings in her beat up Chevrolet as her presence created a buzz that inevitably became public. She sometimes brought one of her gallery employees with her so, if she bought a piece, her name would not be associated with it. This allowed her to scoop up all available paintings by an incipient master. If Savanna was lucky, she'd talk the artist into an exclusive relationship with her gallery.

I was as close as I could get to my Billy Joe painting, trying to read what was on the shiny placard off to one side. I titled most of my paintings and the card said "Dolor's End." (Latin in my previous life?) Underneath was my name and the price of my effort: five hundred dollars.

This was Debra's doing. Crazy Debra. I had to laugh; five hundred dollars? I would've written fifty dollars and felt lucky if someone offered me half.

"Why are you laughing?"

I turned and looked down at a vaguely disheveled woman whose head barely came to my chest. She stared in such an intense way I stepped back a pace. "I was looking at that painting—which I rather like—but nobody is going to pay five hundred dollars for it."

"What about the one next to it. Those magnificent reds. It reminds me of Rubens, the Flemish artist in the Middle Ages who painted with similar color and energy."

That felt good, but made no sense and I wondered why she was patronizing me. "It only got an Honorable Mention."

"It creates a different emotion, certainly, but it's as good as the other one. I think the jury did that so they could give the blue ribbon to a different artist. Spread the joy, so to speak."

The crowd had grown larger behind me and I could hear complements twittering like a flock of sparrows finding sunshine in the early morning.

The woman beside me was persistent and irritating. "I asked you about the red one."

I knew how to get rid of her: "That painting is about a whorehouse on fire." I was telling the truth, but I knew she would take it as an insult and walk away.

"Yes, I can see that. How do you know?"

"Because I painted it." I was mad and gave her a dirty look, pushed through the crowd, and walked away.

When the wretched woman caught up to me and yanked on my jacket, I had no choice but to stop. I had not been brought up to be rude to anyone, much less tiny ladies.

"I would like to pay you a thousand dollars for both those paintings. Do you have any others?"

I first thought it was a joke and she enjoyed harassing novices. I could feel my face flush with anger, but that soon faded away as she continued to stand in front of me, holding on to my sleeve. She didn't look like she could pay ten bucks for anything, much less a thousand.

"I don't think it's worth very much. I'm not a professional and I do this in my spare time. It makes me feel good."

"I am Savanna Golden and am a far better judge of painting than you." She eased the sting of that statement by giving me a big smile and releasing my arm. She knew by the look on my face I had no idea who she was. She wanted to know about each painting and I told her about Billy Joe and the other visions I had when I painted. Then she said, "I own a highly regarded gallery in the city and you've never taken the measure of your talent. You are a gifted artist and I would like to represent you."

"I have no experience with any of this and would like to think it over. I have four other paintings." What I really wanted to do was talk to Debra.

Savanna gave me her card. "I have a reputation for honesty as well as dealing with art of the highest quality. When you decide you want to talk to me again, come to my gallery and bring your other four paintings. In the meantime, I'm giving you a check for a thousand dollars." While she was talking, she had taken out a small checkbook and was writing furiously.

I was too astonished to do anything but accept the check and the receipt. This was ridiculous. Nothing meaningful since I climbed out of the river told me I was a gifted painter. I think great talents start slowly and earn their reputation over years. I wondered if she was an eccentric heiress who enjoyed using her millions in this way. The money was a veritable fortune for me. Now I had much more control over my life. Or so I thought.

Chapter Twenty-eight

Lobo knew something was up. He understood what facial expressions mean. He knew terror and ecstasy, pleading and evading. It wasn't that Big Boy was looking at him in a meditative way or with open hostility, his most ardent admirer wasn't looking at him at all. All sorts of red flags were fluttering in his dark mind. There were little hints since the beginning of the turf wars, especially with his treatment of two members of the Vi*Kings. The Kings were members of a satellite branch of a Chicago mob that was trying to muscle into Big Boy's lucrative businesses. The police thought the name referred to the Scandinavian Vikings, known for their bloody expansions into England and France. In actuality, it had nothing to do with Norsemen. The clue was in the * sign in the middle of the logo which resembled a star. When you beat the crap out of your enemies, they see stars. All the local gangsters knew the actual name was Violence Kings.

Big Boy sent Lobo out to give the Kings a message that they weren't welcome in Spokane. When the enforcer ambushed two of the Chicago thugs and returned to home base, he thought he was being funny when he told Big Boy and the rest of the pack he had renamed the Kings.

"We can call 'em the Humpty Dumptys now. All the Kings' horsemen and all the Kings' men couldn't put Humpty Dumpty together again. They're in pieces, just like Humpty." Lobo burst into hysterical laughter that, after a moment's hesitation, stimulated the rest of the wolves. Only Big Boy sat silent and another of Lobo's red flags started flapping.

Big Boy knew he couldn't count on any of his pack to take Lobo down. The only thing more powerful than fear is love and no one loved Lobo except Snag. The fear he generated in everyone, friend or foe, kept him safe. The boss would have to do it himself and it would be fatal to underestimate an experienced killer. However, before anything else, he wanted Lobo to pay a visit to Pinny. The feds were getting close.

* * *

Pinny was no dummy. He was perfectly aware of the pressure the police were putting on gangs all over the city. This applied especially to the wolfpack since every police informant knew about Lobo's cutlery mania. Lobo had taken to wearing surgical gloves when he did his carving so he wouldn't leave fingerprints. He carried an over-the-shoulder messenger bag to hold his equipment, which went well beyond gloves. Once his victims were immobilized or dead, he put on a bright red barbecue apron which covered him from neck to foot. He didn't want blood spatter on his clothes. A year before, a stream of blood from a severed carotid artery went into his right eye so now he wore a mask and goggles. Lobo was quite a sight when he began his butchery.

Pinny knew it was time to seek a less dangerous environment. He planned to pack up his equipment and take a train to Chicago. He had talked, before Humpty Dumpty, to one of the Kings' members and was told he'd be welcomed with open arms. The timing had to be perfect so his dismemberment would not be an issue. At the moment, he was preparing another ID for Big Boy, and Lobo had asked for one also. He'd finish the job and take off immediately after. Pinny was terrified of Lobo and did not want him to come into his apartment for his ID card. He'd be helpless there and vivisection would be easy. He never fired a gun and felt his only defense was to disappear. It wouldn't be an easy task for a three hundred and forty pound wimp.

The following afternoon, Pinny called Big Boy and Lobo and told them he was on the way to the wolves' cave with the two IDs. Previously, they had always gone to his apartment so Big Boy's antenna perked up. Lobo, on the boss's orders, had planned to eliminate the forger when he went to pick up his finished ID.

Pinny looked massive as he was wearing some of his clothes in layers. He couldn't fit everything into his suitcase as his forging equipment took up a lot of room. Pinny's additional thirty pounds of fabric caused another of Big Boy's antennas to spring up.

"You're putting on weight, Pinny," said Lobo.

"Putting on something," said Big Boy.

Pinny was sweating under all the clothing. "It's still winter, guys and you know I don't like the cold. I did a great job on your IDs and I'd appreciate it if you'd pay me now. I need new photo equipment which will make me number one in my profession."

Big Boy did not want a bloody mess in their meeting place so he paid Pinny and told Lobo to do the same.

"Thanks a lot. Those IDs are worth much more than I'm charging you. I spent extra time last night doing it exactly right. I've got to catch up on my sleep so I'm going home and take a nap."

After the door closed, Big Boy told Lobo to wait an hour, then go over to Pinny's place and tell him you think he made a mistake. He'll open the door for that and you can have a little fun. Leave the notebook you took off the Kings' thugs and the police will think they dropped it at the scene. The cops will take care of the Chicago lowlifes.

Pinny, sweating, walked two blocks and retrieved his suitcase from a dumpster. There was a telephone booth on the corner and he called a limo service. He'd already checked the train schedule to Chicago and he told the driver to take him to the first stop the train would make after leaving Spokane. Pinny mollified the man by telling him his tip would more than compensate him for the long round-trip drive. He shed several layers before climbing into the backseat and took a swallow of Mylanta from a hip flask. Pinny hoped he wouldn't have to use antacids after he reached Chicago. He was right, at least for the first four years he was there. The Chicago police eventually traced counterfeit cards back to the Vi*Kings. Illinois was required to provide Pinny with as much Mylanta as he wanted during the years he spent in prison.

When Lobo returned from Pinny's cleaned out apartment, he was very upset. He hadn't had a good "cut up" for a week or two. Big Boy chewed him out for not following Pinny home right away, not remembering he'd said, "Wait an hour." Checking the airport, bus and train station yielded nothing. It seemed impossible that over three hundred pounds of fat could vanish without a trace.

Lobo did not like criticism in front of the pack and he gave Big Boy the "look." Only his victims received that particular expression and the boss decided his enforcer would have to go now. He thought it best not to give the crazy bastard another day to think about it. Since the five other members of his mob were all present, there was no better time.

"Lobo, my friend, this is a tense time in the city for us all. I have neutralized the Vi*Kings, but it's too late to stop Pinny from talking and the police will be at our door any day. Part of the problem is your fondness for small pieces of human flesh. Because of our long association and my respect for you, I'm going to give you a choice."

Big Boy pulled a Colt 357 magnum out of his belt and cocked the hammer. "We are going to drive you to the train station and watch you board the next train to Seattle. If any of us see you in this town again, we will shoot you on sight. In addition, we're going to get word to the cops you are high on drugs and are looking forward to being the most prolific cop killer in history." The boss punctuated his statement by pointing the big revolver at the rest of his astonished pack and saying, "Right boys? Let's hear it."

The wolves knew exactly what their leader meant and you could hear the hammers of their revolvers cocking. Lobo had his hand near his switchblade but, knowing every gun in the room had a bullet in the chamber, he remained absolutely still.

"Snag and I will drive you to the station immediately, Lobo. If you decide you don't want to go, or try to take off, I will shoot you. I can assure you the entire Police Department will drink champagne tonight to celebrate your arrival in a different jurisdiction."

Lobo's face was scarlet. He had not felt helpless since he was five years old and couldn't stand the feel of it. He was street smart and knew he did not have a choice. Then, a thought settled gently onto his mind and he smiled. Lobo's grin was genuine. If Big Boy and his mob could see into the inky morass of Lobo's brain, they would see the severed head of Thomas Hunter.

"I'm sorry to be leaving you sons of bitches, but I'm looking forward to the hunt. You made a big mistake letting Tom loose in the world and I am going to take care of it. You will owe me. Let's go."

Big Boy tried not to show how relieved he was that Lobo had a score to settle in some faraway place. Lobo handed over his knife and the boss and Snag stopped by his grubby apartment and watched him pack up. When the train pulled into the station, they returned his favorite weapon and watched carefully to be sure he didn't get off before it left the station.

Chapter Twenty-nine

I did not sleep well last night both because of the excitement of Savanna's interest and my deep concern about Debra. A nice breakfast gets me settled down so I cooked two eggs covered with shredded cheddar, a single piece of bacon and an English muffin. This was washed down with cranberry juice and a single cup of strong black coffee. The tastes lingered for an hour and I was able, more calmly, to think about what I was going to write in my note. The woman was dear to me and I was not going to take advantage of her. Besides, her action in showing two of my paintings (which I would have objected to) made me rich. I owed her a better future than watching me die.

My relationship with Savanna Golden was something else. A signed contract would enable me to earn a good living even if I left Dallas. I'll write it so either of us could cancel at any time and I'll use my own lawyer, not hers. Debra is an attorney and I was hopeful, because of our mutual respect, we could maintain a decent business relationship. Our breakup was emotionally difficult and I was glad it would be over soon. My chances were only 25% anyway: there were four ways possible and the only one that could keep us together was a mutual "yes."

I got together with Savanna in the early afternoon and spent a difficult hour. She wanted a binding contract for at least two years. I finally had to tell her I had a terminal illness and would get her as many paintings as possible. Savanna found it hard to choose between her desire to keep me for herself and sympathy with my mortality. I liked her because she was a determined businesswoman who was also sassy and sensuous. One of the last four paintings I brought to her office was one I did after a delirious night with Debra. The colors were dazzling and graphic and there was a fine loopy line running through the middle of it that appeared to have no end. When she saw it, Savanna stepped back, took a deep breath, and put one hand in the middle of her chest.

"My goodness, where did that come from Tom?"

"It's kind of personal, but I was feeling really good."

Savanna looked at me with a sly smile. "I'll bet she was feeling really good too."

I could feel my face turning red so I simply grinned and said nothing.

"If I didn't have strict rules about consorting with my artists, I might try to add a few more lines to your next painting."

"Savanna, you are something else. You'd probably add a few new colors too." When I put an arm around her shoulders and gave her a quick squeeze, she was the one who blushed. I think that exchange did the trick. She got off her high horse and agreed to my terms and I told her I would bring over the contract in a couple of days.

I don't know what made me do it, but the next day I went to the gallery and retrieved the "Debra" painting. Savanna was livid, but she had not paid for it yet.

* * *

I used the Amalfi restaurant as a distraction, although it was expensive and halfway across town. Debra picked me up and we started off, not looking at each other. I didn't want our evening to start like this so I said, "I have some exciting news and I hope you have time to help me with a legal issue."

Debra, without turning her head, said, "I don't make illegal stuff legal."

I took a deep breath in through my nose and let it out slowly through my mouth. I made sure Debra heard it. "There is nothing illegal about this. I am deeply grateful to you for taking two of my paintings to the juried competition. One of mine turned out to be 'Best in Show' and a local gallery owner noticed it. She liked both paintings and bought them for a thousand dollars."

That got Debra to turn around and look at me, wide-eyed. I could see emotions roiling around on her face, but she finally relaxed. "I'm thrilled for you." She reached over with her right hand and grabbed my left. She squeezed and shook it in her excitement and then put hers back on the wheel. "Whose gallery is it?"

"Savanna Golden is the owner and wants to sign a contract with me for all my paintings and anything I do in the future. That's what I need help with."

I was looking at Debra's profile and I could see her jaw drop. "Do you have any idea who she is?"

"After talking with her, I gather she's well known and ethical."

"That hardly covers it. She is a highly respected art history professor at SMU and runs her enormously successful gallery on the side. Mrs. Golden has written three popular books. She is notable, not only in Dallas, for her expertise and honesty. You were lucky she was there."

I put my hand on her shoulder. "I'm lucky for another reason; you put my paintings in the show. I owe you."

The Amalfi was one of those wonderful restaurants whose ambience defined the term, "understated elegance." When I told Debra I received a thousand dollars, I insisted, then stopped and begged which I knew would work better, on paying for the dinner. It was possible this would be the last time we would see each other in a nonbusiness way and I thought Italian might calm our emotions when we opened our notes. We started right off with drinks, Prosecco for her and a tannin rich Cabernet Sauvignon for me.

We split the insalata caprese and then Debra ordered the shrimp scampi while I salivated over the spaghetti with clams, mussels and scallops. I dipped crusty bread into the delicious sauce and we each had a second glass of wine. Debra, who had apparently starved herself, ordered a cranberry panna cotta for dessert. A double espresso was enough for me as I wanted to be fully alert when we exchanged our decisions.

What I hoped to accomplish with the meal, happened: Debra settled back in her seat after her last spoonful and smiled at me. "What a spectacular dinner, Tom. Thank you so much." She paused and her face became pensive. "We came here to make a decision about our relationship and I suppose we better do that before the taste of Italy wears off." Debra reached inside her purse, pulled out a note card, and slid it across the table. I felt my eyes filling and I didn't look at her as I offered my folded piece of art paper. That morning, I drew a picture on the outside of a chocolate cupcake with one glowing candle in the center. She loved chocolate and I knew she would get the symbolism. One to grow on.

I retrieved Debra's note and gave a quick glance across the table. She hadn't opened my folded sheet and was staring at the cupcake. Her mouth was trembling and I saw her close her eyes. Debra's note card was quality stationery; her light blue initials were on the outside. I lifted the flap and read her lovely handwriting.

I have never met anyone so talented, intelligent and kind. On special nights, you sent me to heaven. When you told me you'd only been alive for a few months and were aging rapidly, I didn't believe it until I saw the lines accumulating on your face. You remember things from a previous life here on earth so you're not an alien. Certainly surreal and possibly Kafkaesque. Regardless, the thought of losing you, if unbearable for me now, would be much worse if I'm with you all the way. Please forgive my selfishness, but my answer is, no. With all my love, I wish you happiness and comfort in the time ahead. Debra.

Although this was not a surprise, the finality of it devastated me. Premonitions should make the future easier, but that didn't work for me, at least with Debra. I sat with my eyes averted and my closed right fist pressed against my mouth hard enough to be painful. There was nothing to forgive; she did the right thing.

The sound of gentle tapping shook me out of my reverie. I looked up and saw Debra staring at me. She read my lines and tears were running down her cheeks, dripping off her chin onto the thick art paper.

What the dying need is normal life,
Happy times and not much strife.
That's fine with family and dear friends too,
But not when loving someone like you.

To visit pain on such a friend
Who'd be with me until the end,
I can't condone not letting go.
So, my love, my answer's "no."

Even though we'd made the same choice, it was agony for both of us. It would have been worse if our answers were different from each other. Small consolation. At that moment, our waiter came to the table with the check and saw our suffering. He hesitated and I could see him trying to decide whether to leave the check or give us a few minutes more. In the end, he left the check slightly to my side of the table and left without a word. The terminality of receiving the check at that particular moment was the final blow.

We gazed at each other for a time and then I slid my hand, palm up across the table. I saw the trace of a smile as Debra put her hand in mine. Our fingers embraced and gradually withdrew.

"At the beginning of this delicious, but melancholy dinner, I mentioned the contract I need to have with Savanna Golden. You are the expert but, if it's going to be difficult to meet with me, I can use another law firm."

"I don't see why we can't do business together. Being with you on a different level would be fine."

"Well then, I'll write out the things Savanna and I will need and bring it to your office."

"I look forward to it."

Chapter Thirty

One of Savanna's courses was entitled, The Business of Art. Her expertise was behind the scenes and not obvious to me at first. Later on, she would use the selling of my paintings in her SMU teaching as an example of her marketing methods. Her Rolodex contained a list of her clientele, collectors and anyone else who had taken the least interest in buying from her. She prepared a glowing letter, with a picture of one of my paintings attached, inviting them to come by the gallery and see the other five. Savanna planned to offer my next several paintings at a significantly higher price than five hundred dollars. Fifty percent of the receipts would go into her bank account and the rest into mine. She called the Presidents of the Boards of Trustees of local museums and urged that one of my paintings be included in their next contemporary art exhibitions. She made the same suggestion to appropriate museums in Fort Worth, Austin and San Antonio.

Her next task was to call the art editor at the Dallas Morning News and suggest she come by to look at something very special. That kind of carrot was all it took to get anyone in the newspaper business to jump out of their chair. A week later, she would send a notice out to newspapers in Los Angeles and New York and include the article she knew the Dallas newspaper would write. Savanna called me and said she would be holding a symposium as part of her art teaching. The slideshow would start with Rubens in the Baroque period and end with Pollock, Warhol and Thomas Hunter. The auditorium would hold not only her students, but would include previous buyers, collectors and journalists. Savanna planned to moderate the session, and the dais would have a scholar, an art historian and a knowledgeable art collector. If my paintings weren't enough by themselves, marketing would raise the excitement to fever pitch.

I refused to get involved in the symposium, thinking it was simply a publicity stunt. Savanna was disappointed, but even the presence of a professor could not change my mind. The deeper reason for my reluctance I kept to myself. Lobo had followed me wherever I went and I knew the killer was waiting for any publicity that might pinpoint my location.

Savanna, knowing she couldn't sell any of my paintings until our contract was signed, pressed me to get it done. She already had one very interested collector. The morning after the Italian dinner, I gave Debra the terms and conditions of the agreement with Savanna. She completed it by the early afternoon of the following day and called me to set up a meeting.

"Thanks so much, Debra. This is going to save me money and time. The best part is I don't have to go to an unknown law firm."

"I'm happy to do it for you. Besides, I really want our business arrangement to work out."

I laughed. "Let's shake hands when we meet and I'll introduce myself." Using humor as gravy to cover the marred meat of our relationship seemed to be working. "Can we do this today? Savanna has a buyer already and is really putting the screws to me."

"One of the partners is preparing for a trial next week and I'm going to be tied up the rest of the afternoon and most of the week. I've got homework tonight, but I can stay late tomorrow and we can meet here about six."

I had a problem. The prospective buyer of the painting was coming over the following day with his wife and would write a check on the spot. Savanna said he was very rich and very difficult. If there was a delay, the man would make her reduce the price. I said, "I'll take you out for a quick dinner and we can go over the contract in between bites."

"This shouldn't be done at a restaurant. What if tomato sauce falls on your contract?"

Humor wasn't working for me this time. Debra seemed unfazed so I waited for her to say something else.

"All right, Tom, I can give you thirty minutes at my place. Be there at six thirty."

"Bless you, you've saved my life. I'll bring Chinese and you can have it after I leave."

My phone went dead without another word and I feared I was mistaken about her mood. My day ended at five so I was able to get home and shower. Some of the work at the museum involved a lot of lifting and carrying and I didn't want her making a face before we got the job done. Before dressing, I walked naked into my sitting room and poured myself a glass of old vine Zinfandel. I selected a blue-gray shirt and followed with a swallow of wine. Between the briefs, pants, socks and shoes, I emptied the glass.

On the way out, I picked up the contract and waited for the taxi. I got the driver to stop at the Chinese restaurant and was happy my order was ready. I got enough for two people so when I got back home, I wouldn't have to worry about supper. When I got to Debra's apartment, I was four minutes ahead of schedule. Timing can be everything. Debra was working on her "homework" and answered the door immediately.

It was a long day for her and she looked a little frazzled. Locks of her hair had fallen over her left eye and her shirt was rumpled. I thought she looked gorgeous. I held my hand out. "Good evening, Miss Debra. I've brought the contracts you asked for and appreciate your time."

The serious, and slightly apprehensive, look she had when she opened the door vanished. Debra was feeling the gravy. We shook hands and she said, "Do come in, Master Tom. Take a seat. I need to finish this and then I'll be with you."

I thought to myself, "She's using the diminutive to tease me. I love it."

Debra had been sitting on the couch and working on her coffee table. There were piles of papers and a typewriter with a page still in it. I sat in a hardback chair and watched her get her business composure back. She reviewed the paragraph she was typing and began anew. Her fingers flew across the keys like ten little hummingbirds. I was amazed Debra could concentrate so hard with me in the room watching her. I had never seen her in work mode and it was simply another of her fabulous qualities.

She finished the page and half of another one before she finally took a deep breath and flopped back into the pillows.

"I may have to do a little more, but that's it for now." She paused for a moment trying to find the gravy. It didn't come right away and she said, "Let's have a drink while I clear the trial out of my mind. Then we'll review your contract."

Chapter Thirty-one

I drank a glass of wine at home before taxiing to Debra's place, but another one was probably a good idea, considering we were now only business partners. Debra went into her bedroom and when she returned, she had changed into a light green blouse and combed her hair. Often, when we went out for dinner, we would order a martini. I always had regular olives, but she liked them stuffed with lemon peel or Roquefort cheese. I don't think she meant anything by what she brought me a few minutes later. I truly believe she was still foggy from her homework and old habits die hard.

While Debra was making the drinks, I cleared the coffee table of her papers and typewriter. It would be odd for me to remain in the same chair so I put two coasters on the coffee table and sat well to one side on the sofa. The martinis were on a little tray along with a bowl of small skinny pretzels. We gave each other hesitant smiles as we picked up the glasses.

Something happened to me right then, a reflex I couldn't stop. I raised my glass to Debra and said, "Toast for cheers." I have no idea where that originated, but it was the toast we always said to each other as we *tinked* our glasses together. During that special time, it showed how we felt about our loving relationship. I brought the martini to my lips and looked at Debra over the rim.

Debra's glass was chest high and motionless. She was staring at me with a burning intensity. I didn't drink and began to lower my

160

martini, deciding it was best to apologize before taking a sip. If I erased the toast, perhaps we could drink together and part graciously.

"It just came out, Debra; I couldn't help it. Good memories are hard to forget. You know we'll be friends forever." I must have hurt her badly because her face froze. Only her eyes were alive, lasing deep into my core. I kept my eyes open, letting her probe for whatever she was looking for. My mind searched desperately to find something to say that would let us get past this.

Debra's expression softened and her lips moved. "We forgot to touch glasses, Tom."

Now I was motionless. She had forgiven me and wanted to share our last ritual together so we could keep it as a loving memory. My hand shook a little as I moved the glass towards her. A few drops spilled over the edge and fell on my hand. They felt as cold and painful as our separation.

tink

Debra's, "Toast for Cheers" was so soft that if there was a breeze outside, I wouldn't have heard it. I repeated it, as was our custom, and took my first sip of the clear liquid. We each drank, at first not looking at each other. The gin burned as it went down and I think that was the impetus for both of us to relax and recognize the value of our revamped relationship. Debra asked me about my paintings and I told her I was working on a new one. She told me her firm's big trial was about a major Ponzi scheme and she could never figure out, since there was always a reckoning, how the fools could believe they would get away with it. Perhaps, for them, the few years they lived like kings were worth spending the rest of their lives in a different kind of castle.

We took our final swallow and I steeled myself to be strong. Our eyes met as we raised our glass and tilted our heads back. I took a slow deep breath and stood, holding out a hand to help her rise. We walked together to the front door and I turned towards her. I wanted to give her a hug, but knew I would break down. The hush between us thickened.

Debra whispered, "You wanted to say 'yes,' didn't you?"

I could feel my muscles tensing. Time stretched out. Stretched out. Out. "How did you know?"

"Because I wanted to say 'yes,' too."

The silence and my paralysis probably lasted no longer than three seconds. I moved a step forward and took her in my arms. Debra started sobbing and I joined her, until my hiccups got us both laughing. There was a touch of craziness about our euphoria, because we knew my dénouement was not far away. We moved back from each other a few inches, then I began kissing her, softly at first, and then, because Debra was pressing herself hard against me, it became insistent and arousing.

Finally, out of breath and ragged, we drew apart from each other, not touching. The air around us crackled with the relief of our mutual confessions. We stood for a moment, soaking in the warm oasis of love and desire. Debra brought her hands up and undid the top button of my shirt, then gently took my hand and we walked back towards her bedroom.

Later, when I thought about that evening, it seemed otherworldly. I had the same feeling a person has when they are up to their necks in quicksand and someone arrives in the nick of time. I'm glad we both came to our senses because, at the end, we would have regretted not wringing the last drop of loving from our togetherness.

* * *

It was a small article towards the back of the newspaper, but the name jumped out at Lobo. Tom Hunter was creating excitement in the art world with his vivid freeform color paintings. A man less obsessed would have missed it. Lobo read the sentences over and over until the saliva from his open mouth started darkening the page. After moving from Spokane, he didn't think there was any point in leaving Seattle until he had a lead. He hated his job working evenings and nights as a bouncer in a sleazy bar. Lobo missed the old gang; they were good friends he could drink with, laugh with and kill for. He loved Big Boy who was his mentor, his boss and his support. He was stressed and lonely every day. Not anymore, there was blood in his future again.

Then something intervened, something I could not have imagined. I don't know what caused a sliver of light to pierce through the darkness of Lobo's emotions. Perhaps the weeks of loneliness. The psychopath, riding a bicycle to work every evening, passed the store many times without the least interest. The light rain never bothered him before as he enjoyed water running down his face. Lights turned into rainbows and the blurriness before he blinked masked, for an instant, the wretchedness of his life. Perhaps the small life behind the wet window was the sliver.

Lobo dodged a car, slipped between vehicles parked by the sidewalk and padlocked his bicycle to a meter. He strode to the store and gazed through the window at the dog. Without the cycling wind, his hat shielded him from the rain and he had a clear look at the animal. It noticed the man immediately and was standing with its paws on the glass, bouncing up and down. Lobo walked into the store and, without looking around, approached an elderly man cleaning a cage in the back of the room.

"How much for the dog?"

The man jumped, not hearing Lobo's soft practiced footsteps. "Which one?"

"The one in the window."

The store owner didn't understand the annoyed look on the customer's face. This should be a happy time. "She's fifteen dollars. Do you need food and water bowls? Some doggie treats would be nice."

"I'll give you ten."

"Make it twelve and I'll throw in the bowls and add food for a month. Her leash and the collar I can give you for five dollars"

Lobo was not used to people arguing with him, but he hadn't thought about that other stuff. "Okay."

"The dog is three years old and potty trained. All you have to do is take her outside and she does her business around a tree or a pole. We have plastic bags so you can pick up her poop. You probably want a dog bed, which will be a little extra. You have children?"

What the hell was this idiot thinking? Trying to sell me bags to pick up dog shit? Kids? No way. "I just want the dog, the food and the water bowls. I've got a cushion at home it can sleep on. Don't talk to me about kids and dog shit."

The man began to worry about his sweet little doggie in the window. "Have you ever had dogs before?"

"No I haven't. It's none of your business anyway. The dog's not going to get pregnant, is it?"

"She's been spayed."

"Huh? What's that mean?"

"She's had her uterus and ovaries removed."

Lobo's eyes brightened. "Did they cut them out?"

"Yes, and the vet does it under anesthesia so the . . ."

"That's my kind of dog." He put seventeen dollars down on the counter.

The owner was more worried than ever. He and his wife had three dogs, two cats and a canary at home and pets were his life. "Do you live by yourself? I want to be sure she's going to a nice home."

That was the last straw for Lobo. His switchblade appeared so quickly in his right hand that the man stumbled back against the wall and slid, sitting up, onto the floor. The '*snick*' of the blade coming out was lost in the tumble. "Get your ass off the floor and get me the dog and the other stuff."

The man got up slowly, eyeing the knife and thinking, "He must be psycho. I'll call the police after he leaves." He put the bowls and the food in a bag and took the excited dog out of the window. He offered to carry her to Lobo's car and was appalled when he saw the bicycle. Lobo took a backpack out of the basket on the handlebars and filled it with the bowls and food. He put the dog inside his jacket with her little head peeking out.

Before Lobo opened the padlock on the bike chain, he pulled the owner over by his jacket front. "If the cops come anywhere near me, I will come back and slice your ears off."

The pet owner hastened through the rain back to his store. He locked the door and put the "closed" sign in the window. He felt dizzy and sat down, both hands rubbing his ears. Before he checked the pets and drove home, he looked up the street and yelled, "This is a pet store, for God's sake.

Chapter Thirty-two

Whether Savanna's superb marketing techniques were making my paintings the center of artistic attention or my talent was really special, only time would tell. In the meantime, we were both making money hand over fist. Other gallery owners were desperate to buy because the price was rising so fast they would make money flipping them. What worried me were the articles in newspapers and the few publications dedicated to art. I knew Lobo would have no scholarly interest, but if he happened to catch an article in the mass media, I'd be in big trouble.

My paintings were totally abstract, bold without form, and known for their vivid color. Georgia O'Keeffe had exciting color, but always some form. Mark Rothko's colored bands and Hans Hoffman's mostly sharp edged color blocks were closer to mine color-wise, but had form limits. I was like a piano player who composed without melody using mostly the white keys and, from time to time, throwing in black ones. That piqued interest and was consistent with my mood and motive at the time. My inspiration occasionally came from remembered feelings and flashes of events from my previous life. The green John Deere tractor with the scissoring blades, for instance. However, the vast majority were from everything that happened since I crawled out of the river. My life had about as many downs as ups and at first I was afraid no one would like what I painted when depressed or scared. What I didn't realize was that everybody has good and bad stuff in their lives and my images were not necessarily indicative of theirs. Whatever my mood, a bold and powerful painting might be as attractive to a recent bride as it would be to a dying man.

With Debra back in my life, I wanted to get my own place. Denton was a pleasant and fair landlord, but privacy in my small rental apartment was not one of its features. I now had enough money to rent something nice and even get it cleaned once a week. I felt like a normal person as long as I chose to ignore the dozens of remaining brown hairs that were turning white every day.

I painted daily and was able to turn out a finished work every ten days or so. I had a lot to remember since I first put on Jeff's high school clothes, so my brushes had no dearth of subject matter and moods. The challenge was the first big brush stroke. It had to have the right color and shape to match what was going on in my head.

It was awkward, and sometimes a real nuisance, to live and paint in a small rental house in a busy neighborhood with the owner in residence. I had to pick a time when nothing much moved because I needed quiet to hear and feel my muse. When I started out, I sometimes sat for over two hours without an epiphany before I decided to take a walk. The long delay was a mistake because, when I finally struggled out of my chair, I was mad. That's a mood not conducive to candor on the canvas.

After several of those days, I set my limit at thirty-one minutes. I thought being eccentric with the clock might be stimulating. If nothing came to me by that time, it was seldom dispiriting to get out of my seat. I put on a hat to keep the sun out of my eyes and started walking. Sometimes I met neighbors I knew. Sometimes different aromas outside local restaurants excited me. Sometimes just the act of striding with my head up and my shoulders back made me feel the blessedness of a second life. Besides, it was March and Spring was in the air. When I returned to my room, the tickle of contentment nearly always started my brush moving again.

The trial Debra was involved in lasted nine days. It felt like a lifetime to me because she only had time for two quick dinners and one night. By the time the jury came in with their verdict, I'd rented a small furnished condominium with huge windows in a nice part of town. I showed Debra the second bedroom before I turned it into a light filled studio. It was an opportunity to tease her so, as we came into the room, I said, "This is going to be your room and I want to have it repainted in your favorite color. What would you like? Rose is always nice, and smells good too."

Startled, Debra looked at me with an expression that was half questioning and half incredulity. She saw through my nonsense quickly, perhaps because the serious face I put on was the exact opposite of what my eyes were saying.

She said, "You're close, but you obviously don't know me well enough to get the red exactly right. Scarlet would not be Hester Prynne's choice, but it's mine." Debra took me by the hand and led me to the bed. "I think it's important to show you what a modern scarlet lettered woman can do in such a room."

A couple of hours later, I told her I was going to paint it green, as I would not be able to survive very long in a scarlet room with her.

* * *

Lobo pedaled home in the rain as fast as he could. He didn't want the doggie to catch a cold. He was staying in a decrepit apartment building, which hadn't been refurbished since it was built sixty years before. The day he arrived he was given a set of rules, which he never read. It included a sentence that said the owner did not allow pets. He carried his bicycle up one flight and walked to the last apartment in the back. The dog's face and neck were soaked and he spent time toweling the shivering little thing. He put out food and water, found an extra blanket on the top shelf of a closet, and made a little nest by his bed.

The studio apartment had a kitchenette, a soiled loveseat with a table in front of it, two chairs and his bed, all in one room. There was a tiny bathroom with a shower, sink and commode in an alcove with a curtain in front of it. It was late afternoon and Lobo's excitement made him hungry. The dog followed him across the room and jumped on his leg whenever he stood still. His small refrigerator had a section at the top for frozen items and contained, "TV Dinners." The Swanson brothers started the craze the year before and every dinner was the same, consisting of turkey, peas and mashed potatoes. Lobo ate one every day.

Lobo peeled off the cover, heated the aluminum tray, and set it on the coffee table. The dog jumped up next to him and started sniffing at the food. He found this wonderfully amusing and talked nonstop to his new friend. Freud could not have done better.

"You need to have a name little fella. I'm going to call you 'Boy', after my best friend." Lobo had no clue this was an inappropriate name for a bitch. About three hours after dinner, the dog began to whine. Several minutes later, Boy urinated in front of the kitchenette. Lobo felt his face flush with anger, but it disappeared in seconds.

"I'm sorry, Boy, I totally forgot you had to take a piss. I'm glad you didn't take a crap too." His neighbor heard the laughter.

After soaking up the puddle with paper towels, Lobo put the collar on and attached the leash. There was no one in the hallway or coming up the stairs so there were no pet issues. He walked around the block with his dog sniffing here and there until she found the right spots to mark her territory. She also left a poop, which Lobo ignored, on the sidewalk close to the curb. Lobo picked the dog up and Boy licked his face until, chuckling, he had to put the dog back on the sidewalk. Their bond was instantaneous and growing. Boy, not washed for some time, took a liking to a man with the same habits, Lobo walked her through the door, up one flight and into his apartment, only meeting one older man who had not read the rules either. The dog food was in small pellets that Lobo also used as treats. Over the next week, he became totally involved in teaching Boy to sit and come when called. The newspaper article drifted to the back of his mind, although he planned to head for Dallas when the dog was trained. Lobo was quite sure, with Tom's artistic success, he would be there waiting for him.

Chapter Thirty-three

Savanna had great respect for teaching no matter what the field. It was an act of love and sacrifice, often at the low end of the pay scale. A teacher was supposed to earn and deserve tenure. It was not a device for protecting the jobs of the unqualified and lazy. The fact that Boards of Regents cut courses in the "arts" before anything else upset her greatly. The arts, taken in totality, are vital to instruct and enlighten people and to give them a greater understanding of diverse cultures. It's also a way of understanding history, from cave dwellers' wall drawings, through the Renaissance, to the present time. Art infuses your life with joy and sparks creativity in any number of ways.

Savanna enjoyed teaching, but her real love was her gallery and the works that passed through it. The teaching kept her sharp and up-to-date and satisfied her need to share her success with anyone motivated to listen and learn. Savanna's astute business sense drove her in a direction that sometimes conflicted with her altruism. I was feeling this. Her marketing strategies, which made her buying and selling a success, created pressure on both sides of the transaction. She would be thrilled if I brought her a painting every day as it wouldn't remain in her gallery very long. The knowledge she was also making money for me helped to assuage any feeling of greed, at least for a while.

However, after a few weeks, I felt my impassioned canvases were on a conveyor belt running from my studio to Savanna's gallery. I only needed enough money to eat and sleep, and a little extra to have a nice life with Debra and treat a few friends. No one but Debra knew I didn't have the luxury of years. Strangely, it was the zesty flavors of the Thai dinner I was enjoying with Debra one evening that reminded me there was life outside of the studio.

"You know something, Debra? Cooking is a form of art. Do you think the chef here lives and dies in his kitchen? He's giving pleasure to a lot of people, but I think he would get bored if that's all there was. Isolation and sameness would soon be evident to the customers and business would fall off."

"What brought that on?"

"I love to paint and before I met Savanna, I was doing it for myself. It made this bizarre second life joyful and worth living. Now it's become an industry and I'm doing it for her gallery. For money. You're going to say I'm making the folks who are buying my paintings happy and that is a good thing. However, it's turned my art into a business and I am not pleased with that."

"Tell me the difference."

"What you do and what Savanna's gallery does helps me define it. The legitimate purpose of a business is to make money. Without a profit, a business cannot exist. Lawyers, on the other hand, have years of intensive training to give them the skills and knowledge they need to be of service. Lawyers must pass the bar and there are codes of conduct that guide their professional lives. A life of service can make money, but it's not its essential purpose.

"I'm a little off track now. The reason I brought this up is to see if you could take some time off. It sounds like you've made yourself indispensable which means you have real power."

Debra grinned. "The firm can't exist without me."

I donned a serious face. "Savanna will not be happy, but I'm going to take a week off and go to Hawaii. I picked out a lovely place in Maui overlooking the Pacific with swimming, snorkeling, whale watching, culinary delights and occasionally sleeping. You are number one on a long list of applicants."

Debra was used to my baloney, but she frowned. The idea of a vacation was fine, but she did not appreciate my mentioning other applicants. "How many aspiring vacationers do you think would equal one of me? That's a rhetorical question and it's meant to intimidate."

I needed to get out of this fix. "All of the other hopefuls are men. I'm a one woman man and I'm hurt you forgot that."

I think her twinge of jealousy embarrassed Debra because she set her drink down and leapt on me. We wrestled around on the sofa for a while, until she settled with her head on my chest. She kissed the side of my neck. "The trial is over and we're in a relatively slow spot right now. I've taken no time off for over a year so I'm on."

"Do not . . . I mean PLEASE do not think I'm taking you for granted when I tell you I've already rented a place and have tickets for both of us starting six days from now."

"I'm greatly offended and there needs to be retribution. You will strip down and take your punishment."

* * *

Lobo's life settled into a routine of bouncing unruly patrons out of the bar for ten hours a day. He ate, without charge, at the beginning and end of his shift. That meant he only had to heat TV dinners for himself once daily. He fed Boy twice a day and walked her before he left for work, in the evening and when he got home at 4 AM. He had lunch at midday and took the dog out after he ate. He never picked up the dog's little turds, which led to periodic confrontations.

"Sir, excuse me, you left your dog's poop behind." Whether it was a man, a woman or even a child, Lobo paid no attention. Very occasionally, another man got in Lobo's face.

"Hey buddy, go back and pick up your dog shit."

"Screw you! I don't pick up nobody's shit and I've had enough of yours."

Usually, that ended it. A couple of times, a very large man would start walking toward Lobo. Boy would start barking and Lobo would whip out his switchblade. He'd make a show of looking at the fellow and then at his knife handle before the

snick

sound stopped the man in his tracks. He'd go off muttering and swearing at Lobo, but didn't mess with him.

Lobo hated his job. It meant confrontations every night and occasionally he'd get a bloody nose. He did not dare use his knife because the police would be all over him. He had a record and that meant serious jail time. He'd met several of the local gang members and knew they'd welcome his expertise, but that would put him at risk again. What would happen to Boy if she wasn't fed? Just the thought of it was upsetting and when he got home, he held the dog close and let her lick his face.

Lobo's walks began to extend further away into a gentler part of town. Very seldom did anyone bother him about Boy's poops. Mostly this was because the dog went in the local park or on grassy areas around small trees on the sidewalk. One day, he saw a place with a "Hiring" sign in the window. It was a restaurant, so he knew he could get a couple of meals a day as well as a paycheck. He was a mile away from his apartment and after looking at the well-dressed people on the street, he hurried back to change into his best clothes.

Lobo's "dress" pants were the only alternative to his blue jeans. The worn gray polyester slacks still had a vaguely discernible crease and he located a black leather belt in a pocket of his duffel bag. Seattle is cold in March so he changed into a plaid flannel shirt he'd washed while he was in the shower a couple of weeks before. Lobo always bought extra-large because he learned the hard way that clothes shrank. He debated whether to roll his sleeves up, but decided a more formal look would get him the job. He slipped back into his heavy brown overcoat, patted Boy on the head, and strode back uptown.

Lobo saw himself in the reflection from the glass in the front door and hoped the boss didn't mind long hair. He turned up his collar to hide the spider web. It was the middle of the afternoon and the restaurant only had people at two tables. A middle-aged woman was lounging by the door to the kitchen and he unbuttoned his coat and forced a smile. His plaid shirt was mostly red and he thought that would impress her.

"Hi Ma'am, I saw your sign in the window and I'm looking for a job. I do most anything."

"I'm a waitress. The cook owns the place." The woman flipped a hitchhiker's thumb behind her in the direction of the kitchen. "Hey Gio, your help just walked in. Be nice."

The swinging door opened and a short swarthy man came out, dressed in clean white slacks and shirt. He looked Lobo up and down and said, "You wait tables?"

"Not yet, but I can learn."

"Not good enough"

Lobo could feel his face flush and his pulse start revving up. He put his hand in his pocket, feeling for his knife handle.

The chef said, "How about in the back. I got a machine does the dishes, but sometimes food sticks in the pots and pans. I could also use a hand with the cooking. You do that?"

Lobo hesitated, trying to figure out what to say to avoid losing the opportunity. Then it came to him, "I'm an expert with pots and pans and I've helped with cooking stuff. Snag and I did all that for Big Boy and the rest of the gang." He realized too late that most people did not like gang members.

Giovanni stared at Lobo, trying to figure out what he meant. He didn't see the spider web tattoo. "What's this gang business?"

"There were six of us working in a barbecue joint. They served pulled pork sandwiches and racks of ribs. We did stuff together and called ourselves the, "Half Rack gang." Lobo was getting fired up with his fabrication. "We had T-shirts made with a picture and . . ."

"All right, that's enough. I'll give you a chance. If you're doing well in a week I'll put you on full-time. My name is Giovanni, but everybody calls me Gio." There was a base salary and the employees split the tips. Gio and waiters came in at 10 o'clock in the morning and Lobo would start the following morning with the rest of them.

Lobo was so excited, he jogged much of the way home. He stopped at the bar and told the owner he was quitting the bouncer job. The enforcer ignored the curses for not giving two weeks' notice and hustled out the door. The rush saved the owner the loss of an ear.

Chapter Thirty-four

When Debra and I landed on Maui, we could tell the air was different. It wasn't only the temperature, the Pacific breezes washing over the island gave it a textured vitality that was missing in the middle of Texas. The effect was to have us both turn and look at each other with excitement and anticipation.

I said, "I'd like to drop my carry-on right here and give you a hug."

"I'd like to do more than that."

"Naughty girl."

"Ordinarily, I would poke you for calling me a girl. I'm a woman, but somehow this island makes me feel young again."

"Not a virgin, I hope."

"That's for you to find out."

We didn't have much luggage and the rental car hummed as we drove up the West Coast. The bustle in the southern part of the island slowly gave way to hotels and private homes and an occasional golf course. The ocean, close to the road, teased us again and again as it appeared for moments between palm trees and buildings. Our apartment was on the bottom floor of a seaside villa with nothing but a sloping lawn and a stretch of sand between the surf and us. We dropped our luggage inside the entrance and, touching hands, walked deep into the home, opened the door that faced the sea and stepped out onto the flagstone patio.

"I feel the paint and primer evaporating from my skin."

"The lawyers and the judges are flying into space, their bodies already so small I can't hear their voices."

I drew her close. "What were the chances? We're so fortunate to be who we are, to be born in this country and to have met. I feel truly alive, more alive than I've ever felt in my strange new existence."

Debra lifted her head and kissed me on the cheek. "I'm so glad we said 'yes' so we can be like this for as long as it lasts. We would've died inside; a mere friendship would not have been living."

Our emotions were too full to remain standing and we sat on lounge chairs and relished each other. Debra finally got up and went back into the house. She unpacked her bags, checked all the rooms and ended up in the kitchen. She looked into every cabinet and made a list of things we needed over the next week. She glanced outside and saw me still sitting on the patio and wondered if I'd fallen asleep. She poked her head through the open door. "Saddle up, Tom. I'm going to the grocery store and need a hand."

"Sorry I'm so lazy. I was thinking how grateful I am for this second life. Then I started feeling sorry for myself because it's going to be so short."

"'It is what it is' was one of my grandmother's favorite sayings. Most people don't get a second chance."

I joined her and headed to the car. "You're right. Feeling this way is ridiculous and doesn't honor the gifts I've been given. Let's boogie."

After we put away the groceries, I unpacked. We put on bathing suits and swam for a while before spreading out blankets and lying in the sun. Back in the villa, we brought out the books we'd brought with us and opened a bottle of Tanqueray gin. The tonic water, jazzed up with the juice of real lemons, became something else entirely. I held up my glass. "This is ambrosia, the drink of the gods that confers immortality upon whoever partakes."

Debra turned and gazed at me with soft eyes. "Take me with you, Tom, into your next life."

We sipped slowly and talked about plans for the coming days. It's the most precious time for all vacationers because everything is upcoming, impending, and mysterious. Nothing is done, completed or written in stone. The dining area was lit with flickering candles. Mac & cheese and a side salad waited on the table. Afterwards, Debra and I sat outside for almost an hour looking at the stars and wondering how the cosmos got here. I shifted in my seat and said, "Seriously, I've felt something somewhere been eyeing me for some time, and now both of us."

We went to bed naked and our lovemaking was slow and soft, even at the end.

* * *

Lobo didn't know what he was doing, but Gio admired his enthusiasm and eagerness. The Italian had been dealing with employees for almost three decades and handling each one was different. It became obvious that Lobo was extremely sensitive to criticism and teaching had to appear as if the man was a young partner.

"I'm like you, Lobo. I'd love to throw it in the pot and get on to something else, but boiling water would splatter all over and sometimes burn me. I learned the hard way, my friend, so let me show you what I do now."

Lobo was excited with new stuff. Working for Big Boy, he would plan new ways to get a message across, remove an ear or a finger, or ambush a competitor. Washing pots was a pain, but cooking alongside his new mentor was unique and stimulating. After a while, his 5'7" boss became "Little Boy" in Lobo's mind and anything he said or did was fine. Even in the rare times Gio couldn't hide his frustration, Lobo never reached for his knife.

After three weeks, Gio called him aside. "You've got a real talent for cooking, Lobo. You're learning quickly and taking a big load off my shoulders. You're full time now and I'm adding a dollar to each of your work hours."

Lobo thought if he acted formally, it would impress his boss. "Thank you very much, Boss. I understand and feel good about it. I want to learn more cook stuff."

Gio thought, "This guy is a bit deficient and speaks oddly and, with all those awful tattoos, a little scary. But he does have a knack for the kitchen."

Lobo wasn't the only one learning. "Boy" had already learned to come when called, to shake hands and to stop whatever she was doing when ordered to. The dog enjoyed walking with her master who would occasionally give her a treat for pissing or taking a dump. During the day, she found herself in a noisy place, a room filled with boxes. Boy had a nice blanket and the other stuff piled around smelled good. Her master wasn't the only one who took her for a walk in the afternoon. Sometimes a nice woman would put the leash on and take Boy outside. The lady spent time looking in windows, which Lobo never did.

After that defining third week, Lobo began to think more about Tom. When that happened, he unconsciously fingered his knife and felt his body tense. It was a problem because he liked Gio and wouldn't mind working with him indefinitely. Not only that, Sally, one of the waitresses, liked going on walks with him when he took Boy out. Lobo, surprising himself, started to think about a relationship he didn't have to pay for. Nevertheless, Tom was a task he had to complete. It would be an increasingly bitter burden unless he fulfilled his mission. He wondered, if he could get it done quickly, whether Gio would give him his job back.

Chapter Thirty-five

On their first day in Maui, Debra and I slept late and then walked to the little town where we rented snorkels, fins and masks. Debra picked up a map that showed hiking trails, hotels and restaurants. The clerk said they might see whales migrating if we looked from the high ground. I found binoculars at the villa and scanned out to sea, but there was nothing except motorboats. Later in the season might have been better.

In the afternoon, we drove south to a small lagoon where we gave our snorkeling equipment a good workout. It was Debra's first time and she was thrilled, even with small fish swimming around coral heads. At one point, I swam quickly into shallow water and told Debra I had a vision from the past that shook me up.

"I've never been here before, but the coral and fish wakened something in my head. It was also the noise under the water, the fine tinkles like sand sprinkled on glass. I'd heard that delicate sound before and I saw, in my mind, an entire reef of colorful coral and much bigger fish. I was in the open ocean with the reef behind me. A shark swam up lazily and got between the reef and me. When I turned to watch it, my back was facing the unknown. Finally, the shark seemed to drift away, hardly moving at all, and disappeared into the depths.

"When the vision came back to me, it was so real I looked out to sea expecting to see the shark again."

"Your hands are shaking, Tom."

"Yes, I was in an alien king's realm and I was lucky the monarch wasn't hungry."

"What's this all mean, do you think?"

"I can't imagine. Who gets a second life? Perhaps the shark was reminding me how fragile life can be. Maybe this is my first life and I'm just a guy who got hit on the head and can't remember anything." I tried to make it funny, but it wasn't.

"Are you sure it's your life you're remembering?"

"It's me for sure, in another time and place. And what about my aging? At this rate, my second life is only going to last about a year." I took off my fins and walked to my blanket. I was deep in thought when Debra joined me. She said nothing.

"I went over every moment since I climbed out of the river. I had free will and was not a bad person. Like most people, I probably had some judgment and choice issues in bygone days, but certainly not immoral or unethical. If I was meant to be punished for something I did in a previous existence, Lobo would have killed me by now."

"Who's Lobo?"

Without getting graphic, I told Debra the whole story, including the fact that Lobo followed me to several cities.

"He could be in Dallas right now," said Debra.

"That's why I worried about Savanna's marketing blitz. If he saw something in the papers, he'd be on a plane for sure. After almost three weeks, I think I'm safe." Debra looked so worried I changed the subject. "We were talking about a second life. Wiping out most of my memory and giving me another opportunity for a year sounds like I'm being manipulated. That's what a researcher would do to a rat."

"Researchers aren't trying to harm the rats. They are trying to enhance the lives of the rest of us. Maybe this is to help you in some way, let you know there are existent things beyond your understanding. Anyway, you're much more a mouse than a rat. Come on, let's take a shower and have a drink before we eat."

Under the hot spray, I realized how tired I was and hoped Debra didn't want anything more than a good night's sleep. I opened a bottle of Prosecco and we sat in the dusk for a while before coming in for dinner. We went to bed early and fell asleep on opposite sides of the king-sized bed almost instantly. I thought of Dicker and chuckled to myself as I drifted off.

The next day we decided on a six-mile hike up into the hills above our villa. The start was paved and the rest on trails. We got lost on the way down and ended up having to retrace a half mile. This irritated me and I said, "You probably have a better compass in your brain than I do. I could've sworn this was going to get us back on the main road close to home."

"We decided to take a completely different road back so it was always a risk. Don't worry about it."

"I should have figured it out."

"When the road split, there were no signs and this certainly looked like it was going straight down to the highway. Why are you obsessing about this?"

"I'm compulsive about screwing up. I get stressed."

Debra stopped walking, put her hands on her hips, cocked her head and stared hard at me. Some time went by.

"You're right, of course. It's not a heart attack." I laughed at myself and Debra smiled and nodded. Then she walked over, put her arms around my neck and squeezed until I winced. We held hands and swung our arms as we walked back up the road and took a right at the intersection. That evening, we sat on the patio with margaritas, ate in and went to bed early, once again opting only for sleep.

Every day was different. We snorkeled at new beaches with different reefs, drove south and walked through a couple of magnificent and very expensive hotels, and had lunch at restaurants with ocean views. On the fourth night, I had a surprise for Debra. I drove south for a while and then turned north past the airport.

"It's getting dark, Tom. Do you know where you're going?"

"I have no idea, that's the surprise."

I stopped in Paia, on the north coast in the middle of the island. We walked from the parking lot to Freddy's Fish Boat, a popular local restaurant. The decorations were eclectic, but all native to the island. Fishnets and floats dominated the walls and ceiling. The food and service was excellent and the five courses took over two hours. We each had a small glass of fine port at the end, touched glasses,

tink

and said, "Toast for cheers." It was not the Hawaiian way to rush such a meal.

Debra, on the drive back, said, "You weren't lost at all, were you. What a wonderful evening. Thank you, dear Tom."

"Experiencing that feast without you would be empty and meaningless." We were not intimate that night, but slept close to each other.

By the end of the week, Debra and I were both tanned, but still had deep pink in some areas. Going back to the real world is always bittersweet so we made the last night special. After a light dinner, we sat in the living room chatting for an hour and then went for a swim in the dark and lukewarm Pacific. Still in the water, I slipped out of my trunks and Debra took off her bikini bottom. We played with each other, teasing and kissing until neither could stand it any longer. We laughed as we tried to put our swimsuits back on. The surf would break and the water would push us toward the shore and then back the other way. My foot got caught in the netting inside my trunks and I was tossed upside down.

Debra said, "I'm sorry there weren't more people here to see a killer butt flying out of the surf."

"Yours would be a lot more beguiling." As soon as I got my second leg in the suit, I leapt at Debra and slipped my hands under the back of her bikini. We gripped each other and I said, "Yes, definitely ravishing."

We showered away the salt and dried each other, spending extra time looking for hidden drops. The rest of the night had episodes of sleeplessness and it was fortunate our plane didn't leave until late afternoon. I couldn't sleep right away, thinking about where we might go on another vacation. Debra had no problem drifting off.

* * *

It was time for Lobo to finish the job he started in Spokane. He called the gallery in Dallas and was told there were two Hunter paintings there, but they were both sold. However, there would be more coming the following week. Gio noticed Lobo was in a snarky mood all day, but no reason surfaced. Lobo needed an excuse to get to Dallas, but didn't want to lose his job. Finally, he asked to see Gio in private.

"My brother was in a car accident, Gio. He lives in Dallas and the doctor said it was bad. I need to go see him. I should be back in a few days. Is that okay?"

"Of course it is. I have five brothers and sisters and I'd do anything for them."

"What about my job?"

"I told you it was fine. I have a friend who is a retired chef and she can fill in. Here's the number of a kennel for Boy. They'll treat her like a princess. Keep in touch."

Lobo was worried when he took Boy to the kennel and had a long conversation with the woman at the desk. She reassured him the staff would feed, walk and pamper the dog. In his apartment, he put some clothes in a carry-on and crammed his knife into an open outside pocket.

At the airport, he went through the gate without a problem and he carried his duffel into the plane with growing anticipation.

Chapter Thirty-six

Life in Dallas settled into a less dull routine for me. When Debra and I went to Maui, I brought along a letter-sized notebook for sketches and a traveling watercolor paint box. Watercolor is harder than oil or acrylic because I can't paint over mistakes or change my mind. However, it does have the advantage of serendipity. Something I do today may look horrible, but in the next morning's light, an amazing thing can happen: it's become glorious. It's the brain, of course. After a good night's sleep, I can see things missed the day before.

Restricted to my studio, I mostly paint from memory as surrounding scenery and sensations in a big city have a limit. Inspiration can come from anywhere in the world, but Debra and I happened to go to Hawaii. My sometimes-dozing right brain expanded with the ocean, the flora, the food and the love. I found myself using bigger brushes and more varied colors. The forms of waves, coral, blooms and breasts cadenced onto the canvas with the undulation, flourish and force of flamenco dancers.

Savanna noted this fresh artistic fervor right away and she was ecstatic. This allowed for an uptick in the marketing and heightened interest from collectors. Up went the prices and up went my concern about Lobo. Going someplace else and painting wouldn't do it at all as the already exaggerated publicity would continue and my contract with Savanna would follow me wherever I went. I thought about using my artistic contacts to help me into an analogous line of work. It had to be something that wouldn't mention "Thomas Hunter," but give an adequate income and enough intellectual stimulation to keep me fulfilled and happy. If Lobo tracked me down, he wouldn't be the only one. Savanna was enough of a capitalist to loose beagles on me.

Debra had a funk lasting several days after we got back. Our togetherness finally pulled her, complaining all the way, back into the real world.

"I want to go away again, Tom. I want to be happy with you for the rest of your life."

"Somebody has to pay for that, sweetheart. We could probably do a month or so, but you wouldn't have a job when you got back."

"I've got enough saved up for longer than that. I'm good at what I do and I'd have a half-dozen offers in the first two days."

"Ever the optimist. I truly believe, Debra, that vacations (even honeymoons) are dreams come true. Dreams are fragile. Times like that are truly special and we remember them always. If we were constantly living a dream, we would never have a memorable getaway. I would hate for our dreams to become banal."

Debra made a face and put her head down on my shoulder, hugging my arm as if it was a lifeline. "Time is precious. I'm not going to wait very long for our next dream. No one genuinely appreciates his life until the end is in sight. You, of all people, should appreciate that and let me have my way."

"I think there's a reason dreams last only minutes or seconds. If we spent eight hours of our lives in an alternate dream world, I think we'd need a lot more psychiatrists to keep people in reality. The people who insist on a dream world twenty-four hours a day are called drug addicts."

"I'm trying to maximize my private time with you and you're talking about heroin."

"All right, you know being away together is what I want too. We'll live another dream before my time runs out."

Debra insisted on spending the night with me, although discussing my "end of days" was depressing and dampened my libido. I think she was trying to show me what I'd be missing without vacation time. She was wild and demanding and I had to fake enthusiasm to get through it. Happily, her urgency was strong enough so she didn't notice my little friend took a lot longer to wake up. Anyway, my assurances settled her down and we parted in a calm and loving way.

* * *

When Lobo's flight landed at Love Field, the plane's tires made small squeaking sounds that reminded him of "Boy." He didn't get separation anxiety, he got angry. Lobo figured he would not be in Dallas if I'd been a real hit man. He wouldn't have needed to leave Boy in a friggin' kennel if I hadn't stuck those battery cables into his mouth. Frankly, if Lobo had gone to a plastic surgeon, he would probably speak normally now and, if he'd stop following me, I'd be happy to pay for it.

Lobo rented a car and got a room at a lower end motel. When packing, he jammed the switchblade into an open side–pocket of the duffel and had to push and squeeze it into an overhead bin. An open pocket has shortcomings and he didn't notice the knife's absence until he unpacked in the motel. He spent a fitful night thinking about his lost weapon. He had that switchblade for years and its numerous christenings made it a very personal and emotional possession. Lying in bed, he could feel it in his hand and it made him madder and madder. In the morning, the first item of business was to replace the knife. To his dismay, the hardware store in the area only carried fixed blade knives. He finally found a store, off the beaten path, that carried a variety of strange weapons, including switchblades. The new Italian knife was not like his lost one. Instead of having the blade shoot straight out of the handle, this had the blade folded into the handle itself. Lobo had to make sure his fingers were not in the way when it swung out and locked in the open position. He was not happy and practiced a long time in the evening, pushing the button and not always getting out of the way.

snick   snick   snick

On the second day, he drove across town close to Savanna's gallery. He walked in and looked around, finding two of my newest paintings hanging on the wall. One was sold, but still had the price of seven hundred dollars on it. Lobo was standing with his mouth open staring at the price when Savanna came up beside him.

"Can I help you, Sir? You look a bit shocked. Is that from the price or the beauty and power of the painting?"

When Lobo turned to face her, she could see the tattoo above his collar. The rings in his ears were common among artist types, but the gold-colored safety pins in his eyebrows were not.

"Um . . . I didn't know Tom was an artist . . . he was a friend . . . ah . . . when he was living in another city."

"That was hard to believe," thought Savanna. "Do you like the painting? Perhaps we can come down a little bit on the price."

"The painting is something else. I can't make heads or tails of it. Where are people and trees? Things like that."

"This is an abstract painting. You get the emotion from the shapes and the colors.

Lobo shook his head and glanced down at the price again. He finally remembered why he had come to the gallery. "I'd like to get in touch with Tom. I'm just passing through and we were close in the old days."

Savanna doubted that. "Let me have your name and number and I'll have him call you."

There was a delay while Lobo processed this. He knew he wasn't going to hear from Tom. "I'm staying at a hotel and don't have a phone. Does he come into the gallery every day?"

"Once in a while, but he works in his studio. Give me your name and I'll tell him you came by."

"My name is . . . Gio. Thanks for your time." Lobo waved and headed for the door. He was mad at himself for not being able to think of a good name. He drank heavily that evening and went to bed wishing Boy was with him. The dog made him feel good. He decided the only way he was going to find Tom would be to watch the entrance. He'd have to remember to buy a sandwich and beer so he didn't miss lunch. He got angry when he missed a meal.

The first thing Savanna did after Lobo left was call me. "Tom, there was a strange man in here today asking for you. He was a 'low' type, if you know what I mean. He said he worked with you in the past, which I know is a lie."

I couldn't help it; I shivered. "What did he look like?"

"The man had strange eyes and a tattoo coming up his neck. He talked kinda funny, as if he had a speech impediment. Did you really know him?"

"Before I started painting, I worked briefly in a garage and he was the guy who changed tires. Dreadful man. Something else has come up and I need to talk to you. I'll come by tomorrow."

Chapter Thirty-seven

Lobo drove to the gallery at 8 o'clock in the morning and parked next to the entrance in case he had to leave in a hurry. On the way, he stopped at a deli to get a six pack of Budweiser and a pastrami sandwich to keep them company. He thought that was very funny and he chuckled from time to time. Carrying the bag, he walked across the street and stood on the sidewalk. On that block, there was a residential building and several stores, but no place for him to sit. Lobo knew people coming in and out of the gallery would notice him and he couldn't stand in one place all day holding his lunch. He walked to the end of the block and looked back at the gallery. Lobo remembered Tom well enough that he thought he could spot him from where he was. He sat down on the sidewalk with his back against the building and became "homeless." If he saw a patrol car go by, he stood up and pretended to be looking for something. Nobody hassled him.

At 11:15, he saw a taxi drive up and a man get out of the back. He took a large painting out of the trunk, and went into the gallery. It was Tom for sure. He was so excited he drank his third beer. That was a mistake because, from the effort in getting to his feet, he peed a short stream in his pants, causing his face to twist in several directions. He pulled his baseball cap down over his face and walked quickly to his car. Lobo bent low enough behind the wheel so he would be virtually invisible when Tom came out again. He'd follow him to his studio and take care of business in the wee hours. The only difficulty was Lobo's bladder. After three beers in three hours, the unhappy organ was screaming. In addition, the aroma from his wet pants hinted that another unseemly event wasn't far off. There were shops across from the gallery, but Tom would surely spot him in the street. No one had left the gallery so Lobo, being careful not to jostle himself, opened the car door and stepped out. He walked oddly, like a ballet dancer, to the end of the block and went around the corner. His only hope was the alley behind the gallery so he lurched to the second corner and rounded it. There was a delivery truck behind the gallery with two men unloading a sculpture. It was heavy and they set it down while one rang the bell to get someone to open the large delivery door.

Lobo clutched his groin, waited a moment, and then continued down the alley, hoping the men would get inside quickly so he could relieve himself. It took fifteen seconds before the door opened and the men started to pick up the large bronze piece. A grimacing Lobo stopped halfway to them, grabbed himself, swaying on tiptoe.

"Hold up, Tony. We may gotta problem comin' up the alley."

The other man glanced over his shoulder and said, "Shit! Call security."

The first guy ran in through the doors and yelled something rude. In ten seconds, there were two uniformed armed men in the alley.

Lobo heard the call for help at the exact time the muscles of his bladder overcame his efforts to dam the flow and new drops joined his previous leakage. He turned toward the building, unzipped and whipped his leaking organ into the open air. The stream was impressive, hitting the side of the building from five feet away with hardly a dip. Sir Isaac would've been impressed.

One security guy stayed with the sculpture and the other one, with a drawn weapon, ran towards Lobo. The anticipation was such that the bronze stayed where it was as the two museum men guarding it waited for the inevitable showdown. With the blue uniform now only feet away, Lobo raised his hands and turned directly towards him saying, "I gotta pee, officer. I'll be outa here in a second."

The security man, hosed with a stream of hot maize-colored liquid, shouted "Fuck," and lurched backwards, tumbling onto the concrete. When the hand holding his thirty-eight caliber revolver hit the cement, his grip tightened. This included his trigger finger and the freed bullet ricocheted off the building and struck Lobo on the left shoe.

"Son of a bitch, he shot me." Lobo didn't know the intervention of the building had robbed the bullet of most of its power and, although it hit his leather shoe, his injury was limited to a painful bruise. He fell to his left, the last of his urine stream describing a sparkling arc in the air. The private security officer, thinking he'd killed Lobo when the man collapsed, saw himself on trial for involuntary manslaughter.

Lobo, only dripping at this point, heaved himself to his feet and limped back to the corner of the building. The supine security man, both bewildered and jubilant at the sight of the dead man risen, could only marvel at the benevolence of the Almighty. Lobo, cursing unintelligibly, turned the second corner and headed for his car at the exact time Savanna and I came out of the building.

Savanna noticed him first. "Good God, look at that crazy man."

I turned around and saw Lobo bearing down on us, cursing wildly. His fly was unzipped and his manhood was flailing about with each limping step. "That's him, the hitman I told you about."

Savanna laughed. "I can see why you don't want him hitting on you."

"No, I mean it. He's obviously deranged, but he's a gang enforcer and killed many people. Get inside and lock the doors." I grabbed Savanna's upper arm and pulled her into the gallery. Lobo's car was visible through the glass doors and we saw him open the door and get behind the wheel. He started the car and almost hit a pickup in his haste to get away.

Savanna was desperately trying to keep from laughing at the sight of my supposed killer. She knew I was serious, but something didn't make sense to her.

"I really don't know what a killer is supposed to look like. Hollywood gave me a totally different version." Her efforts at laugh suppression turned into small retching sounds.

I squeezed her arm. "I just spent a half hour telling you something about my past and I guarantee that man will get himself together and come looking for me with a switchblade."

Savanna said, "I believe you," although her body language and eyes totally belied the statement.

I stared at her for a long moment and decided my best option was to get the hell outa Dodge . . . again. "I'm going to pack up and leave town. I don't know where I'm going right now, but I'll keep in touch so you can send me my share. I'll send you more work once I get settled. Do not, under any circumstance, tell anyone where I've gone." My painting days were over as Lobo would notice that right away, but I didn't want to upset Savanna.

Savanna, from long experience, believed all talented artists were a touch batty so she watched me drive away without the least concern. She remembered what Tom told her about his second life and thought, "Tom thinks he's a golem. After all, ashes are pretty close to clay. In a few days, he'll be over it and back painting his marvelous acrylics." Her struggling stopped and she allowed herself a good laugh remembering the sight of Lobo's "winky" swinging in the wind.

Chapter Thirty-eight

After I left the gallery, I went to my rented condo and packed my clothes and other essentials. I was on a month-to-month so I wrote a check to the landlord and told him to keep the room deposit for his trouble in getting rid of my painting stuff. He'd make some money if he sold it. The last thing I did was to take the painting I did after the glorious night with Debra—the one I took back from Savanna—and mailed it to Debra. No explanation needed.

There was food in the fridge and I ate that for dinner and finished the bottle of red wine. In the middle of my third glass, my destination came to me and I phoned American Airlines. The flight left at 9 AM the following morning and would arrive at LaGuardia in New York four hours later. I made a temporary reservation at the Lexington hotel, at 48th St on the east side. I closed my account in Dallas and deposited everything into a branch of the Chemical Corn Exchange bank, headquartered in New York. Even if Lobo found out the city, there were millions of people in New York.

Three days later, I rented a one-bedroom apartment in a nice area of Manhattan's midtown west side. The 86th St. crosstown bus and the subway would get me anywhere I wanted. The first night in my new place was not happy. I thought of Debra and the full impact of what I was leaving behind hit me hard. I called her and, although well aware of my past (including the sociopath tracking me) she was devastated.

"It's too sudden, Tom. We need to have time to adjust to deaths and departures. I feel like leaving my job and moving to New York."

"I would love that, but New York is not easy. Except for Central Park, there's no grass for miles in any direction. The competition is fierce and I gather not everyone is pleasant. I've had no problem myself, but the biggest downside is the expense. You'd have to earn a lot more money than you do now to live the same way."

"I like my job here, and I have wonderful friends. I've never known any place as nice." There was a pause. "Can you promise me your crazy friend won't find you again."

"This city has millions of people and I'm not going to be painting anymore. I'm finally anonymous. If I had a full life ahead of me, I would do more than just ask you to join me. But I'm honest and care about you and it doesn't make any sense to move here for the months I have left."

I heard her quietly sobbing on the other end of the line. It would not be right to ask her to move and I didn't want to leave her up in the air about it. "I'm thinking about the way we're parting, as difficult as it is. Sometimes it's better to cut it with a knife rather than being pulled apart slowly over time. Perhaps Lobo showing up as he did will make it easier for us."

"I ache for you, Tom. I ache for your voice, your humor and your presence in my life. I'm going to hang up now, drink something strong and cry for a while."

"I am bereft, Debra. Remembering us together will give me strength and carry me to the end. The love we share is the best of this life's blessings." I hung up the phone before she could answer. Anything more would be pulling us apart, not cutting cleanly.

Over the next several days, as I walked the streets, I began to feel strangely at home. I got excited passing Carnegie Hall, the Plaza Hotel and the entrance to Central Park. My most vivid past life recollection (which turned into a shakingly wonderful emotional experience) was having New England clam chowder at the Oyster Bar in Grand Central Station. I spent a glorious couple of hours there at midday and the taste the stew, as well as the architectural magnificence of the terminal, gave me goosebumps.

I did nothing during the first week in the city except re-bond as visions came to me. One evening, I saw Victor Borge at the piano with his classic patter and hilarious athleticism. I gave the Metropolitan Museum of Art a good workout and walked down Fifth Avenue, popping into Tiffany's, FAO Schwartz and Saks Fifth Avenue.

I knew I had to get a job before money ran out. What could I do besides painting, bringing patients bedpans, and changing tires? I stopped in a kiosk on the street and bought a Saturday Evening Post, Colliers, The New Yorker, and Sports Afield. I read them all and knew I'd been here before. The Sports Afield had an article about animals in Kenya by a photojournalist named Janet Hutchins. There was a lot of hunting there and a complete absence of controls. Hutchins, obviously an animal lover, was concerned about their eventual extinction. Her prose was succinct and educational and her photographs vivid. I stared at her for a long time.

I began to think about why we should be concerned about a bunch of unfamiliar animals in another continent. The creatures were here long before humans and it seemed to me, and certainly to Janet Hutchins, that we owe them something when we take their homeland and collect trophies. If we don't care about innocent life forms who'd lived, given birth, and died in Africa for countless millennia, wouldn't human creatures be inclined to treat unfamiliar others in far-off places the same way? My vague recollection of historical slaughters would answer "yes." We need a lot more "Janet Hutchins" in high places, and not just for animals

The New Yorker was intriguing because it combined serious writing, poetry, humor and cartoons. Since my rebirth, I'd jotted down a half dozen poems, usually in rhyme, about situations in which I found myself. On the surface, they were humorous, but you could not miss the underlying themes. I showed the best to Debra and she loved them and said I had a knack for words. I sent two of them to the magazine and that's what started my career writing short stories. I did them all in the first person because they were reality to me, but I knew the reader would think I had a good imagination. I wrote several stories about the farm and a couple about the bad boys in Spokane.

My published story about Stanton Mulloy, the dying man in San Francisco, led to a telephone call from one of the editors at The New Yorker. Several hospital administrators and a lawyer had called the magazine to see if this was fiction or nonfiction. They wanted to know the name of the hospital and the patient, but I didn't want to get involved. Fortunately, I used pseudonyms for the doctors, the patient, the hospital and even the city. What I did not need, in my new location, was a slander suit and another visit from Lobo. In retrospect, I should have used a "pen name" instead of Tom Hunter, but it's always easier to see more clearly when we look back.

Mimzy and Debra provided quite different material for the love stories I put into some of my writings. Later, I worried about that. I was afraid, if Debra happened to read the magazine, she would recognize some of the situations and resent me. The wondrous emotional, intellectual and physical connection with Debra left a huge vacuum in my present life. I knew I wouldn't have a relationship like that in the time I had left, but I enjoyed the company of women and yearned for a simple friendship. I was determined to be selective as intimacy was beside the point, especially at my age. I wanted the different intellectual approaches, the varied viewpoints and the emotional reactions that were unique to a woman. Such things were often the butt of jokes from men whose egos prevented them from appreciating the wonders of an alternative chromosome. I didn't understand cultures that limited women to the bearing of food to the table and children to the family. What would be the relative value of nations that insisted on using only half of its intellectual and emotional capacity? The answer was obvious if you spent a little time looking around the world.

Chapter Thirty-nine

I had time in the first weeks I was in New York, to think deeper about my mid nineteen fifties second life. I didn't have the feeling my previous life was a disaster or I was such a saint I was being given an upward rung to climb on the Hindu ladder of lives. The entire thing could be a dream and I'd wake up at my actual age in the future. I thought most dreams are over in a matter of seconds, or a few minutes at most. Can a dream, like a microdot, be so compressed a year of life happens in thirty seconds? Could I truly experience, only in my mind, the complex love I felt for Debra?

Regardless, particularly looking back at the river, I felt there was a journey set before me. I never thought about it this way before, but I occasionally found myself looking around with a feeling of paranoia. You know the sensation when the hairs on the back of your neck stand up and you turn around quickly to see if anyone's behind you. There was never anybody watching and, believe me, I did the 360°, which included everything above and below me. In my peculiar situation, I don't feel it's abnormal to be a little fearful and oversensitive.

On a practical note, I needed to get to work and convince more magazines in the city I was literate and had a modicum of talent. I wrote a half a dozen stories before Collier's magazine accepted a fictionalized story, based on my experience at the farm. Collier's was right up my alley as it began almost seventy years before as a magazine of, "fiction, fact, sensation, wit, humor and news." It also had a reputation for investigative journalism that gave me a bold idea. The maxim, "The best defense is a good offense," came to mind and I started looking into Big Boys criminal activity in Spokane. Although risky, I was tired of running away from Lobo. In retrospect, I should have minded my own business.

The best place to do research on the subject was in newspaper archives. It took a major effort for me to convince the New York Times to help me and they would only do it if I teamed up with one of their top reporters. My being a quasi-gang member with Big Boy's wolfpack finally did the trick. Phil and I met in various places, and a drink helped me to relax and recall details. He was the epitome of an investigative reporter; he wore a snap–brim fedora and had a lit cigarette hanging out of his mouth most of the time. He never drank much, but encouraged me to get a bit sozzled so I wouldn't hold anything back. As Phil and I worked together, his expertise was essential and a partnership would be safer down the road.

At our third meeting, Phil said, "Hearing your story is great, but we need to experience it. The only way the readers are going to get a true feel for what went on there is to describe the streets where the gang walks, the place where they hang out and the bars where they drink. I can't do that from here."

"I can tell you about all those places and where to go. Those are mean streets and it would be best to talk to the police and get an undercover guy to go with you."

"It would help me a lot if you came with me."

"I really appreciate you, Phil, but if any of those boys spot me, I'm a dead man."

Phil was not happy and we had an argument about it. I stood my ground and he finally said he would try to get a cop to go with him. I also told the editor I wouldn't contribute a thing unless he kept me off the byline. I didn't think Lobo read the New York Times, but I didn't want to take any chances. Phil didn't mind getting all the credit.

I worked mostly from home so I was free in the evenings. I soon learned where newspaper guys hung out and decided to make some friends. It wasn't easy at the Times because Phil was the only one who knew me and I was not officially on the staff. I thought The New Yorker magazine was a better fit for this and, after my third poem came out, I made an appointment and was sent to a junior editor named Heather. The magazine was doing thoughtful work and I brought up my experience at the hospital in San Francisco. End-of-life issues were not a big deal, but I suspected, with an aging population, it would become one.

The fact that an oncologist, after he spent some time with his conscience, stopped his treatment of Stanton Mulloy and kept him comfortable was an eye-opener for Heather. It was a touchy subject for others, including the editor-in-chief, but it certainly would create a buzz. Always a good thing for circulation. Heather was younger and happily married so, after our second meeting, I asked her where a single person my age could find some friends. Instead of giving me a list of bars, she did me a much bigger favor. At least I thought so at the time. There was a middle-aged woman in the copy room who had been divorced for several years and was now discouraged and upset. She'd been dating for a while and found men to be untrustworthy, unenlightened and ruttish.

Heather said, "Allie has sworn off men and told everyone to quit setting her up. You seem like a straight-up guy, Tom, and I may be able to talk her into meeting with you on neutral ground. As a matter of fact, my husband Birch and I will go on a double date so she'll feel safe."

"Thank you, but I am not sure about this. I've never been mean to a woman in my life and I'm not a womanizer. I have recently come to New York and would like to have someone to go with me to a show or a restaurant. I'm not interested in intimacy."

"I can't promise anything, but I'll see what I can do. If I've made a mistake in judgment and you mess with Allie's emotions, I'll make sure this magazine will have no further dealings with you."

"This is a new experience for me and I'm nervous about it. You've described a woman who's been treated badly and wants nothing more to do with men. In addition, I've been threatened by one of her friends."

"You know what I mean. I'm serious about this, Tom."

"I'm a decent and ethical man and I'll be taking as much of a chance as Allie is."

"If what you say is true, it'll be good for both of you. I'll let you know tomorrow."

Chapter Forty

Three days later, Heather called me. "It wasn't easy to get Allie out of her shell, but I did it. She agreed to meet you because she trusts me. If you let . . ."

"I know what you're going to say: more menacing words. I'm a good person and I don't think I should meet somebody who is in such a state that you feel it necessary to hang a sword over my head."

There was silence on the other end as she thought about the consequence of such repeated warnings. "I suppose I've been a little much."

"Little?"

"All right. I made a judgment and asked her. We've been friends for quite a while and I couldn't stand to see her suffer."

I understood this was a serious emotional issue with Heather and it's one of the good things about a woman's character. They feel for other people and can get quite involved. Heather could probably issue warnings and talk all afternoon about her friend's woes. I hoped Allie was more at ease with her decision than Heather was.

Our double date dinner was set up for the following Saturday. I was nervous about the meeting because, if she was a flake and unattractive to boot, how was I going to get out of it without insulting both Allie and Heather. I was determined, perhaps selfishly, to make this as easy as possible on myself. I arrived at the French restaurant ten minutes early and chose a seat where I could watch the entrance.

If Allie turned out to be an emotional wreck, I would treat her with the greatest respect and turn it into a "business" dinner, mixing affability with a touch of formality. Neither of them could say I wasn't a gentleman. Birch was an unknown factor, but at least he had a Y chromosome.

Looking back on those few minutes, I knew it was a little silly to obsess about something as basic as meeting a friend of a friend. At least my anxiety sped up the waiting time and I soon saw the three of them walking to my table. I glanced at Allie so quickly it didn't register in my brain. I spent the first seconds greeting Heather and her husband. Heather interpreted my delay and hesitancy as shyness and it turned out to be an excellent way for me to break the ice.

"Allie," said Heather, "this is Tom, the talented gentleman I told you about. He's not as bashful as he seems when you get to know him."

I saw Birch looking at me and knew Heather had filled him in on the tangled situation. He had a slight smile on his face and probably couldn't wait to see how the evening developed. If I could have done it without being seen, a wink would guarantee we'd be on the same page.

"It's a pleasure, Allie. I think Heather is mistaking humility for shyness, but it could've been worse." There was a good laugh and I was especially pleased to see Birch join in. Humor was a great way to start most things and it was something women appreciated. The waiter, as silent as a hologram, materialized at my side to take our drink orders. This was most welcome as it would have been uncouth to order before the others arrived.

During the introductions, I had a chance to observe Allie. She didn't laugh like the others, but smiled tentatively, which I thought was a good sign. She had a pale complexion and features that were just short of pretty. Her most prominent facial aspect, which I rather liked, was dense eyebrows over hazel eyes. She had slightly tangled dark hair to her shoulders, which added edginess to a serious demeanor. She wasn't slim, but had all the right parts.

Fine French restaurants serve a delicacy I really love and I thought it would make a good conversation opener for my blind date. Indeed, when I said "Escargot," Allie turned and looked at me with wide eyes and raised eyebrows.

She said, "I was hoping someone would order that. I'm not into snails, but I do love the garlic and butter they swim in."

"Then you and I will need more French bread for dunking." I waited for a moment. "Incidentally, Allie, you've passed the friendship test. I'm very happy."

That statement startled everyone except Birch, who was trying to suppress a smile. Allie seemed more curious than anything else, but Heather's forehead creased at the thought I had the nerve to test her friend. She said, "Tell us about your 'friendship' test."

"The test only has one question, but passing it is essential. I needed to find out if Allie likes garlic and butter?"

Birch couldn't help himself, he burst out in laughter. Heather took a little more time to get it and Allie looked at me with new interest. Who would have thought snails would have such a noble role? It wasn't long before my no–longer–blind date began dipping her bread into each savory space after I lifted the shell and forked the snail out of its wee home. The conversation was wide-ranging and fun. Allie, after her third glass of wine, started telling me stories about the strange mistakes she found when reviewing a reporter's copy before publication. It wasn't only punctuation, some of the reporters in their haste to finish before the deadline, never read over their own stories. Mixing up bear and bare could be quite titillating.

Birch was a psychologist, specializing in adolescent behavior. His inquisitive mind and offbeat sense of humor undoubtedly made him a favorite, both with the youngsters and their parents. The bottom line was that the evening, from escargot to Crème Caramel, was delightful and productive. Allie and I got along well and I asked her if I could call her for another evening. She said, "Yes, as long as butter and garlic is included." I ran over alternatives to snails in my mind and came up with most things Italian.

Chapter Forty-one

When Lobo got back to the motel after his "open fly" fiasco at the gallery, he was a mess. He gently took his left shoe off and examined his foot. There was a tender bluish spot behind the pinky. He was surprised a bone wasn't broken because it hurt like hell when it happened. He thought, "I coulda been killed. Don't make no sense. I'm not the bad guy here." There was a small bottle of vodka in the fridge and he poured himself a half cup. "I'll shower up and make a plan, give my foot a day to calm down, and then go back and finish things." Lobo began to undress and that was the first time he noticed his zipper was undone and his manhood was hanging out. It looked as depressed as he felt and he pinched it to make sure it was still viable.

Lobo began to feel better with the hot water running over his back and chest. Even his mind settled down: "Tom didn't see me across the street from the picture place so I can go back and wait for him. He makes a good living painting colored blobs so, before I kill him, I'll make him tell me where he keeps his money." Lobo, after he dressed, was so thrilled with this plan he had a full cup of vodka. He walked barefoot about the room for a while and then fell asleep on top of the bed with the TV on.

Lobo woke up at 5 AM and leaned over the side to scratch Boy behind the ears. Not seeing the dog, he panicked for a moment and it took him a while to realize where he was. He got dressed and practiced opening and closing his new switchblade. That put Lobo in a very good mood and he decided to celebrate at the Pancake House. After three cups of coffee, a huge stack of pancakes and six pieces of bacon, the world looked glorious indeed. Lobo drove to the gallery, parked the car by the front door, and walked across the street. He assumed his "homeless" position on the sidewalk and waited. The coffee continued working on his kidneys and after three hours he couldn't stand it anymore. Not wanting to get involved with deliveries behind the gallery, he drove all the way back to his motel room to relieve himself. Lobo was not happy and figured the only way to calm down was to have more pancakes. He ordered a double stack, this time with sausage links.

Lobo missed seeing Tom pull Savanna back into the gallery so he decided it was an opportunity to take a break. He went to a local bar and spent the afternoon there, drinking vodka and annoying anyone near him. He hoped somebody would take offense so he could christen his switchblade, but that didn't happen. Lobo's tolerance for frustration was limited and the hangover he had when he woke the following morning did not help. He couldn't stand to do another stakeout and decided to walk into the gallery, find Tom and carve "Lobo" on his belly. He reminded himself to say, "Hah yoo yeah ya", as he did it.

Savanna was teaching a class that morning so when Lobo walked into the art gallery, he was met by a young woman in tight red slacks and a bulging white blouse with the top three buttons undone. She had a necklace with colored stones around her neck and there was a gnarled wooden piece at the end of it.

"Can I help you sir? I'm Teetsy. A new Hunter just came in."

Both the buttons and the wooden piece distracted Lobo and it took him a while to remember why he was there. "I'm here to see my friend, Tom . . . ah . . . Hunter." Before the woman could answer, he said, "By the way, what's that thing?" pointing at the end of the necklace.

Teetsy's eyes lit up and she reached down and picked up the twisted wooden object. She began fondling it. "It's a penis."

"What kind of an animal has . . .?"

"It's not from an animal and it's not real. It's been carved by a talented artist and it symbolizes the experience and changes of aging. Don't worry though, the form and the lovely grain pattern of the wood means its function is replaced by spirituality."

"Does that really happen? It doesn't seem like a fair trade."

Teetsy rubbed the wood on her cheek. "I don't really know. I haven't been with anyone that old."

"When does it start getting stumpy like that?" Lobo couldn't help himself; he put his hand in his pocket to find out if anything had changed.

The young woman, seeing Lobo squirming about, let go of the wood. "Maestro Hunter has left Dallas and moved on. Nobody knows where. Savanna doesn't know if he'll continue to paint so this is a wonderful opportunity to buy. It's only eight hundred dollars for an exquisite one-of-a-kind Hunter."

Lobo was stunned, both by the price and Tom's vanishing again. Adrenaline flooded his system and his expression became a slurry of hate and rage. The hand in his pocket stopped searching for his "willy" and when it came out, it was holding a switchblade. He pushed the button and the blade swung out and hit him on a knuckle.

"Ouch! Son of a bitch. I'll cut his balls off and then carve him into little pieces."

Teetsy clutched at the phallus dangling between her breasts and backpedaled until she crashed into a wall, shaking loose not only her right boob, but also a large watercolor painting which crashed to the floor, spraying broken glass everywhere.

Lobo, cursing and dancing about, thrust the knife in every direction possible and then ran into the street, still shouting profanities and waving the blade. Teetsy, in a catatonic state, sat rigid among the shards of glass, still gripping the symbolic phallus. Two other women employees, drawn by the noise, sprang into action. One called the police and the other crunched across the glass to her friend and tried vainly to stuff her breast back into the blouse.

The sun's glare shook Lobo out of his ranting and dervish-like gyrations and he gazed with surprise at the "cowboys" staring at him from the sidewalk across the street. There were three women and two men, all with large hats and three of them armed. "Open" carry was against the law, so the three who were packing weapons wore long suede jackets to hide their 45 caliber revolvers. One of the men actually slept with his holster buckled tightly around his PJs. Both men and one of the women, seeing what appeared to be a Yankee accented outlaw stabbing the air in all directions, drew their weapons and began firing. The armed woman, having taken an afternoon training course years before, managed to hit Lobo's car. The cowboys' rounds shattered the plate glass window of the gallery, which was sensational enough to cause one of the men to yell, "Cease fire."

The sudden silence allowed Lobo to run to his car, leap into the driver's seat and take off at high speed. The absence of the museum's window glass enabled the two unarmed women to see into the gallery for the first time and spot Teetsy sitting bolt upright in the middle of glass shards with another woman apparently fondling a breast.

"Shee-yut! You boys done shot a woman in the gallery."

There was silence for a few seconds and the bigger of the two men said, "Twern't me." The other one said, "The Yankee musta did it. Ah'm fixin' to move on." The two weaponless women gaped at each other with open mouths. The smaller one said, "I'm calling the police and tell them to bring an ambulance." She started running back the way they came as there was a telephone booth a block away. Her gait was awkward and she made a loud "pocking" noise with each step as cowboy boots are not made for running.

Her husband, the big man in the front, yelled, "C'mon back here right now, Bedelia Dee. 'Tain't none of yore business." The pockity-pock sped up and the woman turned the corner without looking back.

"Shee-yut!" The remaining unarmed woman looked back and forth between the husband and the spot where Bedelia Dee turned the corner. Nothing more was said and the big fellow holstered his weapon and started walking rapidly away. The other two vigilantes followed him and that left a lone woman sobbing on the sidewalk. It didn't take long for two police cars and an ambulance to arrive. Both women gave the same story about a crazed Yankee dervish waving a sword and uttering threats. One patrol car, lights blazing, raced up the street and found the three armed persons five blocks away, walking fast. The officer called for backup and half a dozen cruisers joined him. The confiscation of the group's weapons resulted in a short, but fierce argument regarding the Second Amendment. The woman tearfully admitted she was the one who might have put a bullet hole in Lobo's rented Chevy. The police arrested all three and they spent the night in jail waiting for arraignment the next morning. An officer called headquarters and put out an APB on Lobo's blue Chevrolet.

Two officers entered the gallery and quickly determined the seated woman clutching the venerable phallus was unhurt. She was simply in shock from the presence of the dervish and the explosion of glass from the fallen watercolor and the plate glass window. In fact, she had recovered enough to begin a seated sales pitch to convince the officers to buy the Tom Hunter acrylic. Neither officer looked at the painting as their eyes were locked on the exposed mammary.

The APB for Lobo went to train and bus stations, the airport and rental car companies. Lobo, in spite of holding his hand over the bullet hole when he returned the car, was accused of damaging the vehicle in a way that suggested criminal behavior. Officers brought him to the police station as a witness in an apparent shoot out.

Although he was mostly an innocent victim, being a Yankee meant he was responsible for the broken glass. This enabled the police to keep him in Dallas as a witness against the vigilantes.

Lobo still had Tom on his hit list, but the recent events put his retribution on hold for the moment. He was frantic to get back to Spokane for the comfort of his dog's companionship and to resume cooking with Gio. It took five days and a lot of questioning before Lobo was able to take an early morning flight home.

Although Lobo's visit to Dallas would appear to be a total disaster, the worst thing for him was the confiscation of his beloved switchblade.

Chapter Forty-two

New York is an exciting place and my guard gradually dropped over the months I remained there. Certain places and events surprised me from time to time as I wandered about the city looking for inspiration for my poetry and prose. Happily, most of my previous life flashes were good. One of the best was a Japanese restaurant on the west side where my mother taught me how to use ohashi (Japanese "chopsticks"). I also recall, as a boy, spending an afternoon watching the Barnum and Bailey Circus in Madison Square Garden. It was an exciting experience involving all the senses, especially smell. What got me into trouble was the cotton candy. I ended up vomiting on the way out of the building and never ate it again.

I saw Allie quite a bit. We had lunch together when her work permitted it, and we went to dinner, a movie, or a lecture once or twice a week. She had never been a beautiful woman, but had tolerably arranged features and she dressed well. The subject of health came up in a conversation a couple of weeks after we met and, after hemming and hawing, Allie confessed something very private.

"This is personal, Tom, so please keep this between us. My closest friends know about it, but it's awkward, especially with a man."

"I don't betray confidences and I can't imagine anything would change our relationship."

We were having a light dinner at a local restaurant and Allie moved forward, looking down at her crispy chicken salad. As I look back on it, she was preparing herself for something negative from me. She took a deep breath. "I had breast cancer and one was removed."

She didn't look up right away so I waited. When she finally flicked shiny eyes up at me, I said, "Thank you for trusting me enough to tell me. How long has it been?"

"Nine years."

"That makes me happy. You'll never have to worry about it again."

"But I'm not a . . ."

"I know exactly what you're going to say. You are going to tell me you're not a 'whole woman.' I realize a breast is an important symbol of womanhood and carries a large emotional load. For that reason, it seems more important than a leg or a kidney. Anatomically, even though it's held in high esteem, it's just another 'part.' For any intelligent and rational person, even if you had both breasts removed, you would still be a person respected, loved and desired. Who the hell cares about the morons?"

Allie looked at me with questioning eyes and I knew she was trying to figure out whether I truly believed that or if I was just trying to make her feel better.

I searched my mind to come up with something that would change the mood and, at the same time, make her believe me. "Which side is missing?"

"The right one."

I was facing her and I moved my right hand up in front her left chest and showed her my palm, opening and closing my fingers slightly. "Wonderful. I'm right-handed so I'd never notice."

There was a moment's hesitation while she figured out what I was telling her. Then she pitched back in her seat and started laughing. She looked up at me, grinning, and more laughter erupted. I couldn't help joining her. I brought my hand up again squeezing my fingers slightly in a slow controlled way that had the same wonderful effect.

After dinner, and on the way to drop her off at her apartment, she was more animated than I'd ever seen her. I told the taxi driver to wait and I walked her across the sidewalk. At the door to the building, she turned around and gave me a huge hug. "Do you want to come up for a while?"

"Tomorrow's a heavy day for me, Allie, but thanks for the invite."

Allie handled it well and simply kissed me on the cheek and walked through the door. On the way to my place, I agonized over what to do in the future. Men had mistreated her in the past and with my future being no future at all, I was determined not to get physically involved with her. After all, she wasn't Debra and I wasn't in love with her. It did not occur to me immediately that my not sleeping with her didn't mean that she wouldn't want to. I decided I had to tell her about my past. I only had a few months to live and friendship was all I wanted. She would surely understand that.

My naïveté would be costly.

* * *

Gio was not happy with Lobo.

"Where have you been, Lobo? You said you'd be back in a few days, a week at the most."

When the sous chef walked into the restaurant, he was stunned to see a woman dressed in white doing his job and forgot it was on a temporary basis. "I was called as a witness in a shooting. The police made me stay an extra week to testify."

"I have a restaurant to run. It's a serious business and this is how I earn my living. Why didn't you call me?"

Lobo had no answer for this as phoning never entered his mind. "I didn't have any change."

Gio, dumbfounded, could only stare at the hapless man in front of him. "Rita is only here on a temporary basis and I'll have her stay until after dinner so you can get back in the groove. Put your uniform on and get ready for the lunch crowd."

This was a lot for Lobo to process. All he heard was he still had a job, his dog was waiting for him at home and life was good again. Tom was still on his hit list, but that flashed only briefly. Lobo wanted to put revenge off for a while. Then Gio began asking him about his trip to Texas.

"I'm really glad you're back, Lobo. By the way, how's your brother doing?"

"My brother? I don't have a brother."

Gio frowned and thought back to make sure he remembered correctly. "You told me your brother had an auto accident in Dallas and he was in pretty bad shape. Isn't that the reason you had to rush off?"

Lobo couldn't remember what he told his boss. His features twisted as he desperately tried to think of something to say that wouldn't reveal his plans for Tom. "I was so upset I guess I said the wrong thing. It was my sister."

"What happened? Is she doing all right?

"She fell down the stairs and broke some bones and hit her head. It was very close but she's doing okay now. Her bones are healing and she woke up from a coma. I won't need to go back."

"I thought you told me it was an auto accident."

"My brother had that, but it was a long time ago. Now it's my sister's accident."

Gio knew he wouldn't be getting any straight answers so he quit asking. He'd keep a closer eye on the man and wouldn't be giving permission for any more "family accident" trips.

Chapter Forty-three

My second life in New York was kind to me for quite a while. I took bits and pieces and made up new stories for the New Yorker and Colliers. I put an underlying meaningful theme into each one. Farmers worked from dawn to dusk and were always at the mercy of Mother Nature. End-of-life issues turned out to be an interest for everyone. I wrote about changing tires and greasing cars as a symbol of "workingmen" everywhere.

However, I eventually had trouble coming up with new material. Even my wanderings through the city didn't help much as an amnesiac loses the advantage of history and experience. Even reading a newspaper confused me since I had no background before that day in the river. I earned a very modest income from writing which, without my painting money, would make a pleasant standard of living difficult.

I needed a break and that's why I was excited when Allie suggested taking a drive out of the city. She wanted to go for a whole weekend, but I knew what that meant. I lied and told her I was attending a church service on Sunday and would be interviewing Dr. Ralph Stockman, a Methodist minister with a nationwide reputation. I could tell by her reaction she was upset and was having more difficulty keeping it under control. I was running out of excuses and it became awkward when Allie invited me into her home, "for a drink," after our dates. One day, she said she wanted to see where I lived and that was easier for me to resist. I told her my deceased mother would lay a guilt trip on me if I showed anyone the mess I lived in. She was well aware of men's habits so she accepted that, albeit reluctantly. The problem of ever having her in my apartment would be getting her to leave. She would probably go into my bedroom and take her clothes off. What then?!

I knew a serious argument would soon arise about our abstinence, but I dared not weaken my resolve. If I told Allie an industrial accident had robbed me of my private parts, she wouldn't believe it. I had no doubt she would wait for an unguarded moment to check it out. In fairness, if a woman gives you the most precious thing she has, namely herself, it's natural for her to assume her partner is making an equally precious commitment. An agreement of celibacy beforehand is essential. A reckoning was coming and I had to discuss it with Allie so she could choose to pull back or breakup.

In the meantime, I couldn't hide my enthusiasm for Allie's day trip. She had an unwashed Plymouth convertible and we left early Saturday morning. We drove up the Saw Mill River Parkway, chatting about one thing and another until Allie again pressed me about what I had done before New York. After the river, I could have been a farmer, a hitman, a garage mechanic, a health worker, a painter or a writer. After a silence and pointed looks from the driver, I decided to come clean and tell her the whole story. I knew this had to happen at some point and it might solve the sex problem.

Similar to the history I told Debra, I kept unsavory and deeply personal things out of it. I emphasized my ashes in the river and my subsequent jobs. I emphasized the good stuff, like my time at the hospital when I made rational patient care a priority. I minimized my painting success and didn't mention Debra at all. I also held off mentioning Lobo as it would scare her. I'd keep that for a rainy day.

When I first started, Allie turned and looked at me with a slight frown on her face and spent the rest of the time staring at the road ahead with a fixed expression. When I finished, I could see a smile starting and then she broke out in unrestrained laughter. For a moment, I was afraid she might run off the parkway.

"Oh my God, Tom. That's the funniest thing I've ever heard. You should write a book."

"It's all true. I wish it wasn't."

"I started to believe you and then realized how ridiculous it was. Your ashes reforming into you?" Tears started rolling down her face and even the car was rocking.

"I'm being totally honest with you. Look at my face carefully and check it out ten days from now." I kept my face serious and Allie could see I was worried.

We'd been driving for an hour and she pulled off at the exit for Bedford Village. It was a charming little town laid on each side of Route 22 in Westchester County. Something in my brain fired up and I concentrated on trying to remember why. Explosions were going off in my head and I asked Allie if they celebrated Fourth of July or had a famous gunfight here.

"No, not that. They do have Revolutionary War reenactments on the green with the colonials lined up against the British redcoats. Black powder is used in the muskets and there's a lot of smoke."

The detonations in my head stopped. Did these particular memories of a previous life appear by chance or on purpose? The blanket of amnesia covering me must have a hole here and there. However, if it was intentional, what would be the motive?

"I've been here before, Allie. I can hear the muskets firing. I have a favor to ask you."

Allie had stopped teasing me and looked worried. She probably thought, after my story, I was loony and having a relapse.

"Of course. What do you want me to do?"

I want you to drive somewhere and I'm going to tell you what might be there. For one thing, it will prove to you that what I told you is real. I also think I may get closer to the reason why I'm here." I paused. "Hickory cured hams and a hay rake."

Allie didn't look at me; she turned on the ignition and shifted several miles, passing Rippowam Country Day school. Red and blue flashed in front of my eyes and I remembered they were the school's colors. Just before the main road made a 90° left turn at a four-way intersection, I told Allie to turn right onto Girdle Ridge Road. (What possessed someone to name a perfectly nice road after a defective shaper for a female body?) We drove for a mile and turned into a narrow dirt road. We only went about two hundred feet before I yelled, "There . . . stop the car."

The car skidded a few feet before stopping. I opened the door and walked across the road and over a low stone wall. No mortar was used between the stones.. There was a small creek, only about two feet wide, and I jumped over it and walked the short distance to a small stone building with a faded red roof. Off to one side was an old rusted hay rake. I painstakingly climbed up and sat in the weathered metal seat. I pulled the large handle on the right with all my strength. It was corroded and didn't move. I looked behind me, remembering the tines of the rake moving up when I pulled the lever. Cut hay would pile up in front of the row of tines and that would release it. The déjà vu put me in a state of euphoria.

The low hand-built stone building was well over a hundred years old. I ducked and went inside. It was empty of course, but I could smell the hickory smoke, hear the crackles of the fire and see the hams hanging from the wooden beams. I rubbed a forefinger over the stones and they came away black with soot. I licked it and tasted the past. My senses were alive with joy and amazement as I slipped back in time.

I stood for a while feeling the heartbeat of a previous life beating in my chest. It was wondrous. Magical was a better term because I had no right to experience this. Someone cremated me and scattered the ashes in the river nine months before . . . unless this was all a dream or a hallucination.

Allie was sitting in the car, staring at me with vacuous eyes. I'm sure she was frightened as the truth of my story began to push on her rationality. I asked her if she'd like to jump across the creek and go into the smokehouse and touch the stones. She shook her head and started the car. We had lunch three miles up the road in Katonah. To honor the past, I had a grilled ham, Swiss cheese and tomato sandwich on rye bread. The chocolate milkshake was delicious and not too thick. I liked to drink it through a straw. Allie said she had a stomach ache, but I talked her into a bowl of tomato soup and iced tea. When we got back to New York, after a mostly silent drive, Allie said, "I have to think about this. You don't seem psychotic to me, but none of it makes sense. It's scary. Have you figured out what's going on?"

"I have no idea how or why this happened, but I believe something fundamental is going to take place. I'll be with it to the end."

After I'd been in my apartment for a while, the smokehouse seemed more mystical than magical. I looked out the window at the traffic and the people. I touched the windowsill and squeezed the skin above my right knee, then sat down in the living room and examined my hands, the palms first and then the backs. Brown spots were scattered on my skin and I stared at them and said, "Speak to me."

Chapter Forty-four

Lobo was not himself for weeks after Dallas. He had failed in his mission to make Tom pay for scarring his tongue. He'd been shot at in the process which was Tom's fault too. Fortunately, Gio hadn't fired him and he was relearning the job and the cook's eccentricities. Lobo was familiar with the learning process, as he followed a similar pattern in his gang work. Big Boy would put out a contract on a rival gang leader and Lobo spent hours stalking the man. He needed to know all of his quarry's habits, especially as he liked to work with his knife.

For reasons he didn't understand, Lobo didn't feel the urge quite as much. The presence of Boy in his life diminished the mad frenzy that could only be relieved by violence. In the past, he looked forward to Big Boy's next assignment. Now, in his rare contract work for other gangs, he worked quickly so he could get home and play with his dog. Boy barked as soon as he heard Lobo's key in the door and jumped on him when he came in. Lobo dropped down on the floor and they would tussle for a while. He didn't know what to think about the situation because, in the past, if a dog licked him, Lobo would cut its ears off. He eventually concluded that Big Boy and Gio only liked him because he was a good worker. His dog, on the other hand, liked him no matter what.

Lobo believed that once Tom was in the hands of an undertaker, life would be perfect. The lying bastard was still hanging around under his skin, like an itch he couldn't scratch. He had to control his temper until the time was right. Gio never threatened him with it, but Lobo knew he was on probation. He started drinking again.

Cooking occupied Lobo's working hours and kept Tom dim in his mind. When he got home, whiskey and Boy took the edge off. However, as the darkness thickened, the itch would start again. He'd take the switchblade out of his pocket and push the little button again and again. Lobo loved to hear the *snick* of the blade flying out and watched the handle as it turned from dead to deadly. He added ice to cheap whiskey and took a swallow every few minutes while he watched I Love Lucy on a black and white TV. He mainly laughed when the scene boarded on the bizarre or embarrassing. Increasingly, during story breaks, he found his mug was empty and he poured himself more. As the days went on, it became a habit. Waking up every morning feeling like dog doo was another itch that was easy to blame on Tom.

On the good side, Lobo was becoming a fine sous chef and Gio allowed him to do many of the simpler appetizers and entrées by himself. The service and quality became noteworthy enough so an article appeared in the local paper describing the restaurant as a local gem. The enforcer loved praise and, having something other than a murder to boast about, was an unusual and satisfying experience.

* * *

I began decreasing the dates I had with Allie. I hoped my history would make her nervous enough to discourage any continued interest. It was done tactfully because I didn't want to make enemies at the New Yorker. Unhappily, that's not the way it turned out. Allie became totally intrigued with me. The thought of becoming intimate with a reincarnated man was impossible for her to pass up. When we went out, she didn't go easy on the booze and her voice went up several decibels.

Sitting in her living room, our time together was more an interrogation than anything else. A worrisome downside of her infatuation was her ballooning interest in sex.

"What's the harm Tom? I'll do anything you want."

"Think of it this way, Allie. If the situation was reversed and I kept pressing you to have intercourse against your wishes, you would not be happy with me."

"I don't understand you. Most men would be thrilled with an offer like mine. Are you gay?"

If I'd been smarter, I would've answered "yes." Instead, a different excuse popped into my mind. "This is very embarrassing, Allie, so I wish you'd stop talking about it. Surely you know when men get older, things don't work as well as they used to."

Allie rolled her eyes. "You always have an excuse. You look fine to me and besides, there's more than one way to please a woman. One night is all I ask."

I couldn't believe how determined the woman was. To say she slept with an alien was obviously her goal and if she kept this up, I'd have to leave New York. In my desperation, I came up with another smokescreen. "I believe I was functioning in my previous life. Maybe I even had children. Now it's totally different. I was reborn without the interest or the means."

Allie had her mouth open and an angry look on her face when a bell saved me. Literally. Phil called me at home earlier when I was rushing out the door. I told him to call me at Allie's later. The phone rang on the table next to her and she recognized Phil's name and passed it over to me.

"Thanks for taking my call, Tom. I expect you're busy over there."

"Actually no, but I was expecting the call and I'm very appreciative."

"I need your help and advice, my friend. Can we get together when convenient?"

"Of course. I understand it's urgent and I can do it now."

"It's not that urgent, but I would like to get it done."

"It's vital for me too. Perhaps we can make it a "quid pro quo."

"Sounds good. I'm still in the office."

I handed the phone back to Allie who hung it up with unnecessary vigor. I wondered what assignment Phil had from the Times that might involve me. Anyway, his timing was perfect.

Allie said, "What's that all about?"

"I'm doing stories with Phil for the Times. They have something they want me to do right away. Beat out the competition and you know how that goes."

"You better get your act together, lover. No more excuses."

"You know what the problem is, Allie. If you don't like me as I am, there are plenty more fish in the sea."

"You're a swordfish and I like the taste. Now, be on your way and dream about our next get-together."

I headed for the door, more grateful than ever for Phil's call. I couldn't resist a final shot before the door closed. "I haven't got a sword."

Chapter Forty-five

Phil and I were sitting in a small restaurant, a block from his office. The New York Times is always bustling and not the best place to talk privately.

"What's up Phil? You called at the right time because Allie is getting pushy and I want to keep it a low-key friendship."

"Most men would like an aggressive woman, at least in the way you're implying."

"Once you start sleeping with someone, it gets very serious. The repercussions can't be exaggerated. If the man moves on afterwards, her friends become bitter enemies and the word spreads. It makes it very difficult to find someone else. Even my own friends might think I've taken advantage. You know Heather and her husband so you can imagine my situation."

"Word gets around and I heard about her vow to never date another man. She probably has major attitude and I'm amazed you've hit a homerun."

"I'm still at bat, Phil, and I'm not even glancing at first. Tell me how to get back on the bench without offending the coach. Heather set this up and I don't want to lose my contact with the New Yorker."

"Cut it off as soon as possible. It will rile her and she may complain to Heather, but the fact you've been a good boy will get you through. I'll support that." There was a long hesitation, with the reporter tapping his right forefinger on his lips. "Of course, she might not be completely honest about it, which would be a problem."

I said, "Guess who Heather would believe. The only way I can prove it is to record a conversation with Allie."

"Sounds like it might come to that." Phil started laughing, thinking I was making a joke. He took a bite of his tuna salad sandwich. "I went to Spokane after reviewing the criminal background on Big Boy. They're into all kinds of things including murder."

I said, "Their enforcer is named Lobo and his targets, as far as I know, are only other gangsters. He's a sociopath who likes to work with a knife. He has a speech impediment because, when he pulled a gun on me, I injured his mouth. He hates me because Big Boy endorsed me, although I was never part of the gang. Lobo has followed me from city to city ever since. Happily, New York is huge and he doesn't know I'm here."

Phil looked at me steadily while his fingers played absentmindedly with a dill pickle. "I hesitate to even bring this up because there would obviously be some risk. The reason I called you was because the local cops urged me not to go by myself. Big Boy is smart and they have not been able to come up with enough evidence to bring the whole group down. It probably makes their work easier if the gangs kill each other off. No innocents have been hit yet."

"You're slick, Phil; I can read between the lines. You didn't get the story and want me to go back into the lion's den with you. Lobo will kill me if he sees me. Are you licensed to carry a gun?"

"The newspaper does not want armed reporters wandering the streets looking for stories."

"The only way I'll go back with you is if Lobo isn't there. Use your contacts with the police to find out what's going on. I think I'm okay with Big Boy. There's a guy named Snag who might be a problem because he's a bud of Lobo's. If we get in and out quickly, I'll do it."

"Okay. If Lobo is elsewhere, we still have to figure out how to approach Big Boy. Give it some thought."

When I got home that evening, I made myself a stiff drink and sat on a straight back chair with my eyes closed. Big Boy was not a psycho like Lobo. He was smart enough to run a well-organized criminal enterprise and keep it as clean as possible. He only used Lobo for defense and was content to keep his territory as it was. I talked to him about this once and he said, "Cooperation is much more successful than competition." Many successful legitimate businesses feel that way too.

Big Boy was not into drugs, but he knew the cops were watching and would use any excuse to arrest him. No matter what the motivation, murdering people is not good publicity for anyone, especially the police chief. If the boss got rid of Lobo, the chief might be willing to go easier on his gambling and prostitution business. Phil didn't know there used to be a warrant out for me and I would get no help from the cops. Probably the opposite.

Two days later, Phil called to say a police informant told the Spokane department Lobo had moved to Seattle and was working as a cook in an Italian restaurant. At first, I thought he was putting me on. Imagine a psycho with an impressive record as a killer working as a chef. It took a couple of days, but the persistent reporter finally convinced me it was true. In a matter of hours, we were on a flight to Spokane.

After we arrived, we rented a car and went to a motel where I made sure we got a room with twin beds. No more Dicker stuff. Over dinner, Phil told me we needed to get the mobster interested enough in what we could do for him to give us a good newspaper story. I'm going to ask about his family history and why and how he became a criminal. It would include most of his businesses and a vague, and probably inaccurate, idea of his profits. All of this would be under an alias. I hoped to get enough information about Lobo that I could give to the police to put him away for life. Lobo was also a danger to the wolfpack as he had a lot of stuff on Big Boy. Perhaps I could spread enough misinformation to get Big Boy to do my dirty work for me.

Phil and I hashed out many worrisome questions. For instance, what would keep Lobo from "telling all" if the police arrested him? The whole pack would be after me. At one point, after our second drink, he wondered if we should both go home. That probably made good sense, but I had the bone in my teeth and was not about to let it go. Lobo had to go. I had a plan that should work perfectly for both of the police and us.

I woke up early and thrashed about in my bed until seven o'clock when we both got up. I was too nervous to eat much breakfast, but Phil talked me into three cups of coffee and an over-buttered English muffin. Phil told the police chief what he was going to do and said he had an ex-criminal "friend" who was going to go with him. He never gave out my name. We took the bus, as a car was identifiable, and walked to Big Boy's cave.

Outside the gang's door, I hollered, "Hey, Big Boy, it's your favorite hitman."

Someone said, "Holy shit, look who's here on a suicide mission."

I expected to have several guns pointed in my direction. Phil and I stood outside the steel door and waited. We were asked to open our coats and unbutton our shirts to show we were unarmed and weren't wearing a wire. One of the thugs opened the door a crack and I heard the boss say, "Let 'em in."

As soon as we stepped across the threshold, the door slammed shut and two men held handguns on us during the search. We went into a back room where Big Boy was sitting behind a desk. He pointed to a couple of chairs and we sat down slowly.

"Well, well, well. It's a good thing Lobo isn't here. You wouldn't get through the front door. Who's your little friend, Tom?"

"This is Phil and he's a reporter for the New York Times. You're a straight up guy, Boss, and I've always liked you. Lobo is something else and when I heard he moved to Seattle, I wanted to do something worthwhile for you and the boys. You are going to like it very much and Phil is going to make it happen."

Big Boy was no fool and he looked at me with a half–smile on his face. "You got big brass ones coming back here. A hitman would not do that. I have an idea Lobo knew what he was talking about. Why would you do anything for me?"

"You are 100% right. I'm a writer, not a shooter. Take a look at the New Yorker magazine and Colliers. You'll see my stuff. You always treated me well and probably saved my life. The police didn't mess with you much until Lobo started cutting up people."

Big Boy took a 357 magnum revolver out of a drawer and put it on his desk. He spun it around until it ended with the barrel pointing directly at me. "Lobo is gone so this conversation is about to end."

Phil said, "Killings are the problem. The police and the public are not going to stand for any more grisly murders in this city. I understand that when your competition gets too close or someone puts a contract out on you, you have to defend yourself. Naturally, you send one of your boys to do some damage. However, you can't run a successful business like that for long."

I said, "Who's your enforcer now, and is he as good as Lobo?"

"Snag's my man, but nobody can touch Lobo. He's the best and if the pressure keeps coming, I may ask him back. Snag tries to copy his hero, but his executions and cut-ups are sloppy."

Phil said, "Good publicity is the key to success, whether it's you or Budweiser."

I stepped in before Big Boy could say anything. "The police chief is getting a whole lot of flak from the mayor and the public. That's why he can be motivated to go easy with someone like you. You're into pimping, bookmaking, loansharking and bribery. You've stayed away from drugs which is a wise decision. The other guys are doing the heroin, cocaine and weed. However, your competition always wants a piece of your business, even if it means killing someone."

"So what! You think I don't know what's going on? Other punks are always trying to hit on me and it keeps Snag busy. I don't think he'll survive much longer. What's in it for me, I'm getting tired of this bullshit."

"Phil had several conversations with the Chief of police and he will let you do your low-key stuff if you quit killing people and continue to avoid drugs. He will go after everyone else in a big way. You'll have little competition. This will make it tempting for you to expand. If that happens, the deal is off." While the air was still, I said, "There's one essential condition: Lobo has to go."

Big Boy's eyebrows shifted up and down as his emotions alternated between annoyed disbelief and surprise. "No police Chief's gonna to do that."

Phil leaned forward. "The election is in three months and the Chief is going to lose his job unless something changes. This is where publicity comes in and I write for the most famous newspaper in the country. Obviously, we cannot have the good guys making deals with the bad guys so I'll have to make it look like the Chief did the whole thing by himself. That won't make any difference to your business, but the murder rate will drop, drugs will become a minor problem, and the other two gangs will disappear from the city. He will get elected again and, if you keep your business low-key, no one will notice it even exists."

Big Boy's lips squeezed together and he started fiddling with the handle of his revolver. He looked over at us and picked the handgun up, pointing it alternatively at Phil and me. When he saw me starting to sweat, he reared back in his chair, put the pistol back in the drawer and started laughing. "You boys wouldn't last a minute in my business. However, you done well with the fuzz. As soon as I hear what you want, I'll do my part. However, if the police touch any of my businesses, the deal's off. How's that sound?"

I stood up and shook big Boy's hand and Phil followed. I had two other things I had to discuss. "Lobo is going to get wind of this and he's not going to be happy. You know he's been cooking in a restaurant in Seattle, but he's also a killer for hire and has done several of those. We don't hear much about it because the mess is elsewhere. The police have nothing on him, but murders appear in the local newspapers. He will eventually be arrested and then, watch out. He knows a lot of stuff. You should seriously consider inviting Lobo over here and get rid of the only possible problem you have with our deal."

"I'll think about it."

"The only thing Phil and I will need from you is a general description of your early life and business history and how you go about it. Don't freak out about this, you only have to give an overview without much detail. Your name will never come up and one of your competitors could be the one talking. Even a lawyer couldn't attach your name to it. Phil will make sure his articles suggest he got the information from your competition."

Phil said, "The general public will be fascinated with your background information and methods. You and the cops know all this, but our readers do not. That sells newspapers and pays my salary."

I could see Big Boy was still not sure. He started chewing on his thumbnail and his eyes wandered around the room. Then he brightened. "Anybody could write this stuff and I'm not going to sign it. Sounds like fun. Come back tomorrow afternoon and I'll have something for you." He laughed. "I'm gonna be an informant on myself, eh?"

Big boy walked with us into the main room where five other men were sitting, itching to do away with both of us. I recognized Snag sitting by the front door with a handgun on his lap.

Big Boy said, "Put it away Snag. There's gonna be big changes in this city and these two gentlemen are going to make it happen. Tonight we celebrate." After we left, I was sure Snag would call Lobo and tell him Tom is here.

We got back safely to our motel, not knowing Snag had already called Lobo.

Chapter Forty-six

Lobo was back with his dog, cooking for Gio, and earning good money. He was more than a sous chef now and normally would look forward to the possibility of a safe and fulfilling life. There were days when he was not aware of the seed lying deep in his belly. But many nights, he felt the hard husk of it and he'd reach for the new switchblade which lay next to the clock on his bedside table.

snick   snick   snick

The sound of it set his adrenaline going and he licked his lips visualizing Tom's blood on the blade. He could smell it.

Lobo knew he couldn't get back to sleep without help. He forced himself to close the knife and put it out of reach before going into the bathroom where he poured himself a half glass of whiskey and swallowed a couple of sleeping pills. He was sweating as he pulled the covers up and he made himself concentrate on the next day's menu before he finally fell asleep.

Weeks went by and Lobo's persistent kernel remained unmoving in its dry sheath. He had no idea alcohol, although seeming to relieve his frustration, was actually nourishing the seed, keeping it alive and ready. When his telephone rang early one morning, he assumed it was Gio, alerting him to some problem in the kitchen.

"Jeez, Lobo, where the hell you been. I been calling for a couple days."

"Snag? What's going on? I'm working every lunch and I don't get home until the dinner crowd leaves. You have to call when I'm home."

"It may be too late now, but you gotta get down here and settle the score."

"What you talkin' about? Big Boy told me to bug out."

"Tom is down here with a reporter. He's suckered Big Boy into talking 'bout his business so the police is gonna go after all the gangs except the boss's."

There was a long pause as Lobo tried to process what had to be hogwash. It was preposterous, didn't make sense at all. "You're putting me on, Snag, and I don't appreciate it. Big Boy couldn't be that stupid."

"I'm telling the truth, Lobo. Tom is here in town and a newspaper guy is writing it up. They're goin' back to New York day after tomorrow."

Ah, rain at last. The moisture began soaking through the kernel's casing causing it to swell and burst. A stalk emerged and wormed its way into Lobo's cortex, bringing feral light into a dark place.

Lobo could see and feel his quarry. "Where is he now?"

"The three of them meet every morning here in the cave. Tom will be here in half an hour."

"How do you know he's living in New York?"

"It's a guess, but the reporter works for the New York Times and they're together."

"I'm on the way. I'll get a train out today and let you know so you can pick me up. It's faster than the bus. Thanks, Snag, I owe you."

* * *

Phil covered most of the questions needed for his story. It was going to be big. He would be revealing the innermost workings of the biggest gang in Spokane. He didn't give a hoot whether the police chief kept his word or not. In fact, he hoped this would get rid of all the criminal activity in this fine city. Back at the Times, his reputation and salary would skyrocket and the editor would give him access to the best stories. He'd finish the first draft in the afternoon and he and Tom would head back to New York in the morning.

"I can't thank you enough Tom. The Times will keep your name out of it so I can't give you the byline you deserve."

"I think we ought to get out of here tonight, Phil. Big Boy is going to get rid of Lobo, but not before we leave. Snag has probably called him already."

"Don't worry about it. The police are sending an undercover guy over tomorrow morning. I'm not taking any chances with our lives."

* * *

Big Boy had been worrying about Lobo for a long time. The psycho loved to kill people and was still doing it. When the cops started arresting criminals, the word would get out to the competition and Big Boy would be first on the hit list. Lobo would get the contract and he was the only guy the boss feared. Tom being down here was great bait.

Big Boy called Snag into his office and said, "I want you to contact Lobo. We need him to off Tom, but be sure to tell him to leave the reporter alone. Phil has to get back to New York and publish his story so we can get our monopoly. Lobo is not in the gang anymore so I won't get blamed for Tom's death. Unfortunately, he is a crazy killer and has to go. It's part of the deal with the police. Get the boys ready to nail him after Tom's out of the way."

Snag blanched and opened his mouth to protest. Lobo was his best friend and he certainly would not be a party to his murder. However, he could see the boss was determined so he changed his mouth to a yawn.

"You bored or something, Snag? If I make you sleepy maybe I should call the boys in here to wake you up."

"I'm not tired, Boss. I'm doing my jaw stretching exercises. If you chew your food real good, you get more nourishment."

Big Boy stared, his upper lip lifting and his eyes narrowing. "What the fuck you talking about, Goofus? Get the hell outta here and be sure to get Lobo here by tonight."

Chapter Forty-seven

I was worried, no matter what protection Phil arranged. Most police officers are well-trained and sensible men with strict rules that govern their actions. However, Lobo was insane, not sensible, and I didn't think anything was going to be done to protect me until I was on the ground with flies in my mouth.

On the way back to the motel, I tried to talk Phil into leaving for the airport to catch the early morning flight. He told me Big Boy wanted a summary of what was going to be written about his activities before he would sign off on it.

Phil said, "We'll be done by 10:30 AM. If Snag called Lobo, he'd have been here two days ago."

"There are only two flights to New York from here and the second one is not until late afternoon. I'm not going to hang around here and be a target."

"You stay at the motel and I'll see Big Boy by myself. When I'm done, I'll pick you up and drive to the airport. We'll be safe there."

At the time, that seemed to be a good plan. Phil went off the next morning and I packed my carry-on, drank coffee and tried to read a newspaper while I waited for his return.

* * *

The last train from Seattle arrived in Spokane at 11:15 pm and Snag was there when Lobo, carrying a small duffel, stepped off.

"Shit, Lobo. I almost called you to say, 'don't come,' but I knew you wanted Tom real bad."

"What you talking about?"

"The newspaper guy made a deal with the Spokane police. Big Boy is off the hook if there are no more killings. After you whack Tom, the gang is going make sure you never leave here."

"Huh? Don't make sense. Big Boy and I go way back and I don't live here no more. He wouldn't make a deal like that."

Snag, driving slowly through downtown, didn't know what to say. He barely got through fourth grade and the only thing he was sure about was Lobo's friendship. "I don't think you should go anywhere near the cave. The boys will do whatever Big Boy wants."

Lobo couldn't recite the times table, but he had excellent survival instincts. "Take me to Kissy's place. I'm not in the mood for nookie, but I'll pay her for the night. Get your car and pick me up at seven tomorrow morning and we'll watch the cave from a block away until Tom comes out. If I can get close, I will use my 45 and then we'll drive to Seattle together. The police will be watching public transportation."

"Don't hit the Times guy."

"Don't worry about that. If it don't work out right away, we'll follow them 'til it's perfect."

* * *

'Red' Olsen had a luxurious vermilion-colored beard and mustache. He was not a uniformed police officer who stood around like a sitting duck. He was a *faux* undercover cop. All the bad guys knew who Red was. Which was the point. He didn't follow the rules, and was capable of anything. Every police department wanted a guy like this.

When Red accompanied Phil to the cave on the final morning, Big Boy and his boys knew not to mess with either of them. After the reporter entered, Red didn't stand outside the door waiting for the end of the meeting, he disappeared. However, everyone knew the apparition was close by. Watching.

* * *

Big Boy was furious. He'd signed off on the deal with Phil, but where was Tom? Big Boy was counting on him to lure Lobo in so he could live up to his end of the bargain with the police. The gang was armed and ready and if Tom died in the process, he could not care less. Snag was nowhere to be found and he hoped he was with Lobo. The problem was Snag idolized the crazy psycho and might not bring him back to the cave for a happy reunion. Big Boy decided to follow Phil back to wherever he was staying with Tom and take care of Lobo himself. He went outside to his Ford and followed Phil at a considerable distance until the car stopped at the Upside Motel. He drove by and parked two short blocks beyond. Big Boy lowered the window and chambered a 30-06 round into his bolt action Remington. There was a 10x scope attached and it would be an easy shot. At this distance, gravity wouldn't matter. Big Boy was sure both Phil and Tom were in the same room and Lobo would eventually show up.

* * *

"What do we do now, Lobo?"

"Sit tight, Snag, I've got it covered." The friends had waited several hours and saw Phil arrive and then leave an hour later. Big Boy, after shaking Phil's hand, got in his car and followed.

Lobo said, "Damn, Tom's not with him so we'll follow them. Big Boy has something up his sleeve.

"Maybe he's waiting for you."

They were in a nondescript rental car and followed well behind Big Boy when he left the cave. Tom would recognize both of them so they stopped and parked as soon as they saw Phil's car in the motel parking lot and the boss pull over further on. Snag was nervous and he kept turning from side to side and drumming his fingers on the dashboard.

"Sit still. You're driving me crazy."

"How're we going to do it?"

"You are going to go into the office, show the manager your gun, and get a passkey. When I walk by the door, give the key to me and wait there. I'm going to go into their room and take care of business. Neither of them will have a weapon."

"What about me?"

"Afterwards, we'll get in the car and take off. They won't have time to see the license number. I'll drive to Seattle and you . . ."

Snag suddenly slid off the seat and crouched under the dashboard. "Holy shit, Big Boy is looking up and down the street."

Lobo quickly covered his face with his left hand and pretended to look into the glove box. Big Boy soon became totally preoccupied with the motel. Then Lobo took out his Colt 45 and slowly swung the barrel so it ended up between Snag's eyes.

"What's this all about, my friend."

Snag hunkered lower under the dash. " I told you before that the cops made Big Boy put you on the hit list. That's why I didn't want you to come down here. He knew Tom would bring you in and he's waiting for you to show up."

"Yeah, you did warn me. Maybe I can get two birds with one stone."

* * *

Red Olson was standing in an alley when Phil left the cave. He had been scanning the area in front and checking the rooftops. He didn't think the reporter was really in danger, but anything could happen with bozos like Big Boy and his groupies. Lobo might show up and he was certainly capable of doing damage. Red knew where I was staying so he jogged to his car and sped on a parallel road with only his lights flashing. He entered the room he'd reserved next to mine and Phil's and, with binoculars, checked out all the parked cars and the trees in the park across the street. He spotted Big Boy in a car two blocks away to his left, glancing toward the motel.

Lobo was in a parking spot a block to the right, but Red didn't see him as he was concentrating on Big Boy. He had a radio in his cruiser, but couldn't leave as he was sure to be spotted. He glanced across the front and then put the binoculars on Big Boy again. "Strange," he thought. Both windows on the driver's side were now open. Even with Big Boy slouching down, he could see the man was looking through the telescopic sight of a rifle. Red let the curtains fall back gently and went over to the wall that separated his room from Phil's and mine. He knocked three times twice in rapid succession that was our prearranged signal. The two men, as Red instructed, went into the bathroom, closed the door and sat on the floor. Red picked up the room telephone to call headquarters to send backup and found it disconnected. The manager only turned it on for paying customers.

Chapter Forty-eight

"Lobo was a pro and he reached into his duffel and took out a pair of binoculars. He checked the motel and all was quiet. This was lucky for Red as he was knocking on the wall when Lobo checked the windows to be sure all the curtains were in place. He got out of the car on the passenger side by crawling over Snag and went into the park. He walked towards the boss's car and settled himself behind a tree. He was now only a couple of hundred feet away and his binoculars had a good view through the car's back window. Big Boy was hunched over something and Lobo didn't know what it was until the boss straightened up and exposed the telescopic sight.

It would be easy, by walking through the park, to get behind Lobo and put a hollow point into his head. However, a gunshot could be heard for some distance and alert everyone. It looked like a stand-off.

* * *

The Upside Motel made Motel 6 look like the Taj Mahal. Only quarter–inch wallboard separated the rooms and probably provided immense entertainment for hot pillow tenants. Red knew the location of the bathroom where I was and he cupped his hands and placed them on the wall. "Tom, either you or Phil call the manager and tell him I'm a cop and have a situation that needs backup. Tell him to have a maid bring a baggage cart to room eight with new linens and pillows piled on it."

I said, "But you're in room seven."

"The maid should first go into room eight for a minute or two and come out with unfolded bedspreads and sheets piled on the cart. Then have her come to my room and I'll get under the 'dirty' laundry. The increase in laundry height will seem like she's added linens from number seven. Make sure she rolls her cart around to the back of the motel and I'll get out and get to the radio in my cruiser. You guys stay in the room."

* * *

Big Boy straightened up, frowning. He saw the maid come out of what appeared to be a storage part of the motel pushing a cart loaded with linens. He watched closely as she went into room eight and came out with dirty laundry. Big Boy had no idea which room Phil and I were in so his plan was to wait until we showed ourselves. The maid went into room seven and came out a bit later with a somewhat larger mound of laundry. Nothing seemed out of the ordinary until she headed toward the manager's office and went around the corner of the building.

That didn't make sense to Big Boy since the fresh linens came from the opposite side of the motel and the washers and dryers were there too. Could the two men be under the bedspreads? No, the pile would be much higher. Something wasn't right and it was time to act.

* * *

Lobo jogged back to the car and rapped on Snag's window. "Big Boy is in the other car with a long gun and telescopic sight. He's waiting for Tom to come out and me to show up."

"Crap! Let's get the hell outta here."

"Calm down, pussy. I got a new plan and you are part of it. Big Boy has no reason to shoot you. The boss doesn't know our location and will think you're going to flush Tom out for me. I want you to cross the street and go into the manager's office. Make the manager tell you where Tom is and get the key. Then cold cock him and drag him behind his desk. Go into Tom and Phil's room and tell them to leave the room. They're not going to argue with a gun."

Lobo could see that Snag didn't want any part of this and it was vital to get him quickly on board. Lobo put the barrel of his Colt into his right eye socket. "You're perfectly safe as long as you do what I tell you. You do not want me as your enemy." Snag nodded and sweat dripped off his chin.

"I am going to take care of Big Boy and use his rifle to make a hole in Tom's head. I want to do it myself. As soon as that happens meet me back at the car and we'll bug out of here. We'll both be safe so give me a smile."

Snag grimaced as best he could and then opened the door. Being careful not to look at Lobo, he started walking toward the motel. Lobo moved swiftly through the park until he came opposite his quarry's car. Big Boy had his right eye pressed against the telescopic sight and he jumped when Lobo wrapped against the passenger side window. The boss, thinking it was a passerby, put an authoritative look on his face and turned to find Lobo holding a large handgun eight inches from his face.

"I will kill you, Boss, if you don't open the door for me. I know you planned to kill me, but because of our long association, I am going to give you a gift. Your life. There is a price, of course, and you are going to do something for me."

Big Boy turned slowly around in his seat. The rifle was useless in such close quarters. "What do you want me to do?"

"Open the passenger door and then look at the motel. Snag is about to go into the manager's office and ask for the key to Tom's room. He's going to open the door and when Tom and the reporter see the gun, they are going to come out. You are going to use that nice rifle to put Tom down. Permanently. Then you are going to give me the magazine and I'm going to leave Spokane. Snag will never harm me, but if you decide to come after me, I will kill you. Now, put your eyeball against that sight and let's see where Tom is hiding."

* * *

Red threw off the bedspread and ran to his cruiser. He talked quickly to the desk sergeant followed by the lieutenant in charge. The lieutenant muttered curses, visualizing the publicity from the small war that was about to start on his watch. He would have to mobilize a dozen officers and give them heavier weapons.

Red had a fully automatic AR 15 with a telescopic sight in his trunk and he took it out and trotted to the end of the motel farthest from the manager's office. He crouched behind bushes and plants, looking through the rifle's sight at Big Boy's car.

* * *

Snag had the key to my room in his hand and the manager was unconscious behind his desk. His hand shook and the large brass disc with the number six on it clanged hard against the key. The church bells of his youth. He stopped walking as a vision of the Church of the Holy Mother materialized in his mind. His choice was Lobo or the Virgin Mary. He rubbed his right eye that was still sore from the pressure of the gun barrel. He muttered, "Shit, I'm gonna burn," and moved forward. When he got to room six, he knocked on the door before he remembered he had the key.

* * *

Phil said, "That must be Red; let's get out of here." We both scrambled from the bathroom floor and rushed for the door.

* * *

Lobo, behind Big Boy, cursed when he saw Snag stop after coming out of the manager's office. Then he saw him resume walking along the row of rooms and knew it was time. He slipped the revolver into his left hand and took out his knife.

Snick

Although Big Boy heard the sound of the switchblade opening, he couldn't turn fast enough to avoid the slice across his neck. Lobo made the cut deep enough to sever both the right carotid artery and the windpipe. The only noise was a bubbly gurgling as the boss's last breath burst through the torrent of blood. Lobo pulled the big body out of the passenger door and settled into the bloody seat. He pulled the rifle closer to him and squinted into the telescopic sight.

Chapter Forty-nine

At the same time that Lobo opened his switchblade, Red heard the jangling of Snag's key and turned to the right. He saw a disheveled man with a room key and hesitated as he thought he might be a legitimate customer. Red looked down the row of rooms, but found it impossible to see which number he was going to. He watched Snag as he stopped in front of a door and knocked. It was strange as he was obviously carrying a room key in his left hand.

Snag's motive was obvious when he reached for something in his pants pocket. His right hand shook as he began to withdraw the revolver and the hammer scraped on the pocket lining. He jerked on the gun just as Phil and I opened the door and rushed out, knocking Snag flat on his back.

Red, seeing that Snag had his hand around the butt of a handgun, brought the AR 15 up for a headshot. However, the head disappeared and he saw the two men he was supposed to protect colliding with their killer.

Lobo, after he saw Snag knocking, knew his plan was in jeopardy and he hesitated. When I rushed out of the doorway, he frantically squeezed the trigger. It was a fraction too late as I was already colliding with Snag. The round hit the doorframe, and splinters flew.

Red knew the tumbling bodies would give Lobo momentary pause so he elected to deal with the immediate threat of Snag's revolver, which was swinging wildly in the air. He put two shots into Snag's head as Phil and I scrambled to our feet. Red whirled to his left and flipped the assault rifle to automatic. There was no time for precise aiming as Red simply wanted to keep Lobo on the defensive. He squeezed off three bursts of three rounds each and then yelled to the pair to hit the ground and stay there.

Of the nine rounds from the AR 15, five hit the car in various spots. One of them went through the open driver's window, passed several inches in front of Lobo's face, and shattered the windshield. Lobo decided it was time to retreat and he ducked behind the car and entered the park running. He was invisible behind greenery and got to his car quickly. Lobo opened the passenger door and crawled over the seats. The key was in the ignition so there would be no waste time in getting away. Lobo saw Snag spread-eagled on the pavement and made a quick U-turn and floored the accelerator just as three squad cars and a SWAT armored vehicle came in from the opposite direction.

Lobo was too far away for Red to fire safely so he jumped up and gestured at the oncoming cars to follow Lobo. The drivers of all the vehicles saw what appeared to be three bodies in the street and an armed man coming at them. The cruiser's front doors opened and the police, armed with pistols, rifles and shotguns, crouched behind them. The green armored SWAT vehicle crossed over to the other side of the parking area and men piled out and took positions behind parked cars.

By this time, Lobo was out of sight and Red put his rifle on the ground, pulled out his badge and walked up to the police lieutenant. He gave a brief summary of the situation and told him to seal off the roads and put men in the railroad and bus stations.

I saw police coming out from behind vehicles and walking towards us so I stood up and said to Phil, "I think you have your story now. I will go back to New York with you and be polite the entire time. However, if you ever speak to me again, on the telephone or in person, I will pay Lobo whatever he wants to pay you a visit." I was in shock when I said that.

Snag was lying on his back with a puddle of blood expanding along both sides of his head. We tried not to look at him as we went quickly back into the motel room to get our luggage.

After our plane landed at LaGuardia Airport, Phil and I gave each other a long handshake. I apologized as I had agreed to go to Spokane, and the fact that both of us were under fire, made us brothers. We took separate taxis and when I closed and locked the door of my apartment, I went into the bedroom and folded onto the bed. It was 10 PM New York time and I wondered if I'd be able to sleep. I stripped down to my boxer shorts and slipped under the covers. The moment I turned onto my left side, the phone started ringing.

It was Allie, making her third call. She reminded me that she suggested a get-together on her first. On her second, she wondered why I didn't call back and became irritated. This time, it was an angry name-calling.

"Hey, I've been in Washington State for three days and couldn't possibly have known about your calls. I got home about thirty minutes ago and this is insulting and hurtful. I'm not the kind of person who can deal with this so it's best to part ways. I wish you all the best."

"Oh my God, Tom. I had no idea you were away. I'm sorry and it won't happen again. I'd like to make it up to you in person. Let me come over now."

"I'm in bed and exhausted. Someone tried to kill me in Spokane and I'm going to be a long time recovering. Good night." It was a serious mistake for me to mention that awful experience. She wouldn't hang up the phone and kept asking, and then demanding an explanation. Finally, after several minutes of agonizing back and forth,

I told her, in a beautifully fabricated slurred voice, that I had taken a sleeping pill and couldn't talk anymore. I hung up the phone and she didn't call back.

The next morning I went through my mail and went out for lunch. I went to a marvelous hamburger joint where the patties were an inch and a half thick and cooked rare. They were so succulent the juice ran down my chin and dripped onto the counter. Mustard, ketchup or relish would have ruined it. On the way back to my apartment, I half expected the phone to ring again. Perhaps Allie felt sorry for me, but I knew curiosity would soon get the better of her. I made up my mind to break up the next day. I'd give Heather a call and stop by her office. If I called Allie from there, maybe I could avoid having her harass me. Besides, Heather surely carried a bigger hammer than I did.

To avoid having Heather turn me down, I didn't tell her the point of our meeting. I gave her a quick handshake when I got to her office and an overview of my trip with Phil. She was stunned by the story and grateful I hadn't been killed.

"I need your help and advice, Heather. Allie and I started off having a pleasant and low-key friendship. I made it clear from the beginning I could offer nothing more. Over the last couple of weeks, I'm getting at least a call a day. She's been suggesting we sleep together and now it's a demand. She called me twice before I got back from my very frightening trip and, in the last one, profanities rained. I didn't hang up on her as I knew she'd go crazy."

Heather was shocked. "I had no idea Allie was in such a state. She obviously needs some psychological help."

"I'm going to tell her we need to go our separate ways. You are a close friend and I want to be sure this will not put her into a dangerous and angry depression."

"I'll talk with her before you have that conversation. Hopefully, I can get her to accept it and maybe you won't need to talk to her at all."

"Thanks so much. I'm still stressed by having a bullet miss me by inches. Trying to keep calm with this added concern is not easy."

I took a bus back uptown to my apartment where I hoped to have a TV dinner and go to bed early. When Allie called me again, I was in the shower and heard nothing. I was clothed and enjoying a gin and tonic when the phone rang for the second time.

"Hello."

"Why didn't you pick up the first time, Tom? I'm really tired of being treated like crap."

"I just got out of the shower and I'm having a drink. You can't hear the ring when the water's running in your face. Have you spoken to Heather?"

"Oh, I'm so sorry. I'm very sensitive about our relationship now. And no, Heather hasn't spoken to me for a while."

Allie was on a roller coaster, going from aggressive to contrite. I thought that might indicate some kind of mental problem, but this crazy woman had pushed me over the edge.

"I am no longer interested in a relationship with you or anyone else. You knew my position from the beginning. You are harassing me now and I'm asking you nicely not to contact me again. If you continue stalking me like this, I will have to call the police."

"I love strong men and I love you, Tom. You don't mean a word of that. I found out where you live and I'm coming over. I'm going to give you the time of your life and you can continue to talk dirty to me while I'm doing it."

Chapter Fifty

I couldn't even try to dissuade Allie as she hung up immediately after her "dirty" comment. If I didn't answer when she knocked, she'd go bonkers. I needed to get away for a while, but halfway down the first flight of stairs, I saw Allie coming up.

"Surprise, lover boy. I thought you might try to run off so I phoned you from the telephone booth on the corner. Good times are ahead."

I ran back up the stairs, desperate to get away. I fumbled for my key and had the door six inches open when she shoved me in the back.

"Hey, quit it, Allie. That's assault and you could be arrested. I told you we were over and I meant it."

Allie was now standing halfway into the room. "I meant what I said too. I'm going to stay here tonight and if you still want me to go, I'll leave in the morning. I guarantee you won't want me to do that."

I knew I could force her out the door, but she'd fight back and it would be a tussle for an eighty year old man. I did not want this to end up in court as there were no witnesses. If I got out and ran down the stairs, she would probably trash my apartment. I had an idea that might solve the witness problem as well as get her out. I stood aside and Allie, thinking she had won, walked into the living room.

Then I stepped back onto the landing and shouted, "Get out of my home, Allie. I will call the police if you don't leave me alone."

Allie's expression registered complete surprise and then changed to a scary mask. She glared at me with her body shaking and her hands opening and closing.

I yelled, "Somebody help. Call the police." Allie disappeared, and I heard a lock clack and my neighbor across the way opened the door a few inches and peeked out.

I turned to her and said in a controlled voice, "There's a crazy woman in my apartment and I can't get her to leave. Please call and get the police over here in a hurry."

When I looked back, I saw Allie turning the corner from my kitchen. She was carrying a ten-inch chef's knife and her eyes were slits. I looked back and my neighbor, a woman I'd never met, said, "Run down the stairs. I'll make the call."

I couldn't believe it. This was the second time in a couple of days someone was trying to kill me. Even if I got down the stairs, she would follow me into the street and, if there was an obstruction or I fell down, I was a dead man. I had to keep her in the apartment until the police arrived. I stepped to the threshold, swung the door closed and held onto the knob for dear life.

Allie went crazy inside, shouting, swearing and threatening. She began pounding on the door and trying to open it using her left hand. After about thirty seconds, I could hear the knife clatter onto the wooden floor and she began pulling with both hands. The door shook and opened an inch or two, but I was always able to close it again. Then Allie did something that changed the tide. She put a knee on the doorjamb, which added significant power to her pull. When the door opened about ten inches, she dropped her leg and tried to shove her shoe into the gap. That gave me just enough time to yank on the doorknob and slam it shut.

I was getting tired and knew she would get her shoe in there in the next minute or so. Once that happened I'd have to let go because she'd go for the knife; I needed another plan.

I held her off after two more attempts, but my hands were played out and slippery with sweat. I held on with my last remaining strength as the door began to open again. I could hear her grunting and straining as if she knew she'd won the battle. At that point, I released my grip and shoved the door as hard as I could. I could see the knife on the floor and I stepped in and kicked it out the door. It had her fingerprints on it. Allie was flat on her back and looked stunned as if she'd hit her head on the floor when she fell. I stood over her and was ready to jump on top if she tried to get up.

At that moment, I could hear multiple steps as the police raced up the stairs. I glanced out the door and saw my neighbor on the landing urging them to come faster. Allie hadn't moved so I was standing next to her when the police came into the room with drawn weapons. I raised my hand and stepped away. My blessed neighbor followed the police in and saved me an explanation as I knew the cops wouldn't know which one of us was the bad guy.

"I saw the whole thing, officers. The lady went nuts with that knife and tried to attack this man. I don't know him, but he lives here and I think she's been stalking him for a while. I heard her on the stairs shouting."

The police instantly turned their attention to Allie, pulled her to her feet, and handcuffed her. One of the officers stayed on the landing and talked to my neighbor and me at length. Allie, in the living room, was shouting obscenities about my betrayal and refusing her overtures. An officer said he might need to come back for further questioning and they led poor Allie away. I felt sorry for her and decided I needed to talk to Heather about this in person. I thanked my savior profusely and then went inside and called Heather, giving her a brief summary of the evening's events, and set up a lunch for the next day.

We ate early to avoid the crowds and I chose a booth in the back of the restaurant. Heather had a sad and worried expression on her face, as she had known Allie for a long time. She apologized for not calling Allie sooner as she was probably on her way to my apartment when Heather was trying to reach her.

"I'm going to be completely honest with you, Heather. If you have any doubts, I have the name of my neighbor who called the police for me as well as the police sergeant who saved my life. You may feel I must have done something wrong to have, within a week, made two people so angry they wanted to kill me."

"I worried about that, but I talked with Phil and he feels responsible for putting you in that position in Spokane. Allie is a different matter."

"I talked to you about her compulsive behavior and that I wanted to break off all contact. I never told her I loved her and never slept with her. It was something she began to demand in increasingly frequent telephone calls."

"Yes, Phil told me you talked with him about it. It's hard to believe someone could be so emotionally unstable that murdering you was the answer."

Allie was Heather's friend and I decided to lighten up, even though I vividly recalled the fury in her eyes. "Perhaps she only meant to scare me."

Heather was looking at me strangely. "You don't look well; are you sick?"

I knew what the problem was: I'd aged half a dozen years since we first met. I decided to give her the whole story.

"I'm aging very rapidly and will probably die in a couple of months. If you have time now, I'd like to tell you about it."

I could see the shock on her face and she struggled to nod. I started with the river and brought her up to date, skipping most of the details. The fact I was almost forty years older than I was ten months before shocked even me.

"Why do you think this is happening, Tom?"

"I've spent time trying to figure this out. It seems to apply only to me, which doesn't make sense. I know additional lives are part of Hinduism, but whatever power caused it has declined to declare itself and it may not have anything to do with religion."

"There's rebirth in Christianity too."

"Surely you wouldn't equate me with Jesus. It's enough to know it's in the bible."

We sat silent for quite a while. Heather's hands were clasped on the table in front of her and she stared at them, every once in a while glancing up at me. I slid my hand, palm down, towards her. "Touch me. I'm real."

Heather moved a hand and then hesitated, calming herself. I felt her fingers on the back of my hand, light at first and then pressing hard, feeling the bones and tendons. She nodded and looked up at me. "What are you going to do now?"

"I'm going to leave New York. Eventually, I have to find the place where I entered the water."

Heather slid her chair back and I rose from my seat. We walked together to the sidewalk and turned toward each other. She smiled sadly for a long moment then put her arms on my shoulders and kissed my cheek. "I wish you well, Tom, now and whatever happens in the future."

Hers was a mixture of disbelief and encouragement and I wanted to send her off smiling. "I hope your next one is long and happy."

Chapter Fifty-one

It was going to be a week or two before I could leave. I was in the middle of a story for Collier's and felt obligated to finish. In addition, there was some damage in the apartment from Allie's temper tantrum and I wanted to save my deposit. I was on a month-to-month lease so there should be no penalty.

The evening after my confession to Heather, there was a knock on my door and, expecting a detective, I was surprised to find my neighbor standing there. She was a middle-aged woman with very dark hair and soft pleasant features. Her eyes matched her hair and her searching gaze had a mysterious quality about it. She wore loose casual clothes: an emerald green blouse with a tan skirt. She had an unusual necklace with some odd symbols hanging from it. Perhaps Egyptian.

"We met yesterday, but it bothered me that we've remained nameless. I'm Duane Dickerson and, after yesterday's events, I wanted to be sure you were okay. Everybody calls me Dee Dee."

"I was going to knock on your door to thank you again for your help. I'm Tom Hunter and you probably saved my life. I owe you more than words. I'd like to take you, and anyone you live with, to an awesome restaurant to celebrate. I apologize for the delay, but I'm still a bit shaken."

"The good news for your wallet is I live alone."

I invited the woman in for a drink and we sat together on the couch and were quickly at ease. Duane was a research biologist working with bacteria at the Cornell University Medical Center. Her interest was in how pathogens worked to cause different illnesses in humans. She had a PhD from Columbia University, but her knowledge and interests were wide ranging. She was divorced for twelve years and had two grown children.

I sipped on my gin martini. "I hope science and art don't mix like oil and water. I've been a reasonably successful painter in the past and decided to try my luck at writing. I'm currently involved with the New Yorker and Collier's magazines."

"For most people, science is something you read and marvel at, but don't actively indulge in. Art, on the other hand, is something we all need to lift ourselves out of the humdrum. How can a bird fly without spreading its wings?"

"I agree and don't understand why it's the first thing shut off when a school needs money."

"Isn't it ironic," said Duane, "that ignorance should be so persuasive in a house of learning."

After a second martini for each of us, we were laughing at nothing and enjoying each other's company. It was amazing how a relaxing friendship could develop so fast. I was a good deal older than she so I wasn't worried about anything more than that. My time with Allie was still an uncomfortable rock in my chest.

"You work weekdays so, if you're free, I'd like to take you to dinner next weekend. I want you to know how grateful I am for your help with my psychotic friend. We were not a couple, but we had been friends for a while until she turned into a stalker. I feel sorry for her and hope a psychiatrist can get her back on track."

"Why don't we get together Saturday afternoon? It would be fun to take a cruise around Manhattan Island and have dinner after that. The New Yorker would approve."

Apparently, I had not paid enough attention to the marvels of New York City. I'd been to Carnegie Hall and the Metropolitan Museum, but had never taken advantage of this option. "Sounds wonderful. I'll get the cruise schedule and make dinner reservations." We parted with a smile and a quick hug. There it was again, the enigma in her eyes.

On Saturday, we took a cab together to the tour boat dock. There were at least fifty other people scattered about choosing seats for the best advantage. Duane knew we'd be going in a counterclockwise direction so we sat on the starboard side. There was a lively cool breeze on the water so it was nice to huddle with our elbows locked together. A personal configuration makes giggling easy. We motored against the wind on the East River, with Duane pointing out New York Hospital where she worked. I held the map we'd been given well out in front because, like most seniors, I'd become farsighted. We rounded the uptown tip of Manhattan Island and saw the George Washington Bridge washed in hot August haze. In spite of the skyline's many towers, I thought the Chrysler building was the most beautiful of all. It was completed in 1930 without a single worker dying, in spite of a frantic construction pace of four floors per week. My love of Art Deco came from something in my past and I mentioned it to Duane.

"Yes, this is not your first life."

I jerked with the shock of it, pulling on her arm enough so she winced. "I'm so sorry. You're right of course, but I didn't know you were psychic."

"I don't like that term. It creates a lot of skepticism and titters. I'm a clairvoyant."

I didn't know what to make of this. "Are you living in the past, present and future at the same time?"

"I'm in the present always, and have only glimpses into the other two."

"How did you know about me?"

"It's your aura. You have an ambience I can see and smell. Did you know different times have different scents?"

Duane's matter of fact discussion of her insight stunned me and I felt uncomfortable sitting so close. We still had our elbows locked and she could feel I was tense. She flexed her arm and drew me toward her, making sure I didn't move away. I sniffed the air. "Can't smell a thing." I was trying to make light of the situation, more for my sake than hers.

"Of course not. I suspect very few people are reborn and not all of them talk about it. By the way, why do you think you were chosen?"

"I have no idea. I was not an atheist; that's the height of arrogance. Maybe an agnostic. That's not so bad and at least it's honest. Faith depends on nothing. It's apocryphal."

"It's a great comfort though. How are you dealing with the end of your life?"

The way Duane was saying these things was not argumentative at all, merely curious. I had no clue what she really believed. "I'm exceedingly thankful for being born or perhaps 'formed' is more accurate. The odds of my original birth were against me, and hugely so. It depended on the date and time of conception—a fraction of a second really—as well as competition for the egg. As I recall, it's three hundred million sperm to one egg. My overwhelming gratitude for winning such a lottery is enough for everlasting peace and contentment."

Duane shifted so she turned towards me. She touched my forehead and my cheek with her free hand and then looked into my eyes. Her gaze was grave at first and then began to soften. Her eyes became unfocused, somehow coalescing with mine. She sat absolutely still, her posture belying what was going on in her mind.

We sat that way, unmoving, for some time and then Duane shuddered and took a deep breath. "There is a path for you, Tom, into the future. You will have a soundless conversation."

I started to pull away, but she wouldn't let me. "What does that mean?"

"I have no idea. All I can do is tell you what comes to me. You will hear and respond."

"Hear something without words?"

"Yes, it's not hard. The words will come to you if you're receptive."

At this point, the boat was going around Battery Park with the Verrazano-Narrows Bridge to the right. Duane could tell our conversation had shaken me and she held me close. We said nothing more until the boat docked and we stepped onto land.

"A nice hot shower at home and a special martini at the restaurant will do wonders for you, Tom. I've never met anyone like you and it's special for both of us."

We walked apart up the stairs and returned to our apartments. An hour and a half later, we walked back down the stairs and hailed a cab. The hot shower worked wonders and I couldn't wait for the martini.

Chapter Fifty-two

I again chose an Italian restaurant because who doesn't like the cuisine. It seemed the safest thing to do as I didn't know Duane's tastes. The waiters were all from the mother country and trained for that profession. We were never rushed and our water glasses were kept magically full without ever seeing the pourer. After our martinis, Duane ordered lasagna and I loved seeing the joy in her eyes as she savored each bite. I had clams, scallops and shrimp over linguine in a savory broth. All of this with a magnificent full-bodied Chianti.

Duane sniffed a few minutes into the meal. "Is all that garlic good for you?"

"Garlic not only keeps the vampires away, it turns me into an optimist."

It's hard to giggle with a mouth full of lasagna, but Duane managed to do it. "I know a couple of holistic types who would love to know about your mood altering secret.

We had a good time together, telling stories about happy parts in our lives. I hailed a cab and told Duane, on the way back, how much I enjoyed her company. I told her we would have another dinner before I left New York. At the top of the landing, we hugged and went our separate ways.

An hour and a half later, I was sitting in my living room with my feet up on the coffee table, savoring the dinner and my neighbor's companionship. The garlic had drifted throughout my body and, now an optimist, the sensation was exhilarating. There was a knock on the door and when I opened it, Duane was standing there in a flowing multicolored gown contained at her waist by a wide sash. She pushed by me before I could collect myself and vanished into the back of the apartment.

"Duane, what's going on? Are you all right?"

I was fighting the obvious, but couldn't help it. In my garlic and Chianti haze, it was a dream I had already fabricated for myself. I felt guilty seeing it come true, but not so guilty I didn't follow her into the bedroom.

It was late and city lights filtered through the closed curtains behind her, outlining Duane's ink-black profile standing in front of the bed. Her shadow-self transfixed me. She moved very slowly as if some power had set the planet into slow motion. Her hands moved from her sides to her waist and I could see the black ends of the sash in her fists as she stretched them outward. The ends fluttered from her dark fingers and her open hands then moved down and inward, disappearing into the blackness of her silhouette.

The silence in the room and the presence of the phantom in front of me was mesmerizing. Time extended into the distance and it seemed much later that black wings, starting at her thighs, moved out from her body. She was Ma'at, the winged Egyptian goddess of truth, justice and morality.

Feathers seemed to flutter to the floor, leaving only bony arms, stretched black against the window. The form turned and I could see a woman's breasts silhouetted for a moment before the umbra settled onto her sheeted nest.

The numinous obscurity in the room made it difficult for me to unbutton my shirt and I fumbled with my belt and shoelaces. It was only when I was naked that I fully realized Ma'at was real and waiting for me. We were transcendent together, ageless and perpetual.

When I awoke in the morning, I was alone. I thought I'd dreamt it until I moved to the edge of the bed, searching for some evidence of the night's apparition. The closed curtains kept the room dark so I felt along the side and under the bed. I touched something that skittered away so I dropped my hand down on top of it. In the dim light, it was a feather.

I never saw Duane again. I knocked on her door several times, but I suppose she was away or busy. I was haunted by that night. The "wings" were obviously the flowing robe she was taking off and the thin fabric looked like feathers as it fluttered to the floor. The feather I found under the bed was undoubtedly from a woman's hat or a child's Indian costume.

* * *

I could have chosen to do something else, something much safer. However, I knew in my gut that my connection with Lobo was not over. He had been a part of me for a long time and would be surprised to learn I was high in the air on the way to Seattle. I needed to find him because, after his efforts to kill me in Spokane, I'm sure the police wanted him as much as I did. Snag made sure to tell me, during my earlier visit with Big Boy, that his crazy friend had given up the murder business. He mentioned Lobo's dog and his job as Gio's sous chef at an upscale Italian restaurant. He said no one with a beloved pet could harm anyone. I knew Snag was setting me up.

I could play the game too. When I got there, I'd tell Gio my name and that I was from the New York Times. I was there to give Lobo the money we owed him for his part in the newspaper article. That was my chum in the water.

I was under no illusions about my ability to confront Lobo. I figured my age to be eighty-two by now and I had no weapon except words. If I only had a year of life, I needed to have faith I had another month or so. The conversation I had with Duane came back to me in a rush. It was between faith and luck at this point.

I located Gio's restaurant without difficulty and parked my rental car as close to the entrance as possible. I wanted Lobo to have a good description when he came looking.

"Good afternoon, Gio. Lobo told me all about you and how happy he was as your sous chef."

"Are you looking for a job?"

"No, I'm looking for Lobo. My name is Tom Hunter and I work for the New York Times. We recently did an article about crime in Spokane and he was very helpful. We owe him some money for his part and we don't have an address. Will he be here later?"

"Lobo doesn't work here anymore. I don't know what he's doing, but it's not here. Are you in touch with the police?"

"Absolutely not. I have a check and I need a signature."

Lobo had obviously told Gio not to reveal anything. "Lobo has moved somewhere else. I'm not giving out his number to anyone."

I chuckled. "Ridiculous, as if anyone would want to harm Lobo. Please give him a call and let me know where we could meet. I'm going to find a place to sleep and I'll get in touch with you tomorrow." Gio agreed to act as intermediary.

I thought the location where I was going to spend the night was important. A high-end hotel would best safeguard me from a nighttime visit. The Arctic Club Hotel was upscale and well situated and staffed. I told the man at the desk not to give my room number out for any reason.

The next morning, I was dizzier than usual. I sat on the edge of the bed for half a minute until the rocking stopped. I looked at my forearm skin; it was loose and wrinkled. I was shrinking, and wondered if this happened in my previous life. I left the hotel and walked to a breakfast place, three blocks away. I ordered coffee and thought about what I wanted for probably the last breakfast of my life.

I decided on eggs Benedict with a spicy Italian sausage patty instead of Canadian bacon. Heavenly.

When I returned to the hotel, I called Gio. He said Lobo was thrilled and suggested I come to a certain street corner in a decrepit and open section of the city where I would be a sitting duck for a long gun. He also requested I bring a doggie biscuit. I told Gio I would be at the South entrance of Woodland Park at 2 PM and we could walk to a mutually acceptable place. I would bring a bag of dog treats. The park fronted on Puget Sound and was over fifty acres. It had several walking trails that would appeal to any psychopath bent on isolated violence. I spent time researching it even before I heard about Lobo's ridiculous suggestion.

Lobo would expect, since the New York Police Department had issued a nationwide warrant for murder, to have undercover Seattle officers at the entrances. I notified the Police Department of the meet and, in a long phone conversation, explored my freaky idea. They were not happy as Lobo would have no trouble in getting into the park unnoticed. I waited excitedly by the phone and wasn't surprised when Gio told me the game was on. I was determined not to underestimate the man.

I still had two hours before heading to Woodland Park and I picked up a bag of beef jerky dog treats at a local grocery. I then headed to the nearest department store and bought a long sleeved yellow shirt and a dark gray baseball cap with a New York Yankees logo on it. When I got back to my hotel room, I roughed up the shirt and cap as I didn't want Lobo to know I'd just bought them. Yellow, even more than red, is the best color if you want to stand out.

I was too nervous to eat much lunch, but I did get a chocolate milkshake. I knew the brain thrived on sugar and the caffeine in the chocolate would keep me sharp. I left my brown slacks on and, with the shirt and hat in place, looked in the mirror. I saw an old man with dubious color taste. Laughing relaxed me a bit.

I left the hotel and headed to Woodland Park's South entrance with only the bag of beef jerky dog treats. I anticipated Lobo would want to get close enough to me to use his switchblade.

Chapter Fifty-three

About thirty yards from the entrance, I made it obvious I was glancing about, searching for Lobo and any undercover cops. I wanted to make sure he was inside the park. There was a homeless woman sitting on the sidewalk by her shopping cart, a park employee trying to install, "Stay off the grass" signs and a van parked on the street close by. They all looked legit, at least by police standards. There were only occasional people entering the park: a couple in running outfits, a group of women pushing strollers, and an older man by himself. I spread my arms with my palms up as a signal to the police that he wasn't there. I knew they had ringed the entire land-based circumference of the park, not just the two entrances. I insisted no one was to follow me after I entered. That met with some resistance, but I prevailed after I said it was my way or no way.

My yellow shirt was a lighthouse. I didn't want Lobo to miss me as I entered the park on the paved walkway. It also allowed the police to identify me quickly if they came searching. I walked fifty yards into the park and stopped, wondering if Lobo had opted out. Unexpectedly, an overweight middle-aged man slid in alongside me and mentioned his name. Gio recognized me even in my peculiar outfit. His accent seemed more pronounced.

"Lobo was an excellent sous chef and I agreed to do him a favor. I have no idea why he is doing this and do not want to know. There is a path ahead off to your left that you can see from here. Take

271

it and he will meet you. There was a pause, and then he said, 'In bocca al lupo.' "

The Italian idiom means, "In the mouth of the Wolf." For your luck to hold, this should be answered by, "Crepi il lupo." It's loosely translated as, "May the Wolf choke to death." Needless to say, I responded quickly. Gio probably had no idea how much of a wolf his sous actually was.

I turned left onto a dirt path and encountered only one other person. Less than two hundred yards later, I saw a man with a small dog on a leash ahead of me. There was another hard-packed dirt trail on his left and he stepped into it, turned around, and looked at me. I continued towards him and he didn't move until I was about a hundred feet away. He beckoned, turned, and continued at a moderate pace on the trail. My right knee began hurting when I took large steps. We continued for a minute or so, keeping a hundred feet from each other until we came to a crossroad. The path on the left looked well used, but the one on the right was smaller and obviously did not have the same traffic. I was tired, aching and increasingly anxious.

The wolf turned around, looked at me, and started climbing up the narrow path on the right. I followed more slowly. After a couple of hundred feet, a glade opened up and he stopped. It was not a large area, but adequate for a fatal confrontation. By this time, both knees were sore, I was breathing heavily, and my left arm was aching. Lobo looked up and down the trail to make sure we were alone and then walked to the far side of the open area. I also looked around hoping, in spite of my agenda, to see someone coming. Even if there was, I couldn't count on the lunatic not slaughtering both of us. I moved off the path and moved closer until we were about seventy feet apart.

Lobo bared his teeth in a wide grin. "I didn't know you were suicidal. Did you bring a weapon?"

"I'm not suicidal and all I brought with me are doggie treats. I followed your instructions exactly."

Lobo frowned, obviously puzzled by what I was doing by suggesting a meeting and exposing myself. "Good. Boy is happy to know she didn't come all this way for nothing." He reached down, unbuckled the leash from the dog's collar, and dropped it on the ground. The dog sat down next to her master without moving.

I opened my paper bag and pointed the open end toward Lobo, showing him there was nothing inside except chunks of beef jerky. I threw a piece that landed about a foot in front of Boy and she jumped on it eagerly, chewing with vigor. Then she sat again, quivering, looking at me expectantly.

"You don't need to kill me, Lobo. You came after me with a gun and I was simply defending myself with jumper cables. You would have done the same thing to me if the situation was reversed. I think we're even now." I threw another treat to Boy.

"You burned my tongue and I've talked funny ever since. *Hah yoo yeah ya.* That's a problem you don't have. You owe me something and money won't be enough."

"I'm dying, Lobo. Maybe I can last another month or so, but then I'm gone forever. You can escape now and there's no way I can stop you. If they find my body here, the police will track you down without mercy. I made sure of that." I looked around the open glen, including up at the sky. I took another piece of jerky out of my pocket and held it so Boy could see it. She rose to her feet, but didn't move.

Lobo said, "The police will never catch me, I also made sure of that before I came up here. Dying by yourself in some other place will give me no satisfaction. You didn't burn me from afar, it was up close and personal. I am going to kill you and it's going to take a while."

The wolf took his switchblade out of his pants pocket, all the time grinning at me.

snick   snick   snick

The maniac took great pleasure moving the blade in and out for me. When the blade remained out and as he was taking his first step towards me, I yelled, "Here Boy, come." I held a treat out toward the dog and rattled the paper bag. Boy took off like a Greyhound. The dog was only a few feet from me when Lobo realized what was happening and started to run. I emptied the bag in front of me and the odor was overpowering. Lobo had covered half the distance toward me and was yelling for his dog to come back. Boy, with a pile of beef in front of her was in heaven and it was easy for me to pick her up. I held her against my chest with my left hand and put my other one around her head, bending it severely to the right.

Lobo knew exactly what that meant: with one jerk, I'd break the dog's neck. He came to a shuddering halt a dozen feet from me. Boy started to struggle, but her position gave her no traction. Lobo's mouth was open and his eyes dilated. "Put the dog down. She's not in this."

"She's in it now. You still have a choice, Lobo. I gave you an out and you didn't take it."

I could see him thinking and knew he'd play for time. "What are you going to do now, Tom? If you don't put her down, I'll skin you alive."

"If you take one step toward me, Boy has a broken neck. To save yourself, throw the knife into the trees and take off running. After half a minute, I'll let the dog go and Boy will follow your scent and catch up to you quickly. If you come back here, I'll be long gone and the police will get you." I could see the torment in his face as he agonized between losing his beloved dog and getting his revenge. If he killed me, he would have nothing left. If he let me go, he could always track me down later.

Lobo took one step to test me and he could see my biceps tense as I increased the pressure. The dog started howling and that did it. He threw his switchblade into the trees and ran back down the path. I moved the dog into a more comfortable position for both of us and retrieved the leash. I hooked it to her collar and started walking back down the path, following my nemesis. I could hear Lobo's frantic footprints fading and tried to pick up the pace so as not to lose him. When I came to a straight stretch without seeing anyone, I took off the leash and let Boy run.

Lobo was at least three hundred yards in front of me by now, and Boy swerved onto a separate trail on the right. Without the dog, I would have missed the turn that led down to the beach on Puget Sound. Now I could tell the police exactly where Lobo had gone.

I walked slowly back the way I came. I was exhausted and fell twice before I got to the south entrance. A police captain, holding a walkie-talkie, helped me to a bench and gave me a drink of water from the van. When I told him the direction Lobo had taken, he said, "We had a couple of officers down there, but when that devil got to the beach, he had a boat waiting. There was a dog with him and he took off before our officers had a chance to arrest him. No worries though, I alerted the Coast Guard. They'll get him for sure.

"I must tell you, Mr. Hunter, we all thought you were crazy to go after that guy by yourself, unarmed. I expected to find your body up there. Don't know how you did it. You deserve a medal,"

I nodded, but knew Lobo was gone. He would hole up somewhere, pet his dog and look for a new switchblade and a new victim. I stood up to him and he'd look for easier opportunities. Surprisingly, in spite of my fear and loathing, I was glad to know Boy was with him.

I gave the police a detailed history of my relationship with Lobo and then asked if someone could drive me back to the hotel. I was too tired to take a shower or go to the dining room. Two aspirin and a bed was the only thing I wanted. As I drifted off to sleep, I knew I'd made the right decision in confronting Lobo. Evil can follow any of us and it is useless to run away.

Chapter Fifty-four

I woke up a couple of times during the night, but didn't get up until almost 10 o'clock the next morning. I was sore all over and my right knee was giving me a fit. It's hard, on a long trek, to keep up with a man half your age. It was time to think about my endgame.

I understood now why demonic Lobo became part of my life, whether I deserved it or not. Unseen and perverse temptations trail all of us. We need to confront evil, in all its manifestations, if we are to survive unsullied and intact. It's close and personal and you have to go up against it, mano a mano, using your head and your gut.

In the end, I remain grateful for both my lives. One life is an opportunity for a worthwhile existence and anything afterwards is a gift, alive with possibilities. I will never forget my chance to give Chinny a better life, the privilege of giving Billy Joe the peace he desired and the comfort and happiness that art can provide. I gave myself to Debra, and she to me, and we experienced the most profound and cherished emotion there is.

The night with Duane remains mysterious. My only conclusion is that rational thought has no answer to what is going on in the universe. Maybe that's enough.

I returned to my room after a light breakfast, sat in front of the window and closed my eyes. I knew that Papi's farm was in northern Idaho so the river was probably the Salmon. When I woke up to my new life by the fallen tree, the cold river water had a familiar feel on my skin, not a surprise since my ashes were in it for a while. More importantly, when I looked upstream, I had a sense that eventual repose was somewhere up there.

Visions of fishing came to me and I had flashes of my mother. I never saw her face directly, but only the dry flies and streamers she tied herself. I probably fished with her on occasion and that would be on the Salmon's middle fork. I could, of course, go back to Papi's farm, retrace my steps to where I climbed out and then follow the river upstream. There was no road alongside the river and I had no idea how far to go. The best plan would be to find the places where fly-fishing people wade into the water. I felt confident I would sense the spot where my ashes were tossed.

I flew to Boise the next day and checked into a hotel. I went over my assets and found, after my last painting sold, I had almost five thousand dollars in my New York bank account. I decided to make a will and dispose of the money properly. I called Debra and told her my time was up.

"What do you mean, Tom? You're NOT going to harm yourself."

"Of course not, Debra, but the day is very close. I'm in my eighties and my joints let me know it. My best friend is a stool softener."

I heard her laugh. Nothing like humor to adjust an attitude. "I've been drawn back to where my ashes went into the water. I have no idea what is going to happen, but I doubt it's an event I'll survive.

"Anyway, the point of this call is to ask you to make a will for the distribution of my assets." I gave Debra the number of my New York bank account and told her to send the appropriate papers to my hotel. Now that I could see the road ahead clearly, I didn't want to linger. It took eleven days and numerous phone calls, but I finally had the documents.

I left thirty-five hundred to the Wellstead hospital for the specific purpose of developing a legally acceptable and appropriate program for end-of-life issues. Transparency and palliative care would be an essential part of that. I gave Debra the remaining funds and she already had the painting I did after an especially loving night with her. I signed the documents with a notary and mailed them back to her. A day later, I rented a car for two weeks and headed north. I knew I'd be leaving the vehicle alongside the middle fork so, after I found the spot I was looking for, I would need to let the agency know the car's location.

It took me about three hours to drive to Stanley. It was beautiful country and I got a room at the Sawtooth Hotel. I sat for a while in my room trying to calm myself. My mind was a swirling stew of excitement, anxiety and fear. The Salmon River itself was only a ten minute walk and I got there without falling. I sat shakily on the bank and listened to the sound of it. The river's other name is "The River of No Return," which was quite inappropriate in my case. My ashes will return to the river and I was sitting on its bank, knowing I would be part of it soon. The splashing, gurgling and swirling noises the river made intrigued me. I recalled my dinner with Duane when she told me there would be a conversation without words. I spent a long time listening and almost fell asleep. I heard no words, but the river's musical voice did its best to relieve my apprehension.

The following morning, after apple juice, scrambled eggs, crisp bacon and a blueberry muffin, I drove to the Salmon's middle fork and searched along its bank. There were numerous creeks where guides would put in their boats for drifting or wading. I drove, sometimes stopping and walking, and explored upstream until a faint scent, a smoky fragrance, stopped me. Whatever it was, it was evocative . . . perhaps hickory. I parked the car and walked down a narrow path that led to an open area. The Middle Fork was in front of me and a feeder creek came in on my left. I was able to walk up the creek for a bit, and it spoke to me in the same language as its larger brother, except with higher notes. I began to stumble and returned to the glade. This cozy place was perfect for trout fishing. Ashes also.

I felt this was the spot as the natural clearing was private enough for a small group to gather by the river. I was going to take my shoes off and wade a bit, but decided against it as I remember river rocks are very slippery. Looking about, I was surprised to see a man casting expertly with a fly rod about eighty yards upstream. I never got a good look at the face, but he had a light brown complexion and longish hair. Why did I say "man"? The figure's graceful motions could easily be a woman's. I stood watching for a time and then crumpled onto the bank, perplexed and frightened. With the water inches from my shoes, I closed my eyes and listened again. As before, the creek on the left had its own little voice, softer than the Middle Fork. The deeper tones in front of me hinted at a rising potency downstream. I began to appreciate that this crystalline stream was going to embrace me tenderly the next day and I stood, calmer and more content. When I got to my car, I looked around for evidence of other vehicles or people. There were none.

Driving back to Stanley, I was in a fugue state, unaware of my surroundings, and even my own self. I drove from memory, preoccupied with the knowledge that I had only a day more to live. How was it going to happen . . . the river seemed no more than a few feet deep. Was I going to fall and drown? Surely, the fishing parties downstream would not allow a body to float the many miles to the fallen tree and the little whirlpool.

Halfway home, I realized what the river was saying to me; I would not be alone anymore. This buoyed me enough so when I awoke from my trance, I began to think about dinner.

Chapter Fifty-five

On my last evening, I felt a strong connection with my river and had a freshly caught trout for dinner. In the morning, I walked for a half hour around the neighborhood, looking at the mountains, the sky and everything in between.

I left all my cash on the bed for whoever cleaned the room and checked out of the hotel. I gave the woman at the desk an envelope to give to the car rental people when they came looking. It contained money and detailed instructions on the car's location.

I began to get nervous again the closer I got to the Middle Fork. My death was certainly unnatural, but the way I was doing it smacked of suicide. I didn't want to leave that way. I hoped whatever gave me this brief second life was going to be nice enough to end it with kindness and dignity. I made the drive so I would arrive at midday, which should give me the least chance of bumping into other people. Indeed, the little clearing was empty and there were no cars on the unpaved road by the river.

At this point, my nervousness became outright fear. I was scared of not only how I was going to die, but also about what death meant. In the beginning, it was only a five-letter word meaning my heart had stopped. Paul Tillich, the early twentieth century theologian, called death "non-being." That brought dying up close and personal. Think about "non-being" for eternity. Calling it, "The Big Sleep," did not help either, but at least it wasn't painful. Of course, not being born at all (the worst kind of bad luck) was also non-being. Anyway, being both tired and grateful at this point was a welcome balm.

I undressed, hid my clothes under a bush, and chuckled wryly at what the finder would think happened in the glen. I struggled slowly toward the river, trying to stretch my life a little longer. I stood on the bank and listened, hearing those soothing sounds again."

I moved closer to the bank's edge and found the water clear and flowing purposely downstream. I thought of the trout I ate for dinner and felt guilty at its removal from this aquatic Eden. I looked upstream and was stunned to find the same person with the same fly rod. This time, the figure was further upstream, at the point where the river bent to the left. The form was motionless facing me, but the greater distance and loose clothes still made it impossible to tell age or gender.

"Non-being" applies only to lifeforms.

I looked around and I was alone. It didn't make sense. I distinctly heard the words. I looked back at the shape standing in the river and remembered what Duane told me. I would have a conversation without words. There were answering words in my mind.

"I am a lifeform."

Existence can take many forms.

I was trying to digest that when I heard a car drive into the clearing, then the high-pitched voices of two young children. I turned back to the river and looked upstream.

Come.

The world around me softened and my dread disappeared. The river continued its reassuring vocals as I moved into it. The water covered my ankles and began flowing across my knees, trying to move me downstream. I stumbled closer to an exposed rock where the current was racing. It flung spray into the sun-filled air, each droplet a prism, rainbow colors winking at me before falling back into the water.

I could hear little steps running toward the river and the children's excited shouts as they burst out of the trail and ran into the clearing.

I thought it was odd, as the river was not that deep, that I was sinking lower and lower. The sensation from my waist down was exquisite. A lover's touch. As the water rose to my chest I looked downstream and there was a line of gray ashes, roiling in the current. Two children were standing on the bank staring at me. In my last moments, I looked upstream and the river was empty . . . must have waded around the bend.

I heard the water's song and there were multicolored lights in the darkness.

* * *

The father said, "We're going to have lots of fun, kids. I'll get your rods ready."

The boy said, "There was a man here, Dad, and he sunk into the water."

The father stared at the river and then downstream. He saw nothing. It was only three or four feet deep and his body would certainly be visible if he had fallen. "I don't see anything, maybe it was a beaver."

The little sister said, "I saw him too . . . colors."

The mother smiled at her husband and said, "Maybe a fish jumped out of the water."

The girl was motionless. "Rainbow wings."

Mom and dad looked at each other and smiled.

* * *

In spite of the current's turbulence, the line of ashes continue downstream, mile after mile. The gray particles, an inviolate line in the center of the current, hesitate for a moment behind a large boulder in the middle of the river and then surge to the right. They float by a whirlpool and a fallen tree, navigate a large waterfall, join the Snake River and then the Columbia.

When Tom's ashes finally enter the Pacific and taste the salt, they find their own way home.

About the Author

Clay Alexander graduated from Yale with a BA in English followed by an M.D. from Cornell University Medical College. After general surgery training at the Columbia Presbyterian Medical Center in New York, he spent two years as a Major in the Army caring for Vietnam War wounded before entering academic and private practice.

Clay has published five fiction novels: *Ultimate Malpractice*; *Time to Die*; *The Wisdom of Seashells* and its sequel *When Seashells Sleep; and The Awakening of Thomas Hunter*.

Clay, and his wife Paula, are devoted to their three sons and five grandchildren and live in Southern California.

Humor will give you extra years of life.

Made in the USA
San Bernardino, CA
11 May 2019